POWER OF THE MEDALLION

THE WIZARD ACADEMIES
BOOK 3

MIKE SHELTON

Power of the Medallion

Library of Congress Control Number: 2020911046
ISBN: 978-1-7335104-8-6

Salem, Oregon

Sign up for my email list to get further news and information on my books and giveaways at:
http://www.michaelsheltonbooks.com

Cover Illustration by Gordon Napier

Map by Robert Altbauer

ACKNOWLEDGEMENTS

This is the final book in my sixth series! What a marvelous ride it has been. I've received so much support from my wife, family, friends, and of course my readers. I'll keep writing as long as people keep reading!

Power of the Medallion is a work of fiction. Names, characters, places and incidents are the products of my imagination and are used fictitiously. Any resemblance to actual events, locales, or persons, living or dead, is entirely coincidental. I alone take full responsibility for any errors or omissions in this book.

-Mike

Books by Mike Shelton

WESTERN CONTINENT BOOKS:

The Cremelino Prophecy:
The Path Of Destiny
The Path Of Decisions
The Path Of Peace
The Blade and the Bow (A prequel novella to The Cremelino Prophecy)

The Alaris Chronicles:
The Dragon Orb
The Dragon Rider
The Dragon King
Prophecy Of The Dragon (A prequel novella to The Alaris Chronicles)

The Dragon Artifacts:
The Golden Dragon
The Golden Scepter
The Golden Empire

The Wizard Academies:
The Mark of the Medallion
The Search for the Medallion
The Power of the Medallion

GEMSTONES OF WAYLAND BOOKS:

The TruthSeer Archives:
TruthStone
TruthSpell
TruthSeer
The Stones of Power (A prequel novella to The TruthSeer Archives)

MAPS

WESTERN CONTINENT
Forgotten Lands
KINGDOM OF FINN
KINGDOM OF ARC
SUR
TWIN CITIES
MAR
WIZARD SCHOOL
THE REALM
TEAN
ANIKARI
WIZARDS CONCLAVE
CITY OF ARC
DENIR
BELOR
EMPIRE OF GILDAN
CYRENE
CITY OF GILDAN
WIZARD ACADEMY
HASARI
TURG
KHAZER
JOR
THERA
BLUE SEA
ISLES OF VORWYTH
MAHLI
AMAN
NORTH SOLSHI
THE CITADEL
ELVYN
RALEEZ
WESTRIDGE
LOR'L
SOUTH SOLSHI
CASSIAN
ALARIS
TILLIMOT
MALLEK
QUENTIS
MARGARID
GAZIR
Bay of Ghazi
WIZARD SANCTUARY
RA
2019

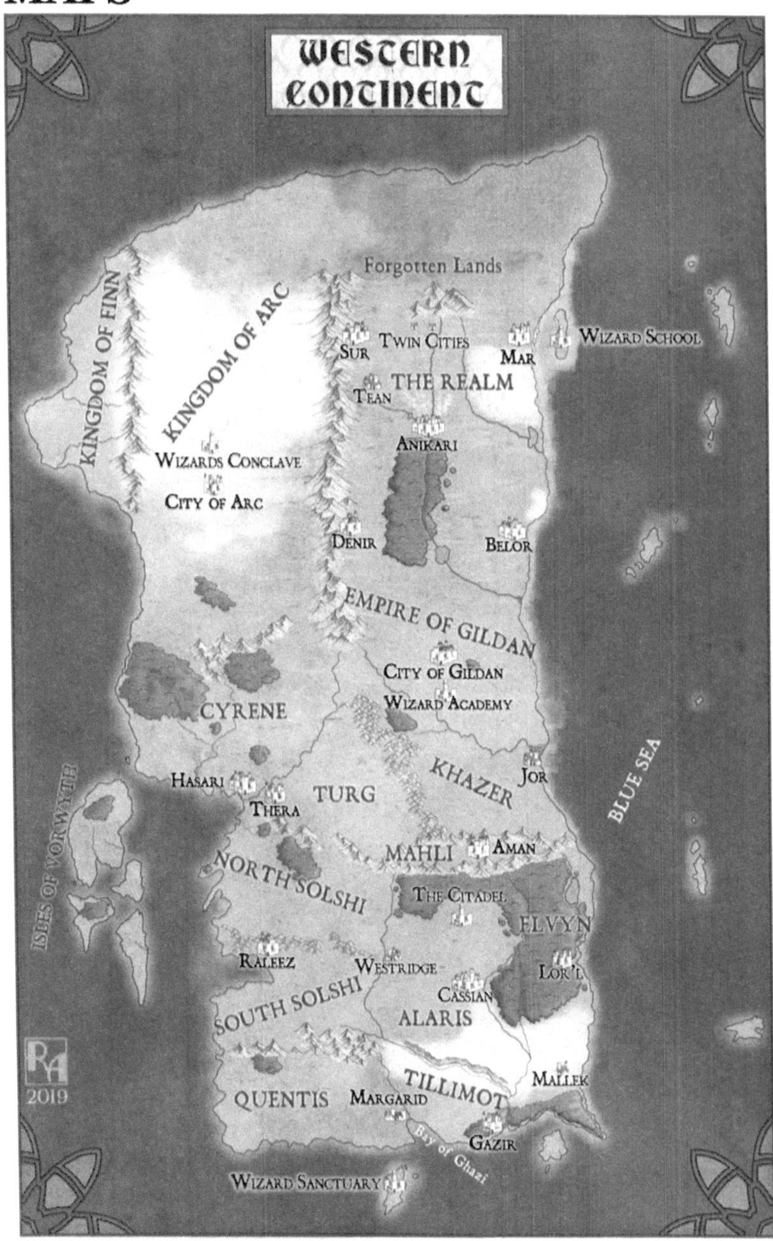

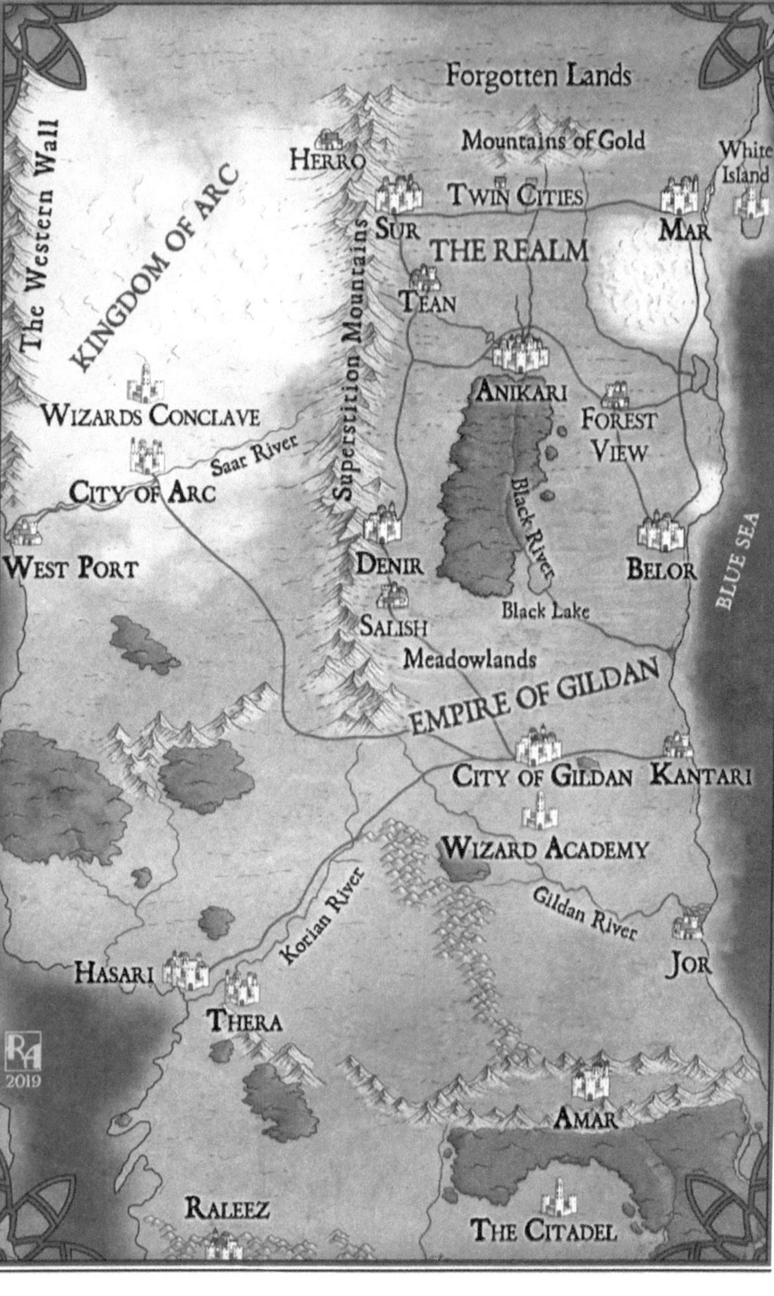
Forgotten Lands
Mountains of Gold
White Island
HERRO
TWIN CITIES
MAR
The Western Wall
SUR
THE REALM
KINGDOM OF ARC
TEAN
Superstition Mountains
ANIKARI
FOREST VIEW
WIZARDS CONCLAVE
Saar River
Black River
CITY OF ARC
DENIR
BELOR
WEST PORT
SALISH
Black Lake
BLUE SEA
Meadowlands
EMPIRE OF GILDAN
CITY OF GILDAN
KANTARI
WIZARD ACADEMY
Gildan River
Korian River
JOR
HASARI
THERA
AMAR
RALEEZ
THE CITADEL
RA
2019

CHAPTER ONE

Sylvonna Hickory ran through ankle-deep lush green grass that tickled her ankles. Feeling the wind against her face made her feel alive once again. A giggle escaped her lips as she tried to catch up with Elise who was racing ahead of her. Puffy white clouds drifted across the azure blue sky and birds called out their morning song as the sun rose gently over the tops of the enormous ancient trees.

Coming to the edge of a pool of water, both women slowed down and then trotted closer to the widening stream. Sylvie took a moment to catch her breath. Off to the right, behind hanging vines and widespread palms, a waterfall could be heard. The closer they got, the louder it became.

"Sylvie, look!" Elise pushed aside a leaf the size of her head and motioned Sylvie forward. "Isn't it beautiful? Just like I told you."

The foaming water spilled down in majestic streams over cascading rocks of varying sizes. The spray filled the air with a light, cool mist. Sylvie watched as Elise moved closer to the water.

The young woman was close to her own age, but physically there were many differences. Whereas Sylvie had shoulder-length blond hair, blue eyes, and a thin body, Elise had straight dark brown hair down to her waist, brown eyes, and pointed ears—enough for Sylvie to know that she and her older sister

Eva were from Elvyn bloodlines. Elise was taller, and although almost as thin as Sylvie, her muscles were toned and her skin held a glowing bronze tint.

Sylvie followed Elise to the water's edge but a sound high up in the trees stopped her for a moment and she craned her head upwards. Past the tallest trees stood a high cliff overlooking the area. She thought she saw something colorful move in its mist-enshrouded heights, but couldn't be sure, and so she turned her attention back to Elise.

"Are you sure we're allowed to be here?" Sylvie asked after catching her breath. "Eva told me not to wander away from the village. Something about it being too dangerous without the use of my memories."

"But don't you feel better, just being out here in the fresh air?" Elise asked, her eyes sparkling with a bit of mischief and joy. "Can't you just feel the magic in the air?"

At the mention of magic, something tickled the back of Sylvie's mind, but she couldn't quite put a coherent thought to it. Elise was right, though; it did feel good to be out here. She had been recovering from the accident at sea for a week now—at least, that is what she had been told. She had been in and out of sleep with a fever the first few days, but her body had healed miraculously fast. There was hardly a bruise or sore spot left. She had Elise and Eva to thank for that.

The two sisters had taken her in and nursed her back to health, allowing her to stay in their small hut with them as she did so. Sylvie had met a few of the other villagers at mealtimes, but this was the first time she had ventured out of the village confines.

Here, not far from the waterfall, the stream widened and the water formed a deep pool off to the side. Walking closer to the water, Sylvie caught a glimpse of sunlight reflecting within and a ray of sparkling colors caught her attention.

"What's that?" Sylvie squatted down for a closer look.

"Gemstones," Elise answered.

"Gemstones?" Sylvie thought for a moment. "I've never seen stones like that before…at least I don't think I have." Her voice rose in irritation for a moment, before simmering down. It was still so frustrating for her. Besides resting and recovering the only other specific memories she had were bits and pieces of the shipwreck, but nothing prior to that. She had been well fed and taken care of, but she felt there must be something more for her.

A soft humming sounded behind them and Sylvie felt herself relax, forgetting all thoughts of annoyance at not knowing who or where she was.

Then a slight rustling of branches behind them made both women jump. Turning around to see what it was, Sylvie was startled to see a young man walking toward them. His mouth was closed and she realized the humming had been coming from him. It was a comforting tune.

"Elise?" the young man said with questioning eyes—ones that were slanted a bit less than Elise's were.

"Jax!" Elise stammered "I…"

Jax sauntered forward. He had long brown hair tied back into a ponytail which hung down to the middle of his back. His eyes, however, were a deep green and his mouth turned up into a slight grin, as if he knew something they didn't. He stopped a few feet away from the women; Sylvie had to look up at him a few inches.

"I heard rumors we had a newcomer on the island," Jax said, his voice deep and smooth, like running over rocks. "My name is Jax Miramenor." The man bowed low with a flourish of his hand.

Obviously, Sylvie had no idea who this man was and glanced over at Elise.

"Jax is considered a cousin. His family lives farther inland and guards the sacred pools of fire."

Sylvie understood the words, but not their meaning. The two seemed uncomfortable around each other.

Jax stood there as if waiting for her to say something so she finally did.

"I am Sylvonna Hickory," she said. "My friends call me Sylvie." The last came out automatically, but she couldn't remember any friends besides Elise and Eva—if you could call them friends. They were more of caretakers. The thought struck her as strange. People should have friends...shouldn't they?

"Something troubling you, Sylvie?" Jax's smile still appeared as if he knew something she didn't.

"Oh, it's nothing." Sylvie waved it off. "My mind's been quite muddled since recovering."

"Ah, I see," Jax said. Then he turned to Elise. "Does Eva know you are here?"

Elise looked down for a moment and then shook her head. When she brought it back up her eyes were more pleading.

"But she doesn't have to know, does she? We haven't done anything wrong. I just wanted Sylvie to see the pools."

Jax moved closer to the water and the two women followed. Sylvie thought she saw another color filtering up through the clear water and leaned down to see more clearly

"You feel them too, don't you?" Jax whispered from her side.

"Feel what?"

"The stones, you can feel their power."

Sylvie looked back to the water and tried to focus on what was at the bottom of the pool.

"Close your eyes and concentrate," Jax said.

"Jax?" Elise said, with new concern in her voice. "She's not ready. This is not your place. You shouldn't even be this close to the village. Go back to your side of the island."

Sylvie had started to close her eyes to concentrate but now opened them back up at Elise's sharp words. This whole place was very confusing. People talked about things she didn't understand, and she saw things she didn't remember, but somehow knew what they were.

Jax said nothing back to Elise, but raised his arched brows even further at Sylvie. With a sigh, she relented—more out of curiosity than anything else, and closed her eyes again. He didn't seem to want to harm her.

She cleared her mind as she had been taught—and then another thought caught her off-guard. She *knew* she had been taught, but couldn't actually remember *being* taught. And taught what?

She pushed the questions away for now as there weren't any apparent answers coming. Her mind went blank and she concentrated on the water. A strange, but joyous feeling rushed up to meet her as her mind seemed to absorb the water. She felt its raw power and it beckoned to her-- and she went deeper. There was more.

Sylvie pushed through the water and felt something else there—the stones that Jax and Elise had been talking about! There was power in the stones. Different types of power and a lot of it. She gasped for a moment then let the water rush over her again. She could feel it on her feet and then seeping up her legs. It was warm and inviting and wanted her. And she hastened to comply. It was almost as if it was part of her nature. She drew more and more of it.

The ground began to rumble and she heard Elise gasp beside her.

"Sylvie!" Elise called out. "Sylvie, stop!"

Feeling a hand on her arm, Sylvie relented and with a disappointing sigh let the water in her mind subside and recede. She opened her eyes to find herself—along with Jax and Elise—standing in mud she didn't remember being there before. Looking back toward the pool of water, she could see slight ripples across its surface.

"I've never seen anyone do that before," Elise said, eyes going wide.

Jax stood silent for a moment and appeared to be figuring something out.

"What did I do?" Sylvie said.

"You brought the water up over our ankles," Jax said, his face now growing darker. "You should not have played around in such a way. The pools of water are sacred. You do not have a right to manipulate them."

"But…" Sylvie didn't know what to say, except, "…they wanted me to. The water called to me."

Jax gave a worried look at Elise. "Take her back to the village," he said with a clipped tone. "And tell no one what she did." He grabbed Elise's arm and held it firmly. "No one. Not even your sister."

"Ow, Jax, you're hurting me," Elise said.

Sylvie reached to grab Jax's hand off of her friend. "Leave her alone. She didn't do anything."

Jax took his hand off and rounded on Sylvie. "You are right. She didn't do anything. You did. You should have been more careful."

"But what did I do?" Sylvie threw her hands up in the air and without knowing how brought a surge of power and the ground shook again.

All three stumbled, trying to hold their balance.

"You must stop this," Jax cried out.

"Stop what?"

"Stop using your power, Sylvie," Jax said, his eyes darting around them as if watching for something.

"But…" Sylvie didn't know what to say. She didn't have any powers—or at least she didn't remember having any.

"But *nothing*," Jax said. "If the others find out about you, you will be in danger. There is a balance to the power on this island, and I'm afraid that you just disrupted that power. Go,

Elise, and take her to the village. Just tell them you were out for a walk and keep her hidden and safe."

"I'm in danger because of who I am?" Sylvie asked. "I don't even really know who I am. Do you, Jax? Do you know something about me that could help me?"

Jax shook his head back and forth a few times as if arguing with himself.

"Jax?" Sylvie said firmly, calling him back out from his thinking. "Who am I?"

"Don't say anything, Jax," said Elise. "A few more days and it won't matter anyway."

"She deserves to know, Elise," Jax said.

Elise pulled her arm back in the direction they had come and Sylvie reluctantly followed. Right before they re-entered the thick foliage Jax called out to her.

"Sylvonna Hickory, I'm afraid you may be a wizard of the earth," Jax said with a worried look. "And a very, very, powerful one at that."

CHAPTER TWO

Kyril Siravan sat outside Emperor Mezar Alrishitar's office, and after pushing back a lock of black hair from his forehead began to fidget with the golden medallion hanging around his neck. Three circles each larger than the last were dissected by six straight lines coming out from the center—the exact pattern found on the mark of his left hand. Three of the lines went all the way to the edge and formed three small semi circles or bumps at the edge of the ancient artifact. The medallion increased his wizard abilities—powers that were relatively weak without it—and also gave him the unique power to transport.

He thought back over the past few weeks and exhaled. Finding his mother's medallion, turning in his mentor, saving the Emperor of Gildan and his son, graduating from the wizard academy as a full wizard of the mind, traveling to the wizard school on White Island, dealing with the chaos there, and finding the second medallion with Joelle. Upon their return they discovered Sylvie may have perished, or at least was lost at sea. It was almost too much for him.

At fifteen years old and from a relatively poor home, Kyril was not used to the attention he was now getting. Meeting with Emperor Alrishitar—the ruler of all of Gildan, widely considered one of the most powerful and popular leaders and wizards on the western continent—was becoming a habit. He would not have guessed this would be his fate when he was a young boy growing up in the shadows of the southern Superstition Mountains in western Gildan.

As he waited, Kyril pushed a lock of his dark black hair off of his light brown face and sighed deeply once again. He was anxious to find the third medallion and stop Gamal Turomi's yearning for more power—and the destruction and unrest that had come with it.

Without any warning, a loud boom shook the foundation of the palace. Kyril jumped up from his seat, ready to use his own powers. The door of the emperor's office came crashing open.

"What was that?" Emperor Alrishitar said.

Four guards immediately surrounded him, ready to protect him from any imminent danger.

Kyril only shook his head and shrugged his shoulders, but both of them moved down the long hallway closer to a picturesque window that overlooked the city of Gildan. A stream of smoke rose from the western edge of the city.

"Inform the captain we are going to the west gate," the emperor said to one of his guards. "Tell him to meet me downstairs right away."

One guard sprinted away on his errand while the other three began following the Emperor. Looking over his shoulder he beckoned Kyril to join him.

"Any idea of what it could be?" Emperor Alrishitar said.

"No, but with Gamal still out there loose there seems to be more and more chaos," Kyril offered up.

The emperor shook his head before continuing. "How could I have been so blind? Why didn't I see this uprising before it happened? The academy headmaster is gone and after what you told me happened at the wizard school on White Island, I'm afraid he may be dead. Gamal had posed as a lowly scribe for years but must have been gathering support. I hate that I don't know which wizards to trust. It's not a good feeling."

Kyril agreed. While using Kyril's previous mentor Targon Quereshi as a front to try and gain followers and find the medallion, Gamal now had more influence and had set his sights on more. And from what he had seen and heard, this extended past Gildan and into the Realm, over to Cyrene, and possibly even up into the Kingdom of Arc.

"And you think Gamal is this Shadow Master from the past?" The emperor appeared worried.

"Yes," Kyril said. "Well, the powers of the Shadow Master seem to have been passed down through time and somehow Gamal has amassed at least some of them and so has convinced others—and supposedly himself—that he is now the new Shadow Master. Either way, his intent is definitely to bring all wizards and nearby kingdoms under his rule."

They came to the main staircase and jogged down to the first floor and toward the oversized front doors. Servants moved out of the way as the captain and his men came in from the other direction. Their boots echoed on the marble floor until they stood at attention awaiting their emperor's orders. Zaidan, the emperor's son came from another direction and with a nod of his head to acknowledge Kyril he spoke to the emperor.

"What is it, Father?" Zaidan said. At fourteen years old the prince was the oldest son, but second child of the emperor. He still stood a few inches shorter than his father, but it wouldn't be long until he was the same height. He had short, dark hair and a thin, but happy face. Kyril had rarely seen him in a bad mood. He controlled his emotions well, and as a young wizard of the mind, kept a cool head in most situations.

"I'm not sure," the emperor said. "Might be trouble with Gamal and his followers again."

Kyril had learned that while he and Joelle had traveled to White Island, there had been more attempts at sabotaging the wizard academy, a break-in into the palace, and other unprovoked uses of magic throughout the city.

Zaiden turned to Kyril with raised eyebrows as if asking for his opinion. Being asked about things by the emperor and the prince still surprised Kyril, but he was somewhat getting used to it. In this case, however, he had nothing else to add for the moment.

"I could take us there," Kyril offered to Zaidan and his father.

The two understood right away. With Kyril's gold medallion he had inherited the ability to transport. At first, it had only been close by and to places he had visited before, but now he was able, for the most part, to go where others had been also, as long as they connected with his mind.

"We don't know what trouble might be waiting for us there," the emperor said.

"But if we don't get there soon we may also lose the advantage of finding out who it is," Zaidan said.

Kyril had thought the same thing but didn't want to presume to know more than the emperor. However, maybe there was a way.

"Sir." Kyril looked up into the emperor's eyes—brown eyes that held glints of gold as a sign of his immense wizard powers. "What if I take Zaiden close to the west gate? We will stay out of sight, but might be able to gather information before you get there."

Zaidan's eyes sparkled bright. Kyril knew he had wanted to transport more and to study the ability deeper. The emperor appeared to be in thought for a moment and then motioned his captain to join the conversation.

"Kyril, if I let you take Zaidan with you, you must also take another guard. Can you transport all three?"

"But Father," Zaidan said, "we'll be fine."

Emperor Alrishitar awaited Kyril's answer. Initially, Kyril had been unsure of his abilities and had only been able to transport himself. However, after the last two weeks and especially on his adventures with Joelle, he had grown in his control and abilities. Being fresh and rested he saw no problem taking all three of them for such a short distance.

"Yes, I can," Kyril answered back.

The emperor spoke to his son. "Zaidan, I am sending Captain Guron with you and there will be no argument. I know you and Kyril are both wizards and think you can handle yourselves, but you are a prince of Gildan and need to be kept safe."

Zaidan let out a puff of air but did not argue further with his father. The captain looked nervous, as if he didn't know what to say.

"I will bring the rest of the men with me on horseback as fast as I can," the emperor said to all three of them. "Keep them safe, Captain."

With those words, the emperor left through the palace door.

"Here goes," Kyril said with a smile. Without even touching the medallion with his hand—something that he had just recently learned he didn't have to do—he grabbed hold of Zaiden and Captain Guron and thought about a familiar inn situated close to the west gate. With all he had learned, Kyril was still limited in transporting only to a place that he had been—or in some cases to a destination that someone he was physically in contact with had been. His medallion flared to life in a golden glow. And with a low grunt from the captain, they transported.

The next moment Kyril stumbled into the side of a building and the other two put up hands to brace themselves against falling. Guron's face was pale and he leaned over and vomited right beside Kyril and the prince.

"Weak stomach," Zaidan whispered with a hushed tone.

"I heard that, Prince," the captain said, but upon straightening didn't seem to hold any malice for Zaidan.

"Don't worry," Kyril said. "Happened to me many, many times."

With only another grunt, the captain motioned the two closer to the west gate. What they saw concerned them. The sounds they had earlier heard from the palace were indeed from here. A raucous crowd had gathered both inside and outside of the gate. A bonfire had been set just outside the gates. People were running around and confusion reigned.

"We need to help," Zaidan whispered to Kyril. "There are not enough guards here to control the crowd."

He moved to go, but Captain Guron grabbed the back of his jerkin and pulled him back behind the corner where they were hidden.

"Your father said to not get involved," Guron said.

Zaidan sighed and relented, but Kyril wasn't so sure he could stay there. Somewhere in the crowd, chanting grew louder and louder.

"What are they saying?" Kyril asked.

They all listened for a moment.

"They are protesting against wizards!" Zaiden said, his slanted eyes going round.

Another explosion rocked the air around them and Kyril put a hand against the nearby wall to keep from falling down. The shaking was followed by the commands of the gate guards to clear the area, but their words appeared to have no effect on the frenzied crowd.

A man jumped up on a wall and began shouting down at the citizens of Gildan.

"Emperor Alrishitar and his wizards enslave you to their will. Stand up and fight. Take your city back!"

The voice sounded familiar to Kyril and he inched closer to try and get a better look.

"Wizard, it's not safe out there," said the captain.

"I'll be all right," Kyril said. "I'm only going a bit farther to see who that man is."

Moving to the edge of the crowd he pushed his way around closer to the wall while keeping an eye on the man there. His face was shrouded by a hood—strange in the hot weather—while a burgundy cloak floated around his thin frame. Moving as close as he dared, Kyril peered up at the man who was still shouting words of sedition.

Another figure jumped up on another wall and started their own speech. This one was a woman, and Kyril would recognize that voice anywhere.

"Wizards protect us," she shouted in response to the hooded figure. "They keep us safe from other kingdoms. Wizards of the mind are compassionate and fair rulers."

"Boo!" shouted someone in the crowd.

"Altia," Kyril said out loud, but not loud enough for the woman on the wall to hear him. She had befriended Kyril and had been part of his mentor Targon's group. But that all had changed a few weeks earlier when Kyril had set a trap for his mentor—and his growing and reckless thirst for power. That's when Kyril learned that Gamal—a man posing as Targon's scribe—was actually the power behind the building rebellion.

What is she doing up there? Kyril said to himself. Her and another wizard, Jordan, had sided with Gamal and should be in prison. And then he remembered the booming sound at the palace and put it all together. Someone must have helped them break out.

Then the man up on the wall issued challenging words and took back the attention of the crowd. A gust of hot wind blew back the cowl from his head and Kyril gasped and slipped farther back in the crowd. The man was Jordan, the wizard who had befriended Kyril at one time but had ultimately thrown his lot in with Gamal's rebellion.

Kyril moved back to where Zaidan and Guron were hidden.

"It seems like Altia and Jordan are out of prison—they appear to be inciting a rebellion," Kyril said, anger building up inside of him. "They are sowing Gamal's chaos once again. I need to stop them."

Kyril's medallion began to glow and he walked back toward the crowd.

"No, Kyril," Zaidan insisted. "Wait for my father."

"If we wait they'll be gone."

As soon as Kyril got closer to the crowd he prepared to transport up on the wall next to Jordan. But someone in the crowd bumped into Kyril right as he transported, and was carried with him. However, instead of landing on top of the wall with Kyril, the stranger landed in the air beside him, hit the wall hard, and fell to the ground fifteen feet below. A part of the crowd rushed forward to see what had happened.

"See what our wizards do?" Jordan yelled out in a clear voice. "They just killed that poor man."

"No!" Kyril answered back. "He's not dead. It was a mistake. He…"

Before Kyril could say any more the crowd surged up against the wall and someone threw a rock up at him. It missed, but leaning away from it made him stumble. He put his hands out in front of him to stop from falling, but Jordan moved in and feigned that Kyril had pushed him. Jordan rocked on one leg and then with theatrics fell off the wall to the other side.

"He's killed another," yelled someone from the crowd.

Kyril peeked over the other side of the wall and watched as Jordan used his own wizard power to provide a soft landing for himself. Glancing up at Kyril he winked, and then a few moments later was joined by Altia who had leaped down from the other wall when people started denouncing her and Kyril. Their goal to sow chaos and confusion had worked.

With long strides they reached a pair of horses and took off to the west of the city of Gildan. Kyril turned back around and found an angry mob glaring up at him. If he transported away that would give the people another reason to dislike him. Before he could figure out what to do, horns sounded at the back of the crowd and the emperor arrived on his white Cremelino horse—one of the rare and beautiful magical horses that bonded with their rider. A contingent of guards followed behind on foot, winded from trying to keep up with the fast horse.

The guards immediately set out subduing the crowd and sending the people back to their homes and businesses. Muttered complaints that wizards were ruining their lives could be heard as the people dispersed. Soon, only the emperor, Zaidan, the captain, and a few guards remained in front of Kyril.

"You can come down now, Kyril," the emperor said with a wave of his hand.

Kyril looked around and with a quick flash transported the short distance off the wall and in front of the emperor.

"What was that all about?" the emperor asked, his face grave and worried. "I asked you to wait until I arrived.

"But…" Kyril tried to excuse his actions. "It was Jordan and Altia…I thought they would leave before you got here."

"And now they are gone, and people seem to blame you—an obvious wizard." The emperor peered at his son. "At least you had the good sense to not get in trouble."

"It's not like I had a lot of choice," Zaidan said, more heated than usual. "The captain held me back! But Kyril was right to go after him. They were inciting the people and putting down wizards."

"There will always be those that don't understand wizards," said Emperor Alrishitar. "That's why we, as leaders and wizards, need to be careful and live by our principles. We have a lot of responsibility and must use it wisely."

"I'm sorry," Kyril spoke. He hated to disappoint the emperor who had done so much for him. The man was one of the most powerful wizards on the continent but was also benevolent, kind, and didn't flaunt his powers. He should learn to be more like him. "I'm sure Gamal was behind this."

The emperor nodded his head. "I agree. And that's why you shouldn't have jumped in. You could have put yourself in danger. We need you to find the third medallion, Kyril. When will you be leaving?"

Kyril sighed. "We were waiting for Bale to get better from his travels in Cyrene with Sylvie and he has refused further healing."

"Well, young Bale needs to learn when to rely on magic and when to not," the emperor said. "If he is not ready then you must leave without him. Understood?"

Kyril nodded. "Yes." He agreed with Emperor Alrishitar. Bale could be so stubborn. Having teased Kyril mercilessly only a short time before, the young spymaster had been helpful in saving the royal family from Gamal's plan, and had slowly been changing in his opinion of Kyril and wizards in general—but not to the point of accepting healing. His pride kept him from accepting the help of others.

"There is too much at stake here," The emperor continued. "You and Joelle need to find that other medallion."

"And find Sylvonna," piped in Zaidan.

The emperor softened his stance. "Yes, and find Wizard Sylvonna if she is still alive."

Kyril grimaced. The last they knew of their friend was from Bale. He said there had been a terrible storm and the ship she was on had been destroyed. They had not heard from her yet.

CHAPTER THREE

"You should have let me heal you, Bale Nabhani," Joelle said. "I don't know why you are so stubborn."

"I'm fine," Bale said. "We should have left days ago." His dark eyebrows furrowed at his two companions.

Kyril tried—and failed—to suppress a grin as Joelle stomped her foot. He watched the exchange between the two with wonderment. Bale Nabhani, a Gildanian of a minor noble house, was darker of skin than Kyril. His shoulders were broad and his stature tall—everything that Kyril wasn't. Joelle El'San was from Belor, a city in the Realm, Gildan's northern neighbor. She had wild, long, red hair, green eyes, and, although she was only a year older than Kyril, was already an accomplished healer.

And she was now the bearer of the second medallion, a companion to Kyril's own.

Thinking of the medallion, Kyril peered down at the golden one that hung around his neck. The pattern on the front of it matched the one on his palm. He still didn't know all that it could do besides augmenting his own power and helping him to transport.

Joelle's own medallion, just recently given to her, was bronze in color with the same pattern. It had given her an increased ability to feel and hear the thoughts and intents of others. It was trying on her at times, and she was still gaining a hold on her increased powers; how to turn the information off and on.

They were two of three medallions that were needed to bring balance back to magic and to defeat Gamal Turomi, a powerful but evil wizard intent on disrupting magic and overtaking the kingdom.

"Kyril!" Joelle's voice rose a pitch and brought Kyril out of his musings. "Kyril Siravan, are you listening to anything I'm saying? What were you thinking about? Do you think Bale is actually healed enough to go? We need to find Sylvie! Did you learn anything else from the emperor? What does he think?"

"Joelle," Kyril said as he exhaled. Listening to his friend sometimes made him feel out of breath. "Hold the questions, please." He glanced over at Bale. The man had been beaten in the kingdom of Cyrene trying to get Sylvie to safety, and then had ridden straight through to return with the information to Emperor Alrishitar, all the while thinking that Sylvie had died in a shipwreck. But none of them could believe it. Bale had rested for a week, denying healing by the wizards, hence the argument between him and Joelle.

"I am ready," Bale said, mouth held firmly.

Kyril nodded his head at Bale. He knew that on their recent trek to Cyrene that he and Sylvie, their other mutual friend had become close. Out of all of them, she was probably the one that needed the least amount of protection and help, as she was a powerful wizard of the earth—with skills far and above most of her peers.

"He looks ready to me," Kyril said to Joelle. "And yes, the emperor has provided supplies and money for our journey and insists that we leave right away." He sighed. "The question is: do we try and find Sylvie—or do we go to Arc ourselves and try to find the other medallion before Gamal does?"

"Sylvie," was all Bale said. "The three medallions are meant to be together and I suspect that since you two have the others, she is meant to find the third one. If we find her, we will find the other medallion."

Kyril understood his reason and his own heart led him that direction also, but… He turned to Joelle for a moment. Tears came to her beautiful green eyes and Kyril put a hand on her shoulder.

"Sylvie has to be alive," Joelle whispered. "She has to be! But…"

Sylvie was a young wizard, the same age as Joelle, whom she'd befriended at Gildan's wizard academy. While Joelle had been a visiting wizard from the Realm, Sylvie was a visitor from the Kingdom of Arc, a mostly desert land to the northwest. They had become fast friends and both had befriended Kyril, when no one else would.

"But what?" Bale said. "She's your friend. Don't you want to help her?"

"Of course I do!" Joelle said, louder than she intended. Putting a hand over her mouth, she peered around the small courtyard beside the wizard academy where they now stood. "But…" She glanced at Kyril and he knew he was thinking the same thing she was.

"But," Kyril finished for her, "we have a duty to the emperor—no, to all our kingdoms—to find the other medallion before Gamal does. He must be stopped above all else. He is trying to disrupt the power in our lands."

"I couldn't care less about your wizard powers and who is more powerful," Bale spat. "If Sylvie is still alive we must find her."

"Bale, as part of the spymaster's office, you work for the emperor and serve the entire Empire of Gildan," Joelle continued for Kyril. "As much as we all want to find Sylvie and hope that she is…" She choked up. "…And hope that she is well we have a larger duty as holders of the medallions. Please try and understand. If we don't stop Gamal, it's not just wizards he will rule, not just our power that will be thrown into chaos—it will be all of our kingdoms that he will try and exercise dominion over. He is already raising an army in Cyrene and giving favors to their king. Finding the medallion and defeating Gamal is the best way we can save not only Sylvie, but everyone. We have been given a great task. We've seen his influence in Gildan and the Realm; you said he was in Cyrene, and I'm sure he is headed toward Arc. I think we need to find the medallion first and then Sylvie. I love my friend, but this is bigger than all of us!"

Joelle wiped tears from her eyes, clearly wanting to find her friend, but feeling pulled by duty. The same duty that drew Kyril to the same conclusion.

Bale stood still for a moment, conflicting emotions crossing his face. His hands were held tight and he paced back and forth. Kyril could tell he was tortured inside about what to do—they all were. Eventually, his eyes softened, his fists relaxed, and he stopped moving.

"I cannot imagine the weight you two must feel," Bale said.

Kyril breathed a sigh of relief at his words. Maybe Bale would finally let go of some of the noble arrogance he was known for.

"And Sylvie is a powerful wizard of the earth," Bale continued. "So if anyone can survive it's her."

"Thank you, Bale," Joelle said. "This is hard for all of us."

"It seems that you two need me more than she does, or you wouldn't be begging me to go…"

"Begging you?" Kyril said, now his fists clenched. How dare he speak that way? "We are not *begging* you."

Bale flashed a toothy white smile and cocked his head to the side. "Sounded like that to me. And I accept your petition. You obviously need me to protect you and help you on your important quest. So when do we get going?"

"Just like that?" Joelle said, then squinted her eyes at Bale.

"Get out of my head, wizard," Bale said to Joelle.

But instead, Joelle just smiled. "It's nice to know you really do care."

Bale growled, but Kyril put his hand up to stop further argument. Bale had shown his loyalty to their empire and was a trained fighter…something they might need before it was over.

"And so you both know," Bale said seriously. "You may be mighty wizards of the mind and heart with powerful medallions, but if Gamal had anything to do with the disappearance of Sylvie, he is mine. Do you understand? Mine!"

Kyril shook his head. "I understand Bale, but I'm afraid it will take more than your fervor for revenge to defeat him. It will take all we have at our disposal."

There was silence for a moment as the wind picked up around them, bringing little relief to the heat and humidity of the day. Kyril looked toward the back of the school where the library was and saw that the windows and wall had already been repaired from the fire that Gamal and his followers had sent as a diversion to kidnap—and most likely kill, the headmaster of the Wizard Academy during the graduation ceremony. He knew that Sylvie had been instrumental in stopping its threat at great physical cost to herself. He wondered briefly what crucial and ancient information had been lost—and whether they had enough information to find the other medallion and destroy Gamal.

"What are you thinking, Kyril?" Joelle said. "You do tend to go off on your own more often of late. Is that the way with wizards of the mind?"

"Yes," Kyril said with a half-smile. "Although I'm not always the best at it, our power comes from reasoning things out. We must have a plan of attack."

"We've done enough thinking and talking," Bale added. "It's time to act."

Joelle nodded her head in agreement. Kyril knew that wizards of the heart acted on impulse, on their emotions. That's what drove their power. But there had to be a balance.

Finally things clicked into place. "We leave at first light," he said, turning toward the academy. "But I think we may need one more person with us."

"Who?" asked Joelle.

"Hasani. His memory of things could be vital to our success."

"Great," Bale mumbled. "Another brainy wizard."

Joelle laughed. "He's not all that bad. I like Hasani."

Both Kyril and Bale smiled at Joelle as she began to blush profusely.

"No, no, no," Joelle said, growing more embarrassed and defensive. "I didn't mean it that way. You two are horrible."

Both Kyril and Bale were thrown back by the force of her words—and stumbled to stay standing. Kyril's heart pounded with fear for a moment until Joelle took a deep breath and it all went away.

"Sorry," she whispered. "Sometimes I get carried away."

Kyril was glad that Joelle was on their side. Her power over emotions had been growing since receiving the medallion. The medallions augmented a wizard's natural abilities, and Kyril had felt his own abilities to concentrate and decipher things develop and flourish more also.

"You're a dangerous person, Joelle El'San," Bale said. "Dangerous indeed."

CHAPTER FOUR

Sylvie sat in a hut and heard a group of people arguing nearby outside. She heard her own name mentioned more than once. For the past day she had not been let out of her room. Only Elise checked on her, and when she did she was very tight-lipped and quiet. Moving closer to the wall, she tried to pick up the rest of the conversation.

"You know the rules," said a man she didn't recognize. "All newcomers are to undergo the ritual. It is the only way to ensure they forget their past lives and stay and serve the stones here."

"But she already doesn't remember who she is," said Elise. "There is no point to the ritual."

"Eva," said the man. "What do you think? What does this woman remember of her past life?"

There was a short pause before Eva answered.

"Elise is right, she doesn't remember anything about her previous life. She could be a great asset to us. We don't get newcomers very often and the stones need to be guarded and protected…but I have a strange feeling about her. Something is different."

"Different?" Elise forced a laugh. "What do you mean? She's perfect to begin training to become a guardian like us. The rumors say there is chaos on the continent, and we need to protect the stones of power to keep the balance."

"Silly girl," said a woman that Sylvie hadn't heard speak before. "Where do you hear these things? Are you listening to stories from the suppliers again? You know you are not supposed to be talking with them."

"Mother," said Elise, "there is no harm in talking. I know my place. I know what I have to do. But a bit of company…like Sylvie…is nice once in a while. Why do we have to stay so cut-off from everyone?"

Sylvie was trying to put together what they were saying. She still didn't know where she was, but by their talk and the look of things when she had been allowed out for walks, she thought they were on an island somewhere. She tried to remember her geography, but like everything else, nothing came up. She remembered her name and knew how to do automatic things like talk and walk and she mostly understood words, but besides that…nothing. But what had she done the previous day at the stream? She had used some type of magical power. And Jax had called her a wizard. The title meant something to her, she was sure of it, but with another shake of her head she went back to listening to the others.

Elise was speaking again.

"Jax said…"

"Jax?" said the man. "You are not supposed to be around him or them. You know that. Their group guards the fire pools—that is all. They can't be trusted near the stones." He stopped for a moment. "Now, where is this girl? I must see her for myself to determine if the ritual is needed or not."

Ritual? Sylvie panicked. She didn't know what that would entail, but it made her feel uneasy. Frantically, she slipped a pair of shoes on and ran to a small back window. She pulled a chair up under it and squeezed through. Luckily, she was thin. Even so, she scraped her hip bone on the windowsill. Clenching her teeth she pulled herself through, dropped to the ground, and with a quick look to the right and left took off running into the closest crowd of trees she could find.

Not knowing where to go or hide, she tried to remember the path they had taken to the pools the previous day. Hearing shouts behind her from the small village, she pushed herself faster, but tripped on a large vine and found herself suddenly face down on the ground. With a quick thought—and without knowing how--the vines slid off of her and she jumped back up only to wince at a tingling in her ankle. After wiggling it a few times, it felt better and she took off running again.

The sound of an animal scurrying off to her right and birds fluttering through the trees put her on high alert, and she jerked around frantically trying to figure out which way to go. Off in the distance she thought she heard water, so she followed the sound. A small animal path zigzagged through the thick jungle foliage. Large leaves bigger than her face slapped against her as she ran blindly down the thin path.

She stopped once to catch her breath after emerging from the thick jungle. Ahead of her was a tiny meadow and a pool of water. She listened for pursuit, but couldn't hear anything, so she walked to the pool, where she found a small stream feeding it. She walked along its bank where the trees were thinner. At one point, she startled two deer and they ran off, leaping over the stream and prancing back into the trees.

The trees thinned enough for her to see up ahead and she spied a small waterfall, no more than ten feet high. Above it was a hill that dipped away, but farther behind rose the large mountain she had seen before.

Beside the waterfall, Sylvie found a place to sit on the ground, with a large boulder at her back. Pulling her legs up against her body and wrapping her arms around them, she pondered her options. Tears came to her eyes and she angrily brushed them away.

Now is no time to cry.

But it was hard not to be frustrated. She suddenly felt very alone.

Absently picking up a few pebbles in her hand, she wondered how she could get away. But where would she go and what would she do?

"I told you to be careful with your magic," came a voice behind her.

She jumped, but at the same time realized that four rather large pebbles had been circling the air in front of her. They dropped to the ground as she stood up and looked behind her.

Jax, the young man she had met the previous day, jumped down from the rock she had been leaning against. He had a bow slung across his back with a quiver of arrows and his silky hair hung loosely rather than tied back as it had been before.

"Did you even know what you were doing?" Jax looked down at the pebbles.

Sylvie followed his gaze and shook her head. "I was only trying to think about who I was and how to get away. I didn't even realize they were in the air until you spoke."

"So you really don't know who you are?" Jax leaned back against the rock and folded his arms across his chest.

His attention made Sylvie uncomfortable.

"Why are you here alone?" Jax looked around to make sure. "Where is Elise or any of the others?"

"I heard them talking about a ritual," Sylvie said. "I was afraid and ran."

Jax's eyes sparkled with mirth and his lips took on a slight curve. "I bet that surprised them."

"What is the ritual?" Sylvie asked. "They said something about taking my memories away. But I don't *have* any to take away."

"But they would be afraid you would remember someday, and if you did you wouldn't want to stay and be a guardian."

"What's a guardian?" Sylvie couldn't keep up with all the new terms. "I've heard Elise and Eva mention it."

Jax let out a deep sigh and shook his head. "I'm not sure I should be telling you this. I could get in a lot of trouble."

Sylvie stood up in anger. "No one wants to tell me anything. I'm the one who was hurt and shipwrecked here. I'm obviously different from the rest of you." She was the only one with blond hair that she had seen on the island so far, and she definitely didn't have pointy ears like everyone else. She wiped tears from her eyes. "I don't even know where I am!"

With her last words a swelling of power surged up through her. The bulky rock that Jax stood next to cracked down the side and water sloshed over the bank of the stream next to them.

Jax rushed to her side and grabbed her shoulders with both hands. "Stop this, Sylvie! Stop it now!"

Sylvie still wasn't completely sure how she did what she had done but with a deep shudder she tried to calm herself down. She took a step back from Jax and his arms fell down to his sides. Continuing to breathe deeply through her nose, she saw fear in Jax's eyes.

"They'll know where you are now," Jax said. After ten seconds of pacing he appeared to come to a decision. He stopped and scowled at Sylvie. His emerald green eyes met her blue ones and she felt a buried intensity trying to escape. "You're too dangerous to stay here. We need to get you away from here."

He reached to grab her hand, but she pulled back. "Not until I know where *here* is."

"We don't have time for this," Jax said, his breath quickening.

When Sylvie didn't move, Jax let out a long puff of air.

"Fine," he said. "It's not as if the others like me anyway. You are on Vorwyth, west of the western continent."

"Vorwyth?" A faint echo of familiarity ran through her mind. "The Isles of Vorwyth. Somehow I know that name…and I didn't think there were any people living there."

The sound of leaves rustling and footsteps growing louder drew both of their attention toward the trees.

"Well, there obviously are," said Jax in response to her musings, "so you've been mistaken or misled. Now, unless you want to go through the ritual, I suggest you come with me."

He reached his hand out toward Sylvie and after only a short hesitation she grabbed it. He pulled her toward the stream below the large pool of water and they started to run through it to the other side. The tropical weather had warmed the water and she sensed a strange but comforting power surge through it and into her. She stopped and turned toward the waterfall. The breeze sent a spray of water in their direction.

"Come on!" Jax tried to pull her the rest of the way. "What are you doing?"

"The power," Sylvie murmured. "There is so much power here."

Suddenly in front of them, just at the edge of the deep pool of water, a group of stones rose up in the air and hovered over the water. Red, blue, white, orange, and pink shades caught the reflection of the sun and spread an array of color up and over the water.

"Oh, no," Jax gasped next to her.

Voices called out from the trees as a group of villagers emerged, Elise and Eva among them. Sylvie hardly paid them any attention as she gaped at the colors of the stones. They were beautiful—and so powerful.

"Sylvie," Elise called out. "Let the gemstones go. We'll help you."

"Those are sacred," said a man that Sylvie surmised, based on his looks, was Elise and Eva's father. "You have no right. And Jax, you should know better too. What are you doing here? You are not allowed at the pools here."

"You scared her with your talk of the ritual and the guardians, Lhoris," Jax said. "She is too powerful to stay here. We need to let her go back to her home."

"You know the rules, Jax," Lhoris said. "No one can leave the island. That's the way it has to be. That's the only way the Stones of Power stay protected. Now bring her to me."

Sylvie watched the exchange between Jax and Lhoris with curiosity. She was so lost, but didn't like the idea of having to stay anywhere. It should be her choice.

"Why are you helping me?" Sylvie asked Jax.

"I…I'm not sure," Jax said, still holding onto one of her hands. "It just seems like the right thing to do. You are not meant to be here. It was an accident."

"What about you?"

Jax shook his head. "I don't have a choice."

"We all have choices, Jax," Sylvie said. "Even you. I can tell there is a difference between you and them. You don't belong here either."

Jax's face twisted in frustration. His lips held tight as they both watched the small group of people move closer to the edge of the water.

"Are you sure?" Jax whispered beside her.

Sylvie nodded her head but didn't say anything as Jax dropped her hand and moved slowly toward the stones that were still floating above the water.

"No, Jax," Lhoris called out and started running through the water toward his nephew. "You know the rules."

The rest of the people came toward Sylvie, but they never reached her. Jax reached his hand out toward an orange stone, then the next thing Sylvie knew, Jax's hand was in hers again and pulling her out of the water and along a winding path. The sounds of yelling faded from her ears and they moved faster than she thought possible, the branches whizzing by their heads and their feet scarcely touching the ground.

They left the trees and came to a stop at the edge of a white sandy beach. Small white waves crashed into the shore and blue water filled her vision for as far as Sylvie could see.

"What just happened?" Sylvie let out a breath of air.

Jax gave her a lopsided grin and held out the stone in front of him on the palm of his hand. "I just used an orange garnet SpeedStone, Sylvie. Now we both have to leave this island as quickly as we can."

CHAPTER FIVE

Sylvie put a hand to her head and tried to will away a growing headache, but it wasn't working. She felt that her life, what little of it she could remember, was spinning out of control. Jax walked down the shore and Sylvie followed him. It was growing hot, and the sand's reflection of the sun was burning her face.

"What is a SpeedStone?" she said, only one of a multitude of questions racing through her mind. "And how do we get off the island?"

"There are a few boats hidden somewhere around here," Jax said, walking toward a bulk of bushes where the sand met the tree line. "I know the villagers use them to meet traders."

Sylvie caught up to him and started searching the foliage for a boat. "How long until they get here?"

Jax laughed. "I have no idea. If they have to walk normally, or even run, I would say we have only thirty minutes or so."

"So the…SpeedStone, as you called it, how…?" Sylvie didn't even know how to ask her question.

Jax scrunched up his face as if trying to figure out how to explain. "Islands like this all over the world house pools and ponds of powerful gemstones. Each stone has special abilities associated with it. Those of us of Elvyn descent, or at least of mixed race"—he scowled at the clarification and Sylvie wondered why—"have been given the responsibility of being guardians over them, and hence also have the ability to use them."

"What about me?" Sylvie asked. "I'm obviously not an elf and I felt them and at least lifted them out of the water."

Jax shrugged his shoulders. "I don't know much about the world out there. But I do know you have wizard powers. Maybe that allowed you to do what you did?"

"Could I use them?"

"I don't know," Jax admitted. "But if we don't find a boat and get away you won't find any answers to your questions."

The two continued looking for another ten minutes. Finally Jax called out to Sylvie from thirty feet away.

"I found them," he said and began pulling away the brush that had hidden them.

Sylvie joined him and saw that there were three small row boats tied together, with a set of oars in each. After a few more minutes they had one uncovered. Jax took out a small knife hanging from his side and sliced a rope that held two of the boats together, then began dragging it toward the water. Sylvie moved behind and started pushing.

As she did so she thought about the power that she had used at the stream and how it had shaken the ground and even cracked a rock. She felt power build up from the ground once again. It seemed to flow into her from the sand, the dirt, and even the water.

"Hey!" Jax jumped to the side. "Watch out."

Before she could stop, Sylvie had pushed the boat the rest of the way effortlessly and now it sat in a few inches of water.

"I see you're learning to control your abilities better," Jax said. "We might need them before this is all done."

Jax motioned Sylvie into the rowboat, pushed it out on the water a bit more, and then jumped in with her.

"Are you sure about this? What about your family?"

Jax's eyes went dark. "My family is shunned and kept to the middle of the island. Lhoris and his people have never treated us well. Elise is the only one that has ever been a bit friendly to me, and as she gets older she'll become like the rest. I've been looking for a chance to get away for a long time."

"But why?"

"The people you met are full-blooded elves. Years ago, they say, two generations before I was born, another stranger came to the island, not of Elvyn blood. He befriended one of the elves and eventually they had a child—a half-blood elf. The child eventually married another elf and had children. At that point, the full-blooded elves separated themselves and vowed to keep their blood pure as it affected their ability to care for the gemstones. I've never liked the arrangement myself."

Yells from the shore stopped his explanation. Running out of the trees were Lhoris and the others—and another man. He had lighter brown hair reaching his waist and shielded his eyes as he looked out at Jax and Sylvie, who were now a hundred feet from shore.

"Jax!" called the new man. "Come back and we can work things out."

"Row faster," Jax ordered Sylvie and started to do so himself.

"Who's that?"

"My father," Jax said. "He doesn't understand. He still thinks it's an honor to watch over the fire pools, but it's just an excuse for the others to keep us away from them. It's a minor task, and my contribution won't be missed. "

"But you've never been off the island," Sylvie said. "We don't even know where to go."

Jax turned and looked behind them. "They're not letting us go easily."

The other two boats from the bushes were now moving toward them. The rowers knew more about rowing that Jax and Sylvie did and were quickly gaining on them. One of them stopped rowing, pulled out a bow, and shot an arrow at them.

Sylvie pushed Jax to the side to avoid being hit but in doing so his oar dropped out of his hands and began floating away from the boat.

"No!" Jax yelled and tried to catch it, but he missed and soon they were past it. The other boats were getting closer and another arrow splashed into the water next to them.

"They could hit us if they wanted to," Jax mumbled. "They're only trying to scare us into turning around."

Sylvie had the remaining oar and moved it from one side of the boat to the other to try and keep going straight, but her arms were not very strong and she soon tired.

"Give me the oar," Jax yelled.

Sylvie handed it to him and watched as he took the SpeedStone out from his pocket. She didn't understand what he had in mind.

"Touch the stone to my leg while I row," Jax said giving her the orange stone. "I'm not strong enough to use it without it touching me."

Sylvie peered down at the beautiful stone. She could feel its power pulsing in her hand and wondered for a moment again if she could access its power. A sound on the pursuing boats shifted her attention back to them. One of the men pulled back on his bow again.

"Now," Jax yelled out. "Hurry and put it against my leg."

With her head facing the back of the boat, Sylvie caught sight of an arrow leaving its bow. She prepared to dodge it if she needed to, but once again Jax used the SpeedStone, this time to turn the oar in the water, and the boat jumped up out of the water for a moment. When it came back down it took off. The speed almost threw Sylvie into Jax, but she hung on with one hand and kept the orange stone on his leg with the other.

Jax rowed like a madman for at least fifteen minutes then dropped his arms and let the oar clunked to the bottom of the boat.

"I can't do anymore right now," he said, clearly exhausted.

Sylvie brought her hand down from his leg. The shore of the island they had left was now too far back for any of their pursuers to do anything about them leaving. They must have covered miles in only a short time.

Jax barked a laugh and Sylvie smiled.

"You did it," she said.

"We did it," said Jax, then his face grew serious as he looked around the empty sea. "But what did we do? Where to now? You have no idea of who you are still or where you were going before the shipwreck, do you?"

"I still can't remember anything," she agreed with a shake of her head. "I know what things are and how to use them, but I can't remember who I am or where I came from."

Jax thought a moment before speaking again. "Well, we know you have powers and we know you are not an elf. If we can get to the mainland we might be able to determine who you are. So, let's row east."

"And which way is east?"

"I think it's that way." Jax pointed straight ahead. "Just let me rest a few minutes and then I'll row again."

Sylvie sat thinking for a moment and wiped the sweat off her forehead. It was getting very hot. "What do we do about food and water?"

Jax scooted back in the boat. Sticking his arm under the last seat he pulled out a small bag. Sylvie gave him a questioning look and he smiled. He opened the bag, reached in, and began to pull out a few items.

"In case the rowers get caught at sea or in a storm," said Jax.

He pulled out a waterskin, a small wrapped package of jerky and dried fish, and finally a smaller, heavier-looking bag. Jax pulled a drawstring open, smiled, and then held it out for Sylvie to see.

"Gold," Jax said. "Looks like they were preparing to buy something on the next trip. Good luck for us."

"Gold…" Sylvie murmured. "I know what gold is. It's used to buy things."

"Well, hopefully it's enough," Jax said.

For the rest of the day Jax took turns rowing and resting. Sylvie had asked once if she could help row, but Jax wasn't sure that was a good idea. He didn't know how the gemstone would react with whatever other abilities she had. Sylvie was disappointed but understood.

As daylight began to wane they saw a landmass in the distance. They were about to use the Speedstone again, but a ship, quite a bit bigger than their own, came into view heading in their general direction. With a few waves of their arms they alerted the ship to their presence and soon it pulled up next to them.

A stern-looking man glared over the edge at them. "What are you two doing out here?"

"We got lost," said Jax before Sylvie could say anything.

The man huffed, but then motioned for another to lower a rope to them and one by one they climbed up the rope and into the ship. A sailor secured their boat to the side.

"Good thing we came along when we did," said the man. "You don't want to be caught in the straits during the night. Tides will pull you all over the place."

Sylvie didn't understand what he meant, but she nodded her head. "Thanks."

"My name is Anders," said the man. He was tall and muscles bulged through his thin shirt. His hair and beard were a medium brown, and his hazel eyes were kind. "We're sailing from Raleez to West Port in Arc. We're not stopping anywhere in between and if you stay on board you have to pull your share of work."

Sylvie felt lost still and a few stray tears filled her eyes.

Anders, taking her bewilderment for fear softened his gaze. "Ah, don't worry, miss. Nothing bad will happen to you out here. My crew's all upstanding men." He glanced around and caught a few of his crewmembers' eyes. "Right, men?"

They all nodded their agreement.

"By the looks of your blonde hair and fair skin," Anders said looking at Sylvie, "you're headed to the Kingdom of Arc anyway, I would guess."

Sylvie just nodded her head in agreement. "Arc."

Anders appeared puzzled and then turned to Jax. "She doesn't seem to talk much."

"Been out on the water a long time," Jax said.

That seemed to appease Anders. "But I can't place where you are from, son. Got a strange accent. By the look of you, part Elvyn I would say."

Jax's face grew red and his lips tightened.

Anders held up a hand in the air as if to stop any retort from Jax. "No judgement here, young sir. It's supposed to be lucky to have an elf on board. And I say half luck is better than none at all." Anders laughed at his own joke and Jax appeared to relax.

After shouting at his crew to get back to work, Anders led them farther into the ship and to a small storage room.

"There's not much room left on board—all full of goods I'm delivering to Arc, but there's a few blankets and you can sleep here tonight. Now, what are your names? I can't call you Arc and Elf." Anders laughed again.

Sylvie joined in the laughter; it felt good. She was beginning to like the captain of the ship. And Arc was as good a place to go as any if that was where he thought she was from.

"I'm Sylvie and this is Jax," Sylvie said.

"Well then, Sylvie and Jax," Anders said while patting a doorway, "welcome to the Rapid Rose. The quickest ship on the western seaboard and named after my beautiful daughter."

With the introductions out of the way, Anders showed them around the ship, then returned them back to the storage room.

"Two days to port, my new friends," Anders said as he left them with instructions for a few chores before dinner.

CHAPTER SIX

After their evening meal, Anders informed them that they would be dropping anchor for the night and would go through the straits in the morning. Pointing to his right he said, "That's the Kingdom of Cyrene over there. Most of their people live in Hasari, their capital, and the rest are scattered around on farmlands. They raise a lot of sheep and cattle there. Wouldn't mind settling down there someday; got some proper rivers for fishing."

Sylvie didn't hear much after Hasari was mentioned. A memory pricked in the back of her mind, but she just couldn't seem to grab hold of it. Next thing she heard, Anders was talking about the land to their left that had been growing bigger for the last few hours.

"Now that's the Isles of Vorwyth. It's rumored that pirates live there. If you sail too close to it, they sneak up on you in the middle of the night, climb on board, and steal your food and such," Anders said with a shake of his head. "And then they leave a bag of money for your trouble. I've been sailing these waters for ten years and never seen them. I think it's all just a myth. Can you imagine someone stealing your goods and then leaving you money for it?" He shook his head. "I don't think anyone lives out on those islands if you ask me."

Jax turned his eyes toward Sylvie and she shook her head not to say anything. Was that what Lhoris and his people did to survive? Stole from others? But if they left money, then they weren't all that bad. She didn't know what to believe.

Lying down that night in a corner of the storage room Sylvie fell asleep within a few heartbeats. The gentle rocking of the ship was a comfort to her and she felt any uptightness and difficulty from the day ease out of her.

* * *

Sylvie was awakened by a not-so-gentle rocking of the ship. Her stomach lurched and she hoped she wouldn't get sick.

"Jax," she said, gently pushing him. "Jax, wake up."

He lifted his head and pushed back his long hair out of his face. "What?"

"Something's wrong," Sylvie said.

Jax opened his mouth to argue, but then the ship rocked again and he understood her meaning. They got up and walked out into the narrow hallway. They had to jump back in their room to keep from being rolled over by crewmen running down the hallway. Once they passed, Sylvie and Jax followed them up the short stairs and to the deck of the ship.

By the light outside, it was an hour away from dawn, and what little light would normally be there was covered by thick gray clouds. The ship swayed again and Sylvie fell into Jax, who only stayed upright by grabbing hold of a wooden pole. Looking up, they both saw the mainsail going back up.

"You two should not be up here," shouted Anders, coming closer to them. "This storm will be a bad one—quick but bad. We're going to try and get through the straits before the worst of it hits us. May not be the smartest thing to do, but

I don't want to be holed up here all day. My products need to get to Arc on time. I am known for my quick deliveries."

He shooed them below but then was quickly on his way to the other side of the ship to bark orders at his men. The two of them didn't heed his warning, but tried to stay out of the way. Neither was keen on sitting in a small storage room without any windows while the ship rocked around. Finding a small place under an overhang, they sat down together with their backs against a cabin wall.

The wind was blowing from the other side of the ship, so for the moment the two were sheltered. Once the rain hit, though, it would be a different story. They sat silently watching the crew run around.

"So you're from someplace called Arc?" Jax finally said. "Sounds like a funny name to me."

"And your people are pirates," Sylvie said with a hint of a chuckle.

"I don't believe it," Jax said, but not with a lot of conviction.

"Don't worry," Sylvie said. "I won't tell."

Jax grunted, but then smiled. "Are we crazy for doing this, Sylvie? I mean, you can't remember anything and I know nothing about the world out there."

Sylvie didn't answer. She really had no answer for him. Without her memories, she didn't know if this was a crazy thing to do or not.

Soon, the ship was underway and they watched as they grew closer and closer to the strait. Land rose up on both sides of them and the water grew rougher. It started to rain and the two stood up to go back inside when a crack of lightning lit the sky and then struck the top of the mast.

"Fire!" yelled a crewman.

"Let the sail go!" shouted the captain.

A crewmember began to argue but the captain gave the order again. "Let it go now before it catches the other sails on fire!"

Ropes were cut with a small hatchet and soon the sail went flying through the air. Eventually, the fire was snubbed out by the wind and rain. Now, though, they only had two smaller sails to keep the ship upright—and going forward and it didn't look like they were going to be very successful at it.

Sylvie stood next to Jax and shut her eyes for a moment as if listening to something. The wind, waves, and rain seemed to call to her. Without thinking, she stepped out from the small overhang and headed toward the bow.

"Sylvie!" called out Jax over the growing tumult as he grabbed her hand and pulled her back. "We need to get below."

"No, I can help," Sylvie said, feeling that somehow she could but still not knowing how.

The ship twisted to the side as the tide and current began carrying it through the strait sideways.

"It's gonna roll!" cried out one of the crewmen.

"Steady on the sails, men!" Anders bellowed. "Stay the course!"

But Sylvie tended to agree with the crewmember. The ship was moving almost sideways, and with each wave men were tossed back and forth, unable to hold on. Sylvie grabbed onto a railing with one hand and Jax with the other.

"I need to see where we're going better," Sylvie said.

Jax glared at her a moment, then nodded his head and pulled her along with him. They moved slowly from pole to bench to railing, grabbing hold of anything they could as they moved down the ship.

"Hey, you two," cried out Anders with anger. "I told you to get below!"

They needed the ship back straight before they crashed. They were too close to the high cliffs on the shore and moving sideways through the water.

"Hold me steady," she told Jax as she lifted up her hands into the air.

She felt Jax's arms around her waist. As his warm breath touched the back of her neck, a tingling sensation went down her spine. Jax held both of them against the railing and she turned her attention to the weather around her. She emptied her mind and felt the power grow within her. She almost felt giddy with delight as she drew power from the wind, the clouds, the rain, the waves, and reaching farther out, from the land on both sides of them. To the west she felt a different power from Vorwyth—*the gemstones!*—but she turned her attention away from them, as she didn't feel right about using their power.

In the back of her mind, she heard a whisper telling her to relax and become one with the wind and water. And she did. It was wonderful and beautiful. The wind carried such power with it, but it didn't have any direction, no consciousness—so Sylvie gave it some. She became the wind and took control of it. She now floated over and around the ship and saw the billowing black and gray clouds.

She spoke to the wind and told it to turn the ship back straight. She pulled wind from one side and pushed it from the other until she felt—and then saw—the ship turn forward, facing through the strait.

Now she gathered power from the water beneath her, smoothing the waves in front of them while pushing them off to the side, and then, from the back of the ship she pushed it forward.

"Sylvie, be careful," Jax said in whispered awe.

Sylvie opened her eyes and looked behind the ship. A cresting wave was coming up fast—she had made it too big. With a pull from her hand in the air she beckoned the wind instantly to her command and pushed back on the growing wave. The ship bumped and lurched, but stayed steady, then surged forward and directly through the narrow strait.

Sylvie sensed the building power of the beginnings of a lightning strike. With both fists up in the air she grabbed the tip of the strike and—

Her intent was to throw it away from the ship, but the amount of raw power in the lightning sent a roar of pain through her body and she yelled out. It overwhelmed her for a moment, and it was all she could do to push it just to the side of the ship. The air crackled with an instantaneous *boom* of thunder causing everyone on board to jump.

The ship lurched and Sylvie felt herself sliding to the deck. Jax somehow kept her standing, but her power was gone.

She felt empty and hollow inside, where only moments before she had been one euphoric combination of wind, rain, water, and air. She struggled to stay upright—she wanted to see this through.

"Look!" Jax pointed ahead. "We're almost through it."

The rain lessened and blue sky poked through the fading clouds. The ship was still moving faster than it should have been moving on its own, the force of Sylvie's wave behind them that Sylvie had created still propelling them to safety.

The wind died down and for a moment there was only the residual splash of the sea against the hull of the ship—then a loud handclap sounded. Sylvie straightened up and twisted in Jax's arms, though he still held a hand behind her back and one on her elbow. The captain walked toward them with a huge grin on his face as his claps grew louder. Soon the entire crew joined him in applause followed by a fair share of whooping and hollering.

"You didn't tell me you were a wizard, Sylvie," Anders said with a broad smile. "That's even better than having a lucky elf on board." He bobbed his head at Jax. "No offense, of course."

"None taken," Jax said, his own smile beaming across his face.

"That was the most amazing thing I have ever witnessed in all my days at sea," Anders continued. He patted Sylvie's shoulder. "I am in your debt. If you ever need a ship or a crew, we are yours."

Sylvie felt slightly self-conscious with all the attention and a bit lightheaded. She swayed a moment, but Jax was at her side to hold her up.

"I don't really know where that came from," she said weakly. "Who am I?"

"Someone quite amazing I would guess," Jax said, with a light blush creeping up his cheeks.

Sylvie didn't know how to take it all in. What she did had been amazing—and by the reactions of others very rare, but she really didn't know how she did it. She had only acted on instinct.

Were there others like her? Were people really this powerful? It boggled the mind. She had controlled the weather.

"What if I was a bad or evil person?" she said with a soft voice. "With all this power, I could do a lot of things.

"I don't believe you were a bad person," Jax said.

"Neither do I," Anders added. "Now, why don't you get below and get some food and some rest? We should have smooth sailing the rest of the day and will be in Arc by tomorrow morning, thanks to you. Don't worry about any chores—you've earned your fare many times over."

Sylvie agreed with both the food and rest. She was famished and exhausted. But she worried about what would happen when they landed on shore. What was awaiting her in the Kingdom of Arc?

CHAPTER SEVEN

The next morning Sylvie and Jax stood at the front of the ship as it was escorted to a slot in the docks at West Port. Jax stood silently as he surveyed the mass of people and ships around them. Sounds of gulls squawking overhead, captains yelling commands, and dock workers carrying goods to and from ships filled the air with a din that made it hard to think. He had pulled his long hair back with a band; Sylvie thought he appeared quite handsome as he stood at the railing surveying the port.

The day had dawned clear and sunny and the water lapped gently against the shore. Behind the docks, a city sprawled along the coast, bisected by a blue river that poured its water into the bay. There weren't many trees and most of the houses were built out of rock or brick with only a few taller than two stories high. Off to her left Sylvie could see a range of mountains fading into the distance. The air here was much drier than on the island where Jax was from.

"Are you all right?" Sylvie asked, concerned by how quiet Jax was.

He shook his head a few times before turning to her. "It's so big. So many people. I...I...knew there were others in the world but could never guess there were this many."

"This many what?" came Anders' voice from behind.

"People," Sylvie answered for Jax.

Anders' laugh came out as a loud boom. "Oh, West Port is a decent size for a port city up north, but you should see Raleez down south in Solshi, or even Margarid in Quentis. They make this look like a small village. Where are you from, anyway?"

"Nowhere," Jax mumbled and Anders didn't push it.

Sylvie wiped sweat off the back of her neck. It was going to be a hot day. The crowds of people didn't seem to bother her as much as Jax. She supposed that wherever she had been from, she had seen this many people before. And as luck would have it, many of them had light hair and skin similar to her own. Could this be her hometown?

Soon their ship was tied off and they prepared to disembark. Jax put a smile on his face that Sylvie could tell was partially forced.

"I suppose you'll be heading to the Wizard Conclave," said Anders.

Both Sylvie and Jax gave Anders a questioning look. She didn't understand what he was saying.

"Wizards Conclave?" Sylvie felt so confused. "What's that?"

Anders burst out laughing. "Oh my! I'm not sure what you two are running from…"

"What makes you say we are running from anything?" Jax interrupted.

Sylvie noticed him rolling something around in his hand. The sun caught a corner of it and she realized it was the SpeedStone. She didn't understand how they worked, but she could surmise the value of something like that. Even as a normal gemstone it would fetch a hefty price.

Anders put his hands up in the air to placate the two of them. "Look," he said politely. "I can tell when two young people are in trouble. I haven't asked what you are involved in and I won't. It's none of my business. And you were mighty helpful during that storm. I meant what I said about owing you."

A line of men carrying crates of merchandise began filing onto the ship and the captain pulled the two of them to the side. Sylvie slapped Jax's hand with the stone and he got the point. He put it back in a pouch and into a secure pocket in his clothes—clothes that after a few days at sea were not looking much better than her own.

"With that power you have," Anders spoke carefully and quietly, "you'd better be careful. Arc is accepting of wizards like most kingdoms around here now, but there are always those that will want to do away with you or use you for their own doings. There's been trouble brewing the last little while all up and down this coast, they say. Someone's causing trouble. If you're a part of that, I wish you good luck."

Jax peered over at Sylvie, but she just shrugged her shoulders. She was as lost as he was.

"Either way," Anders said, "the Wizard Conclave is where they train wizards around here and it's as good a place as any to find what you are looking for."

Sylvie relaxed a bit when she realized that Anders really was trying to help them. "You're a good man, Anders."

He smiled and scratched his beard in embarrassment. "Just be careful, you two."

A dock master came on board and Anders excused himself to take care of business.

"You ready?" Sylvie asked Jax.

"Of course," Jax said. "Why wouldn't I be?"

Sylvie chuckled and grabbed his hand and pulled him along off the ship and onto the docks. She felt him stiffen next to her as the crowd grew thicker around them, but, to his credit, he continued walking and didn't outwardly appear to be worried.

The people here were varied in appearance. Although predominantly light skin and blond or brown hair prevailed, there were enough brown and even darker-skinned people that Jax didn't stick out. Soon, they were off the main docks and onto a bayside street lined with shops and offices that serviced the harbor. A few street vendors tried to grab their attention as they hocked their wares, but the two of them walked right by.

Coming to a street corner, Sylvie saw a small contingent of men walking down a side street headed in their direction. They were uniformed and their faces stern. Jax pulled Sylvie behind a building before they got too close.

"I don't like the way they look," Jax said.

Sylvie agreed. They were different from the rest of the dock people. Peeking around the corner of the building, she saw the group of eight men, all with medium-brown skin, dark brown hair, and crisp blue uniforms. A sword hung at the side of each man.

"We've been here a week, Captain," said one of the men, "with no sign of the girl."

"The king gave his orders," said another man, eyes peering carefully around the crowds.

Sylvie slid back behind the corner before they looked in her direction. Her heart began pounding and she didn't know why.

"I don't like the man our king was with," said a third man as they passed by the corner where Sylvie and Jax stood.

If the guards turned in their direction they would be seen for sure. She pulled Jax toward the door of the nearest shop, opened it, and stepped inside.

"What was his name again?" said one of the guards as the door began to close behind Sylvie and Jax.

"Gamal," came the reply. "Master Wizard Gamal."

The door closed and she missed the remaining part of the conversation, but something about the man's name was familiar. Something resonated with her deep inside and she felt the stirrings of her power. She gulped and closed her eyes briefly, and tried to get it under control, but the ground shook a little in response to her power and she stumbled into Jax.

"Are you all right?"

"Yes," Sylvie lied, her heart thumping hard. "I'm fine."

A man in the small store had grabbed onto the edge of a shelf and looked around with surprised eyes.

"What was that?" he said. His hair was the color of Sylvie's, but hung a bit longer than hers, down over his shoulders. He was in his forties or so and wore a colorful and—Sylvie guessed—stylish outfit of loose silk pants that ballooned out from his sides and tightened at the ankles. His shirt was also loose and he wore a colorful vest over it.

"What do you mean?" Sylvie tried to control the shaking she had caused.

Voices outside the shop were raised, and peeking through racks of clothes and two mannequins in the window, she saw the guards had stopped walking. She had a bad feeling about them and moved closer to the back of the store, pretending to look around at the men's wares.

"It's a clothing shop," said Jax, his jaw open as he turned around in a complete circle. "I've never seen so many clothes in my entire life."

"Now, listen here, you two," said the shop owner. "I don't want any trouble. You don't look like you can afford what's in here. So run along."

Jax just shrugged and moved toward the door, but the guards were still outside. They seemed to be looking for someone. Sylvie turned back to the man, took one of his hands in both of hers, and improvised.

"Sir, we are so sorry to bother you." Sylvie tried to pull herself up as tall as she could. "We just came off my father's ship and are only here for a few hours. We heard your shop made the best quality clothes on the block."

"You did?" the man said, looking skeptical, but also beginning to look somewhat pleased at the compliment.

"Now, I know we aren't much to look at, but we've been on a ship for a few days…dreadful things, if you must know. We would be happy to pay you well for your assistance as long as you close the shop while we are here."

Now the man did look suspicious. He peered out the window and must have seen the guards, because when he turned back his face had turned darker.

"Are you two in trouble with the law?" he asked. "Now, I'm not a fan of those guards from Cyrene being here—they've got no business in our land, but I don't want any trouble either."

Sylvie reached into a pocket and pulled out their pouch of gold. She had no idea what she could buy with it, but it had to be able to get them something. As she opened it she turned away from the man and motioned for Jax to pull the blinds and lock the door.

Before she had even opened the bag, Jax was standing next to her again, and the room had grown darker.

"How…?" the shopkeeper said as he turned back toward the window and door.

"He's fast," was all Sylvie said, shooting Jax a look. He had used the SpeedStone.

He just smiled at her and moved up next to her. "It seems like the good man here doesn't need our gold."

"Gold?" said the man, turning his attention back to the bag that Sylvie now held open in front of him. He squinted down and his face went white.

"Too much?" asked Sylvie.

The man tried to stutter a response but couldn't get anything out. Jax reached into the bag, pulled out two golden coins, and set them on a counter.

"What can we get for these?" Jax said to the man.

"What can you get for these?" the man repeated, clearly surprised. Then he laughed. "You two are quite the jesters, aren't you?" Then, turning to Sylvie, he said, "Does your daddy know you have all that gold there? I don't want some ship captain coming and telling everyone that I ripped him off and took his gold." He took one coin and placed it back in the bag and then held up the other one. "For this I'll get you each two outfits and a pair of shoes…best you've ever seen."

"We have a long journey to make," said Sylvie, thinking about the Wizard Conclave. But then she remembered the story of being the daughter of a ship's captain and quickly tried to amend her statement. "I mean on the ship. I want sturdy clothes and shoes."

The man laughed again and glanced once more toward the front window of his store, now dark with drawn blinds. "Well, come on in the back. I have a few things already made that I can alter for you. I'll be missing business with you two in here it seems, so let's get going."

He headed through an opening and Sylvie and Jax followed. He came up next to her and leaned in and whispered, "That was fun."

"This is not a game, Jax," Sylvie said. "Those guards were looking for me. Did you see their swords?"

Jax frowned. "And why do you think they were after you? Who are you, really, Sylvie?"

Sylvie shrugged. The answer was always the same. "I really don't know. But based on how I look, it seems like the Kingdom of Arc is where I should be."

The man began to dig through some clothes. "You want a dress or pants and shirt?" he asked Sylvie.

"Pants," she said.

"Shame," the man said as he pulled out a beautiful long dress. It was blue cotton—a color she instantly became drawn to. It had laces up the front and was tight around the waist, and then flared out with a slit running part of the way up one side.

Sylvie knew it wasn't serviceable for traveling overland, but…

"Take it," Jax said.

"What?"

"Take it," he repeated. "It will look nice on you. A bit more coin won't hurt."

Sylvie wasn't sure if either of them truly knew the value of the coins they had, but she did really like the dress.

"Yes, I'll take it along with the other things," she told the shopkeeper.

He smiled and began rummaging through the rest of the clothes, pulling out different options from time to time to hold up to Jax or Sylvie. After a few additional measurements, a small pile of clothes sat on a chair in the middle of the room.

"Give me an hour and I'll have it all ready."

Sylvie and Jax looked at each other. They didn't know where else to go and she didn't want to go out front and face the guards again. Next time, she might not be so lucky in escaping them.

The shopkeeper sighed and motioned them toward a back door. "You can go out here. Turn left and go down three doors. Open it up and call for Jacques. He'll fix you up a tasty meal."

CHAPTER EIGHT

The day had started off sunny and warm and Kyril figured that they could ride quite far before sunset. They began descending into a small valley with the southern tip of the Superstition Mountains to their right. Kyril was riding out in front, with Joelle and Hasani following. They rode side by side with Joelle asking questions and Hasani doing his best to answer. Kyril smiled at the conversation. Hasani definitely had more patience than he did with Joelle's chattering.

Holding to the rear of the group was Bale. He called it the "defensive position"—a role he proclaimed he had to take on with the three inexperienced wizards. The fact of the matter was that in his recent adventure to the Realm, Kyril had done more traveling than Bale had done. But he let the man play his part. He was the only non-wizard in the group.

Without warning, a rumbling of thunder was heard in the distance, and soon thick gray clouds began approaching from the west.

"I'll scout out a place to find shelter," Bale said as he raced up in front next to Kyril.

Before Kyril could say anything the man moved past him on his tall black horse, its hooves kicking up dirt into his face. Wiping a speck from his eye, Kyril felt the wind picking up. Turning around in his saddle he noticed Hasani's long, multi-braided hair wrapping around his face like small snakes, and

Joelle's hair wasn't faring much better. The ground rose and wound its way around an outcropping of rock and then turned and started back downhill.

Stopping for a moment, Kyril looked out over the grassy plains, and could barely see the small range of mountains that divided Cyrene from the Kingdom of Arc to his left. He wondered what they would find once they arrived at the Wizard Conclave. First, though, they would need to find shelter from the storm moving in quicker than he had thought possible.

"Someone's there." Joelle pointed down the road from them.

Sure enough, three travelers on horseback were riding frantically up the hill toward them. Kyril, Joelle, and Hasani took their horses to the side to allow them to pass. Kyril did a quick look around for Bale but didn't see him. Hopefully, he would find a place for them to escape the brunt of the rain and wind soon.

"You'd better find shelter!" shouted the man leading the three. He motioned his arm toward the storm. "They roll in off the Blue Sea and don't stop until they hit the mountains. We're going to get drenched.

"Pa," said a young man around ten, "look, up there."

All six of them turned their heads toward where the young man pointed. Not too far up into edge of the Superstition Mountains was a dark hole.

"It's the cave, Henry," said the third person, a woman.

"So it is," said Henry. "Good eye, Remi." He then turned to Kyril's group. "There's room for all of us if we hurry."

A little annoyed at having missed the cave themselves, Kyril gave one last look around for Bale, and then nodded his head to Henry. Joelle opened her mouth, obviously to ask about their friend, but for some reason Kyril didn't want to mention him and gave a shake of his head to Joelle. She knew him enough to not make a scene, but she was obviously not happy.

On the way up a narrow animal trail there wasn't much conversation. It took all their concentration to maneuver the rocky path with their horses. Kyril found out that the woman, Amie, was Henry's wife. They had been living in Arc with her family for a while. They seemed like pleasant enough people and so Kyril followed them, with Joelle and Hasani pulling up the rear.

The rain began before they got to the cave and the ground became slippery but Henry continued leading them up.

"We've been here before," explained Remi, who rode directly in front of Kyril. "We traveled to Gildan to meet my grandparents a few years ago and the same thing happened. The cave is warm and dry. We'll be safe."

Kyril nodded his head. But a moment later, Remi's horse stumbled and slid sideways on the mud. Remi fell from his horse, grunting hard as he hit the ground. While he was trying to roll to safety, lightning flashed and the horse spooked and went wild-eyed. In its attempt to run, it stepped on Remi's leg. The sound of bone crunching was followed by a loud wailing.

"Henry!" called out Amie.

Henry stopped and turned around. His face immediately fell as he saw his son on the ground writhing in pain, blood oozing from his smashed leg.

Kyril jumped from his horse and made his way over to the boy. He had begun shaking violently.

"He's going into shock," Joelle said, joining Kyril next to the boy. "Hold him still," she said to Kyril before bending over him.

Henry kneeled down on the other side of the boy, while Hasani and Amie held the reins of the remaining horses. They reared and wanted to follow the other one, but Hasani spoke some reassuring words to them and they soon settled down.

Henry began to move his hand toward Remi, but Joelle's hand snaked out and grabbed his wrist.

"Hey, what are you doing?" Henry pulled away. "I need to sit him up. I can carry him to the cave."

"I know you think that's the right thing," said Joelle, "but if he sits up right now, too much blood will run down into his leg and he could bleed to death before I can heal him."

"Heal him?" came Amie's voice from the other side of her husband. "You're a wizard?"

"Yes," Joelle whispered and reached both hands over the boy's legs.

Her bronze medallion began to glow and Joelle sucked in a quick breath of air.

"Be careful, Joelle," Kyril said. He knew that Joelle's tendency to want to help everyone made her tempted to access more power than she should—something that the medallions made even easier. Doing so could burn her out and even kill her.

Joelle didn't answer him. Closing her eyes, she placed her hands tenderly on the boy's leg. A bronze glow from the medallion around her neck shot down to her hands, and immediately Remi's leg began to reshape itself—but he passed out in the process.

"You're killing him," Henry said, trying to push her away.

Kyril moved behind him and pulled him back. "Let her do her work."

"But she's too young, she might not know what she is doing," Henry said. "She'll kill him. Let me carry him the rest of the way."

"She's very good," Kyril said. "Watch."

They all stood and watched as the bone reformed and strengthened, then tendons reattached, and lastly new skin grew back over, leaving the leg looking as good as new. Finally, she pulled her hands away and dropped back on her bottom in the middle of the muddy trail.

Remi's leg was healed, but his eyes remained closed.

"He needs to rest," Joelle said.

Henry reached over once again to pick up his son, but looked at both Joelle and Kyril first, his eyes lingering on the medallions hanging from both of their necks. His eyes went round with surprise…and something new entered his gaze. To Kyril it looked akin to greed. Joelle must have noticed also as she stuffed her medallion back under her shirt. He had a hard time tearing his focus away from them.

A gust of wind turned Henry's attention back to his son and the storm. He picked up Remi and stumbled.

"Don't drop him," Amie yelled out and came to Henry's side, but the horses she had been holding bolted away from her.

In the span of a mere moment, Kyril called upon his own medallion, transported downhill in front of the horses, and grabbed their reins. He brought them back up and both Amie and Henry stared at him.

After handing the reins to Joelle and Hasani, Kyril put his hands under the boy. "I'll transport him to the cave. I can see it from here, so it should be fine."

"Should?" said the man, his face growing more suspicious.

"Well," Kyril stumbled, "I'm still kind of new at this."

Henry reached his hands out to grab his son back, but lightning flashed, followed by a very close rumble of thunder. The horses got spooked again and tried to run.

"I need you with the horses," Kyril said. "I'll take care of your son. I promise."

He didn't leave Henry any time to argue and with one look to lock in his destination he transported to the cave. He laid the boy down and then stood at the opening and watched the others complete the rest of their climb. He walked back into the cave a dozen feet and noticed it went back farther than he could see.

Off to one side were a small pile of animal skins and three bundles of dried wood. Kyril rearranged a soft goat skin underneath Remi. By the time he was done the others were arriving in the mouth of the cave. They brought the horses in and tied them off around a heavy stone inside the cave, while Amie fell down on the ground next to her son.

After everyone was settled, Hasani quietly went to work building a fire. After setting the wood in order he brought forth a small spark of magic and lit it.

"So, you're all wizards?" asked Amie. Then, to Hasani, she said, "Where's *your* magic jewelry?"

Hasani shook his head. "I don't have one."

The woman's face fell slightly.

Kyril walked to the edge of the cave, wondering where Bale was. The day had grown darker with the storm clouds and the rain was now coming down in sheets. A rock overhang stopped most of the water from getting inside, but Kyril wiped a few drops of spray off of his forehead.

"He'll be all right," Joelle said from beside him.

"Who?" Kyril asked, noticing that Joelle had her staff in hand. As a healer she enjoyed healing and helping others, but Kyril had also seen her in a fight. She was quite dangerous with the staff.

"Bale," she said. "That's who you were thinking about, right?"

Kyril let out a long breath.

"It's fine to care about him, Kyril," Joelle said. "I know he teased you mercilessly before. But he's changed now."

Kyril grunted. He wasn't sure how much Bale had changed, but he did appear sincere about helping them.

"Are you expecting trouble?" he asked Joelle, eyeing her staff once again.

After a few moments of silence, Joelle lowered her voice. "I don't trust these people, Kyril. Something is going to happen."

"Are you feeling their intentions, or are you just nervous because of the storm?"

"The way they looked at our medallions," Joelle said with a quick glance behind her. "I don't like it."

"But what can we do?" Kyril asked. "We can't go back out in this storm."

"I know. Just be careful."

CHAPTER NINE

Kyril agreed with Joelle's assessment of the situation. Something wasn't sitting right with him either. These days he found himself always having to be more careful. Was there no one he could trust anymore? It was becoming a hard way to live. He supposed, if needed, he could transport Joelle and Hasani back out into the rain.

Kyril and Joelle warmed their hands by the fire, then went to their horses. Taking a brush out of his waterproof pack Kyril began brushing down his horse as he thought about their mission.

Kyril could hear the soft whispers of Henry and Amie behind him, but he tried to concentrate on what he needed to do.

They had two of the three medallions, but Gamal always seemed to be a step ahead of them in sowing chaos. They had to find the third medallion, with Sylvie or not, before he did. There was no telling what Gamal would do with that much power. Unless they found a way to transport there, it would take them at least another three days before they reached the Wizard Conclave. He hoped to find answers there.

The smell of roasted meat made Kyril's nostrils twitch, but before he returned to the fire, he made sure the horses had a few handfuls of oats. They would be able to get more grass on the plains tomorrow.

"Come and share a meal with us," invited Henry.

Amie brought the three wizards sticks of roasted venison, and Kyril took a bite. Juices rolled down his chin and he smiled with delight.

"Mmm, good," Kyril said to Amie. "Thank you very much."

She nodded but wouldn't meet his eyes. She returned to Remi's side, and soon the young boy began to stir. She helped him sit up. For a moment he appeared confused.

"She healed you," Amie said to her son, while pointing at Joelle.

"You mean, she's a wizard?" His eyes grew round.

"They all are," Henry said in a low voice.

Henry's eyes were on Joelle as if he could see the medallion under her shirt. Kyril brought his own hand up to his chest, making sure that his was still tucked underneath his clothes. He was beginning to sense the same trepidation that Joelle had of these people.

Amie began spreading out the additional skins around the fire for each of them. Talk turned to the rainstorm outside with assurances from Henry that it wouldn't last long.

"We'll all be on our way at first light, I'm sure," Henry said. "These storms are fierce but quick."

"Have you traveled much?" asked Hasani. "What brought you on the road this time of year? Summer's a bit hot for traveling."

Kyril smiled grimly at Hasani's questions. He also must have been worried about the newcomers. Travel between Arc and Gildan in the summer was usually only limited to caravans and traders. Spring and fall was more of the time for personal travel.

Henry glanced at his wife before answering. "Going to stay for some time in Gildan with my relatives. Arc's a hard place to live in. We needed a new start."

Hasani nodded his head, but Kyril could tell that the librarian was thinking hard about something. "You don't travel with much," he simply stated, voicing Kyril's own concern.

Henry's eyes grew dark and his brow furrowed.

"We've had a hard life," Amie pipped in. She put a hand on her husband's knee. "Henry was hurt a few years back and couldn't work much. This is a new start for us and our son."

"Can I take a look?" Joelle offered.

Henry shook his head. "No, I'm fine."

"But she healed me, Papa," said Remi.

"I said I'm fine!" Henry stood up suddenly and went over to his horses and spent some time rearranging something. "We should settle down for the evening. I'm riding out as soon as the sun is up."

Kyril caught a look from Joelle who was sitting on the other side of Hasani. Her eyes were round and she glanced around nervously. She put her hand to her medallion and moved it back inside her clothes.

Henry came back to the fire and threw some powder on it causing it to flare and crackle for a moment before settling down. Soon a sweet, fruity aroma began to fill the cave.

"Incense," Hasani said. "It is used to help people relax and sleep better." He yawned and settled himself down on the skins.

"Yes, it will help you sleep well tonight," Henry agreed. "We should all get some sleep.

"But why did Hasani tire so quickly?" Remi wondered out loud. "*I'm* not tired."

"Hush, boy," Henry said.

"Just lie down, Remi," Amie said, "and stop talking."

Yes, why *did* Hasani tire so soon? wondered Kyril to himself. But before he could finish the thought, he too was yawning and lying down himself. It had been a long day of riding.

"I guess I'm more tired than I thought," Kyril said.

"Kyril!" Joelle called out weakly from a few feet away. "Kyril, they're going to take our medallions."

Joelle's voice pushed through Kyril's foggy mind. He could feel her urgency, but he just couldn't keep his eyes open. He was so tired. He brought a hand to his chest to make sure the medallion was safe and immediately fell asleep.

***

Kyril heard whispering before he opened his eyes. He tried to sit up but found his feet and wrists were bound, with the latter behind his head. His mind was still foggy and he fell back asleep for a while before he became more aware of light around him. He slowly opened up his eyes and lifted up his head a few inches. Both Hasani and Joelle lay next to him, also bound. Amie stood off to one side arguing with Remi, while Henry was closing a pack on his horse.

Joelle groaned and lifted her head. Confusion spread across her face before her eyes went wide with fear.

"My medallion," she whispered. "It's gone."

Kyril mentally checked for his as well. "Oh no, not again," he groaned. The emperor and so many others counted on him to stop Gamal and bring balance back to magic, but he seemed to keep getting his medallion taken from him. He shook his head at the failure he felt once again.

Hasani stirred between them and he blinked a few times before struggling against his bonds.

"They took our medallions," Joelle said to him.

"Ahh, you're awake. Good," Henry said. "It's almost time to leave. I told you we were leaving at first light."

"What have you done to us?" Joelle said. "And where are our medallions?"

Henry's eyes swept across his packed bag. "Safe for now. Now get up." He kicked Kyril in the side with his boot."

"Papa," called out Remi. "Don't hurt them. She healed me."

A moment of hesitation spread across Henry's face at his son's words, but soon he hardened once again and kicked Hasani this time.

"Keep your boy quiet, Amie," Henry said. "These three and their medallions are our ticket to freedom for the rest of our lives."

Kyril struggled with his ropes. "Kind of hard to get up without the use of our feet."

Henry grunted. "If you try and run you won't get far." He patted a sword and a dagger at his hip.

But the three of them still had their wizard powers. Henry would be no match for them. Kyril eyed Hasani and Joelle and tried to get them to understand they could still get away. But Hasani shook his head.

"He's poisoned us," Hasani whispered with a lick of his lips. "Something to take away our powers, if I had to guess."

Kyril tried to summon his powers, but Hasani was correct. It felt a lot like when he'd been imprisoned in the dungeon at the wizard school. He could tell that his powers were there, but he couldn't access them.

Henry laughed. "You're a smart one there," he said to Hasani. "And you are right. A few drops was all I needed to bind your powers."

"Where did you get such a horrible concoction?" Joelle said as Henry loosened the ropes around her ankles. "This is how you repay me for helping your son?"

Before anyone could react, Henry smacked Joelle across her lips, drawing blood. "Shut up and just do what you're told and maybe you'll live. The medallions are worth more than all three of you, but the little extra to deliver you in person won't hurt."

Tears formed in Joelle's eyes, and as soon as Kyril's ropes were loosened he kicked out at Henry and caught him in the knee.

With a loud bellow of pain he cursed and drew his sword and held it at Kyril's throat.

"No, Papa!" Remi said.

Henry grunted and instead used the hilt to hit Kyril hard on the head. Blackness overtook him immediately.

* * *

The next time Kyril awoke, he saw the ground moving by slowly in front of him. His head was pounding and he squirmed to try and sit up.

"Stop moving," came Henry's voice from above him.

"Kyril, are you all right?" Joelle asked.

Kyril tried to twist around but couldn't see her or Hasani.

"If you'll stop moving I'll let you sit up," Henry said, then proceeded to pull Kyril upright from where he'd been flung sideways across the horse.

He took a moment to get his bearings. The sky was clear, and they appeared to be riding in a small valley between the Superstition Mountains and the smaller range that marked the southern tip of Arc. Henry sat behind him on the same horse.

"Keeping you out ensured your friends' cooperation," Henry said. "Do I need to knock you out again?"

"No." Kyril shook his head. He needed to stay alert in order to find a way out.

Joelle sat on a horse with Amie, and Hasani rode with Remi. The two of them seemed to be engaged in a friendly conversation about the wildlife in the air. Kyril shook his head in puzzlement.

"Hasani, are you enjoying yourself?" Kyril said with a bit of sting to his voice.

"Yes, quite well, Kyril," Hasani said with a smile. "I've never had such a grand adventure. There are so many things to learn around here. Did you know that…"

Kyril put his hand up to stop Hasani. He didn't have time for all of this. He needed to stop Gamal. "This isn't a vacation, Hasani. These people have kidnapped us, while we are on a direct mission from Emperor Alrishitar. They will be lucky if they are only imprisoned for the rest of their lives."

"Henry?" Amie said. "Maybe we should let them go. The man only requested that we get the medallions."

"What man?" Kyril was getting more uncomfortable with the situation.

"None of your business," Henry said with a slap to the back of Kyril's head. "Now shut up, all of you. When we get paid for the medallions and the wizards, we will be rich enough to go anywhere."

"But Pa, I don't want to go to prison," whimpered Remi, and he began to cry.

Henry retied Kyril's hands—this time in front of him. With a final warning for the others to not cause any trouble, he pushed the horses harder. The three horses with people jumped out in front with the two others—Joelle's and Hasani's—following behind.

Hours went by without seeing anyone as they rode through the short grass plains of Southern Arc. Periodically they saw groups of trees or a rock formation sticking out from nowhere in particular. Besides that they rode hard and fast farther into the Kingdom of Arc. At least, Kyril thought, they were going in the same direction as their original intent.

The trotting of the horse had lulled Kyril into a semblance of sleep when he was suddenly awakened by something. Lifting his head, he looked around. Racing up from behind them came a lone rider.

"No problems here, you three," Henry warned, "or your friend Kyril gets the end of my dagger." He jabbed Kyril in his lower back to emphasize his point.

Kyril stiffened, not wanting to get poked. At the same time he felt a warming in the palm of his hand—the medallion was close enough for his scar to recognize the power. But where was it? Kyril hoped that whatever poison Henry had given them would wear off quicker for a medallion holder.

At least that was one bit of hope.

The second came only a few moments later, as the lone horseman raced past.

"Good afternoon, gentlemen and ladies," said Bale. His mouth curved up at the corners and there was a glint of mirth in his eyes. "Mind if I ride by you? I'm in a hurry."

Henry waved him on, but Bale paused for a moment.

"Everything all right here?" Bale asked.

"Just fine, son," said Henry.

Kyril prepared himself for Bale to make a move to rescue them. But the opportunity never came.

"Good day, then," said Bale as he moved forward. "Perhaps we'll see each other at the next town."

Kyril couldn't believe it. He jerked his head back to see Joelle and Hasani. Their faces mirrored his surprise. But then, Bale turned around in his saddle and winked. Suddenly, Kyril understood. At least he hoped he did—he still couldn't tell with Bale. There were lingering doubts in Kyril's mind still about the man's motives.

"What was that?" Henry said, pushing the dagger a harder into Kyril's back.

"I'm sure I don't know what you're talking about, sir," said Kyril. "You're the one that has this all planned out so well. Maybe the man just wants to buy you a drink at the next inn."

"And where would that be?" asked Joelle.

"I told you all to be quiet," Henry shouted again. "Just ride. We'll be there before nightfall."

CHAPTER TEN

Without horses and not wanting to spend all their money the first day, Sylvie and Jax now found themselves on the road from the coast to the capital city of Arc. From there, they decided they would go to the Wizard Conclave, where wizards were taught and trained.

Sylvie hiked up her pack a bit on her shoulder. Filled with three changes of clothes, including the soft dress and some food, the pack was already growing heavy. The weather was warm—bordering on hot—and, as they moved farther from the coastal city of West Bay, the air grew drier and the breeze died down.

The roadway was crowded with people, horses, carts, and wagon trains traveling in both directions. Boats sailed up and down, what she learned was, the Saar River—a waterway that flowed from tall mountains to the east, past the capital city, and eventually dumped into the Blue Sea at West Bay.

"Many of them look like you," Jax said.

Indeed they did. About half were blond, and most of the others medium brown hair. Most seemed fit and were tan—most likely a byproduct of traveling on the road. More than once, people, usually children, would stare and point at Jax with comments about his long hair or partially pointed ears.

"What's an elf doing so far from home in this hot waste?" said a rather beefy man, leaning out of his carriage.

"Just traveling to the Wizard Conclave," said Sylvie.

"Ah, magic users you are?" he said, wiping his brow with a white silk cloth. "Why don't you ride with me for a while? I would like to hear your story."

Sylvie's chest beat with panic. She knew they didn't have a reliable story that would pass more than a few questions. And Jax appeared nervous. She was about to tell the man that they were fine when a few of his horsemen riding behind the carriage came out next to Sylvie and Jax.

"I insist," the man said with a flourish of his meaty hand.

"Thank you, sir," Sylvie said, not wanting to cause a scene.

The carriage stopped and the two were ushered inside. The two benches that faced each other were wide enough for at least four people, yet the man was the only one inside. He directed them to the seat opposite him and then motioned his driver to continue. Before saying anything else, he pulled a basket out from under his seat and reached inside. He pulled out a bright red fruit and offered it to Sylvie and Jax.

Jax took it and turned it over in his hands, apparently not knowing what to do with it.

"It's a pomegranate," Sylvie said, the name of the common fruit of the area coming instantly to her. "Here, let me show you." She took a knife from her pack and slit the fruit in half.

Jax's eyes went round as Sylvie held up the red seed-filled halves, one for him and one for her. She proceeded to take out a few seeds and pop them into her mouth.

"Mmmm," she said. She couldn't remember when she had eaten one last, but the taste seemed familiar to her. "Very good." She handed Jax a few.

"I grow them myself," said the man. "But where are my manners? I am Master Elan Flint, merchant of Arc."

Sylvie eyed the interior of the carriage. There was not one tear in the seat or stain on the wood. The armrests were gilded in gold.

"You do quite well," Sylvie said with a smile as she wiped some pomegranate juice from her lips.

Elan shrugged his shoulders and placed his palms out in front of him. "I do like the finer things in life. Now who, may I ask, are my two passengers?"

Jax let Sylvie take the lead once again. "I am Sylvonna, Sylvie for short, and this is my friend Jax. As we said, we are on our way to the Wizard Conclave."

"And which of you is the wizard?" Elan's grin grew bigger.

Both Jax and Sylvie froze for a moment.

"Ah, I see it's Sylvie," Elan said. "I can sense these things."

Sylvie looked at him with surprise, but then he laughed again, his voice booming and deep as it shook his sizable frame.

"I could tell by the way Jax looked at you from the corners of his eye," Elan admitted. "I am no wizard myself. But I have employed a few from time to time. Really very handy to have around. Now, what tricks do you do?"

Sylvie was becoming increasingly uncomfortable with this line of questioning. She peered over at Jax. He had a hand in his pocket. She knew what he was thinking. He wanted to whisk them out of there using the SpeedStone…but for some reason she didn't think that would be a good idea. She gave him a shake of her head and turned back to Elan.

But before she could say anything, loud voices and stomping of horse hooves came up behind them. Master Elan stuck his head out of the window and beckoned one of his riders.

"What is the commotion back there?" he called out. "The dust they are stirring up will dry out my sinuses. See what is happening."

While the rider went to check things out, Sylvie had hoped that Elan would have forgotten his question. But he did not.

"You were about to tell me what you can do," he said.

Sylvie took a deep breath and decided it was better to minimize her abilities. "I'm not so sure—that's why we are going to the Wizard Conclave."

Elan just sat and watched her, but his eyes grew darker. "Don't play with me. You're too old to go to the Conclave as a new student, you travel with an elf, and speak like a wizard. Who are you?"

"I...I..." Sylvie faltered for a bit, wiped a few tears from her eyes, and decided to be honest. "I don't know, sir. I know my name is Sylvie and yes, I do have some wizard abilities, but I was in an accident and don't know who I really am."

Elan silently studied her. The horseman came up to the window again and Elan leaned out to speak to him.

"The Cyrenes are looking for a young wizard from Arc," he said as his eyes flickered inside the carriage. "The young king of Cyrene is offering quite a large reward."

Elan thought for a moment and nodded his thanks, then called out to his driver to pull over up ahead in a small village, down a side street, until they stopped in front of an older inn.

Sylvie's heart was pounding and Jax gave the impression that he was about to bolt.

Elan leaned forward in his seat and waggled his finger at Sylvie. His jowls moved from side to side as he shook his head. "Seems like you've been a naughty girl, young Sylvie. Now what would the Cyrenes be doing looking for you here in the great Kingdom of Arc?"

Sylvie closed her eyes for a moment and wiped a drip of sweat from her forehead as her anger grew. Why was everyone after her? She clenched her teeth and her fists tightened…and then the rumbling began again.

The carriage shook violently. Was Elan trying to destroy them? What was happening?

"Sylvie!" Jax touched her shoulder.

Her eyes popped open and he jumped back.

 "Stop," he whispered.

She realized then that she was the one causing the shaking. She turned to Elan, who was still leaning forward, staring at her. His face was filled with a mixture of awe and fear.

"Sir?" came a voice from outside. "Is everything all right in there? What's going on?"

"We are fine," Elan said without moving his eyes from Sylvie.

Taking a few deep breaths, she unclenched her hands and the shaking ceased. Then the three sat in silence for a moment before Elan spoke.

"I'm an influential man, Sylvie. I own houses in three kingdoms, run trade routes on land and sea, have hundreds of people working for me, and have more gold than I can spend in my lifetime. Some would say I am powerful even…but I've also got an eye for power in others. I would guess that what we just saw was only a fraction of your potential."

Sylvie only nodded, not knowing what was going to happen. Her quakes would draw the men from Cyrene to her once again, she supposed.

"I have a deal for you," Elan offered.

"A deal?"

"We could just go, Sylvie," Jax whispered from beside her. She flicked a quick look at him and saw he was now fingering the orange SpeedStone.

Elan furrowed his brows as he watched the stone roll around in Jax's hand. "Quite a gemstone for you to have there, son. I see both of you may be more than you appear at first. So for my deal: I will get the Cyrenes off your backs and you can travel to the Wizard Conclave."

"And what do you want in return?" Sylvie wondered now what she was getting herself into.

"Aaah, you catch on quickly, young wizard." Elan sat back in his seat. "What do you have to offer?"

Sylvie caught Elan's quick glance over toward Jax and the SpeedStone, but that was not Sylvie's to give—nor would she do so even if it was.

"How about a lucrative trading deal?" Sylvie said.

Elan raised one brow. "I understand you are a powerful wizard, but somehow I seriously doubt you have those kinds of connections, my dear."

"Have you heard of the Rapid Rose?" Sylvie asked.

Elan sat forward on his bench, apparently eager to hear more. "Yes. It's one of the quickest ships on the western sea. It's highly competitive to get cargo on that ship. The quicker our products get to market the quicker we get our money."

"Go to West Port and find Anders," Sylvie said. "Tell him I'm taking him up on his offer."

"Who is Anders, and what offer is this?" Elan said. "Come, now, Sylvie we don't have much time before those men catch up to you. What exactly are you offering?"

"Anders is the captain of the Rapid Rose," Sylvie said. "He owes me for saving his ship. Tell him that you require his services for a month, exclusively."

For the first time since they'd met him, the rich merchant was ruffled and speechless. After a moment, however, he regained his composure.

"I have no love for Cyrene and her young king whose men appear to be looking for you. I have no reason to give you up to them. If what you offer is real, it would be lucrative indeed."

"Enough for you to help us get away?" Jax said. "She is telling the truth, sir."

"Yes. Yes." Elan nodded his head. "I suppose she is. No one would make such bold claims otherwise. Something is going on here in Arc that I don't like. And above all, I am loyal to my kingdom. And I will not see Arc—my kingdom— destroyed by the Cyrenes or anyone else bent on it."

Sylvie had to contain herself from rolling her eyes. He came off as a man more loyal to himself and his own riches than to a kingdom. But she let him talk.

"All I have and all I am is because of our great kingdom here. As a fellow Arcanian, I can promise you that I will help you escape the clutches of these men who are following you."

"Do you really think I am from here?"

Elan laughed hard. "Oh, young wizard, look at your hair and fair skin. Do you know of any other kingdom in the western continent that produces such beauties?"

Sylvie felt her face heat up and turned to Jax.

"What do you think?" She wanted Jax's input. "Do we trust this man to help us get away?"

Jax shook his head. "I do not know your ways, Sylvie. Already I have seen enough to understand the importance of what my people do, though." He hung his head in shame. "I do not deserve for them to ever take me back."

"Oh, Jax," Sylvie said, placing a hand on his arm. "I couldn't do this without you. We'll figure it out."

"How can you be so positive, when you don't even know who you are?" Jax said, bewilderment all over his face.

"Because, I surmise, she is more—much more—than we see here, young elf," Elan said, leaning an ear out the window. "Now, you have a story too, I would suppose, but if I hear right, you need to leave quickly."

As if in response to his words, shouts and the pounding of horse hooves were again getting closer. Elan clapped and a man opened the door for Sylvie and Jax. They stepped out and looked around at the back of the small inn. There weren't many places to hide.

"Go," Elan said. "I will distract them until you get away. I promise you will get to the Wizard Conclave."

The two ran behind a building, then Jax held the SpeedStone out in the palm of his hand.

"I don't know if that's a good idea," Sylvie said. "We don't know where we are going."

Jax wrapped his hand around the stone and a bright orange light escaped through the slits between his fingers.

"She's close by," yelled a man, and dogs began to bark.

Elan's carriage pulled out in front of the men, forcing a collision of horses and carriage. Screams and yells filled the air.

Jax grabbed hold of Sylvie's hand and with a flash, they sped through the streets, past the carriage and the horses, and back onto the main road. Horses, carts, and people flew by in a stream of light as they raced faster and faster. They passed through one village and then another, losing track of time.

"Stop!" Sylvie said, noticing they were coming up too quickly to a significant city—a very large city, and might crash into the city walls.

Jax pulled her off the road as they slowed to a stop, both of them tumbling to the ground. Luckily there was no one around them. Jax lay still, breathing hard, and Sylvie got up on her knees and looked ahead.

Not far from them rose the tall sandstone walls of Arc— the largest city and capital of the Kingdom of Arc. Rising high over those walls were square buildings with tall towers, all in the same sandstone color.

It was beautiful and hauntingly familiar in the setting sun.

CHAPTER ELEVEN

That night, Sylvie and Jax stayed in an inn and she had the first real bath in…well…since she could remember. She was sure she'd had them before, as she couldn't imagine herself *not* having one. She sat in a metal tub and let the hot water soak off the grime that had accumulated since she had left the island. She had instructed Jax to do the same in the men's bathing room. He had been nervous to leave her alone, but she had been adamant about him not being in the same room with her as she bathed. That was not an option.

She leaned her head back, closed her eyes, and thought about Jax. He had been quite amazing to her. She couldn't imagine how he felt in the crowded cities, considering the sparsely populated island he had come from. It was all so new to him, and though he was quiet most of the time, he seemed to be handling it well. Sylvie, on the other hand, felt like she was on the verge of tears at every moment. Oh, she knew she hid it well, but it was so hard knowing things around her, but not really remembering them.

And her magic abilities—well, that's what made her the most afraid. Elan had alluded to the fact that she was very powerful. And it had scared Jax enough to help her leave the island paradise behind. There were so many questions that raced through her head. Most of the time she shoved them aside because there were no answers and only blank holes.

The Wizard Conclave was her last hope. They trained wizards, right? They could help to fix her. Maybe they knew her family or friends. She knew she *must* have them, somewhere.

After a while the water grew cool and she got out, toweled off, and dressed into one of her new outfits. She put on tight blue hose over her legs and a long blue shirt that cinched with a belt at the waist. Then, she pulled on gray boots. She hoped she looked all right. She smoothed down her wet blond hair before packing her old clothes into a pack.

Walking back from the woman's bathing room she met Jax in the common room for a hot meal.

"Feels good to be clean," he said.

"I agree," Sylvie replied. "Now let's eat.

After eating they retired to their room early. They would journey to the wizard school the next day. Even though she was both excited and nervous about what lay ahead, Sylvie fell asleep quickly.

* * *

The road north from Arc to the Wizard Conclave was thick with people. It had already taken them much of the morning to maneuver their way through the bustling, crowded city. As the sea captain had said, it was much bigger than East Bay. Hawkers sold their wares on every street corner, and Sylvie found herself trying a few hot delicacies that made her mouth water.

Outside of the great castle at the edge of the city, few other buildings rose higher than two stories tall. But the sprawl seemed to continue out forever. With desert all around, there were no geographical barriers to curtail the growth of the city.

The river split the city in half, resulting in a dozen bridges connecting the two sides.

Crossing one of the bridges, Sylvie stopped and gazed down. The churn of the river mirrored the feeling inside her. She felt her mind drawn to the water and could sense its power and speed as it washed over pebbles ground to sand over the years.

"Sylvie," Jax said. "What are you doing?"

She peered around and found herself standing on the first rung of the railing. Shaking her head to clear her thoughts, she stepped back down.

"I don't know," she admitted. "The river called to me. I wanted to be part of it."

Jax reached over and took her hand. "Don't think like that."

"Oh, no," Sylvie tried to clarify. "I was not thinking of jumping. It's just that…well, it's hard to explain, but I was almost melding with it—becoming one with the river."

"We need to get you to the Conclave," Jax said. "From what I have heard, there are very powerful wizards there that can probably help you."

Sylvie agreed. After walking over the bridge they finished making their way to the north part of town. They passed through three different walls and gates, signifying the growth of the city over time. Arriving at the last gate, they saw carts for hire lining the road heading to the Wizard Conclave.

One man motioned them over and offered them a ride for a price that Sylvie thought seemed fair.

"It's a deal, I promise you," said the cart driver. "Many of the students go home for the summer, so there is not as much work for us now."

"But the Conclave is still open, right?" Jax asked with a nervous look at Sylvie.

She hoped they hadn't made this trip for nothing.

"Oh, yes!" The man's face brightened as he took their bags and helped them into the cart. "There are students there all year, and…" He leaned forward as if sharing a secret. "If you ask me, you get better training in the summer and more attention from the teachers. I even hear there is a new master there."

"A new master?" asked Sylvie.

"Seems the former headmaster is not feeling well and so a new fellow showed up to help run things," the man said with a shrug. "But what do I know about wizards? I'm just a driver."

The man closed the door to the cart and went up front. Two tan horses began pulling the carriage, and Sylvie and Jax settled in for a trip that they were told would be only an hour.

"What will you do when we get there?" Sylvie asked Jax.

He was sitting opposite her, and in these few moments of relaxation realized how handsome he really was. With a thin face and soft features and a slender—yet toned—build, he looked ready to pounce at any moment. But his smile was big and contagious.

"I'm not sure," Jax said. "The world is so big. Maybe I'll stay there and study for a bit…that is, if they'll let me." His face fell at that.

"Oh, Jax," Sylvie said. "I'll make sure they let you."

Jax laughed. "I'm sure you could. I don't know what they'll think about me…a half-breed elf."

"Don't be so down on yourself. You're a wonderful, caring, and handsome man."

Jax raised an eyebrow at that and Sylvie felt her face heat up.

"Let's just wait and see," Jax said.

Before they knew it, the cart was slowing down. Sylvie pulled back a curtain and leaned out of the window and gasped.

"It's huge!"

Jax joined her, and together they gazed at the Wizard Conclave for the first time. Sturdy stone walls of a dark tan seems to go on forever. Tall buildings three and four stories high rose up inside the walls, and there was an enormous and more ornate building in the center with towers impossibly high. Soon they came to an open gate but were stopped by a guard.

"I think I have a new student for you," said their driver, "and an elf, it seems."

The guard approached and peered inside their window. His fair face grew even paler as he inspected Sylvie. He stuttered a few words of greeting and motioned the cart through the gate. Sylvie watched him lean over and whisper something to a younger man, not much older than Sylvie herself. The man turned in her direction with narrowed eyes and then took off running toward the largest building.

The guard waved for them to continue inside the compound. Sylvie couldn't believe the transition of the grounds from outside the walls to inside. Here, hundreds of palm trees were swaying in the slight breeze. Other plants dotted the landscape intermixed with rock gardens and fountains spewing water. Benches and walkways wound around the garden area and eventually led to the many buildings that surrounded it. Sylvie's heart ached at the sight and tears came to her eyes.

"What's wrong?" Jax asked.

"Oh, nothing," Sylvie said. "Nothing at all in fact. I just feel like my heart is going to burst. I'm just so…so happy. I don't know why, but this place…"

She didn't know how to describe how she felt. Memories seem to fade around the edges of her mind, but nothing clear enough for her to grab onto. And the tears she cried were ones of joy. She knew this place. She didn't know how she did. It was like finding that a place in your dreams actually existed.

"I'm home," she whispered, knowing deep inside the truth to the words.

The driver drove the cart around a curved driveway to the front of the main building and stopped. He opened the door for them and retrieved their few bags from the top of the cart.

"Good luck here, miss," he said to Sylvie, "and to you, sir." He smiled at Jax. "I hear they take real good care of you here."

Sylvie wiped her eyes once again, the dry air taking care of the rest. She stood with bags in hand and looked directly up at the tallest tower. She could almost visualize what it held. Almost.

A door opened and five men and women rushed out. Two were dressed as guards, while the other three wore robes of distinguishing colors: a man in blue, a woman in green, and someone—a broad shouldered individual—came up the middle clothed in a flowing burgundy robe with the cowl pulled up over their head.

The other four appeared to let the one in burgundy take charge. Sylvie noticed they did not smile and stood stiffly as if expecting trouble.

"Welcome to the Wizard Conclave, Sylvonna Hickory," came a low, calm male voice from under the hood. She could just see his shadowed face under the blue hood. "We've been looking for you everywhere, and here you are! Where have you been?"

"Looking for me?" Sylvie asked, remembering the guards from Cyrene that had almost caught them twice. She looked at Jax, who appeared ready to grab his bow and nock an arrow if needed. "You know who I am?"

"Of course we know who you are," the man said, his voice growing harder. "Now stop playing games with me. Where is the medallion?"

Sylvie was totally confused. "I…I…don't know what you mean," she stuttered. "I don't know about a medallion. I was in an accident and don't remember who I really am. I was told that maybe the Wizard Conclave could help me. I…" She didn't know how to say what she needed to. What if she wasn't right? What if they couldn't or wouldn't help her? "I…"

"She's a wizard," said Jax. "And needs help finding out who she is and in controlling her powers."

Sylvie was thankful for Jax jumping in. It didn't seem as strange for someone else to say she was a wizard; she still wasn't completely comfortable with the idea of it.

The man, his hands folded in front of him, peered back and forth between the two and then took a few deliberate steps forward, ending up directly in front of Sylvie. She looked up into his hood and found black beady eyes—and for the first time that she could remember truly felt fear.

Was this how they treated their students? Scare them as soon as they arrived? If so, she didn't know if she wanted a part of it or not.

"Maybe this is a mistake," she said to Jax, then turning back to the man, tried to smile and be polite. "Maybe I don't belong here."

"You really don't remember anything?" the man asked, his voice growing lighter and raising an octave. He clapped his hands together a few times. "Oh, this is rich. Rich indeed."

Sylvie was confused by his reaction and truly didn't know what they should do, but before she could decide, the man waved a hand around the yard of the Wizard Conclave.

"Welcome to the Wizard Conclave," he said. "We will indeed help you to remember who you are and regain control of all your abilities. I have a feeling that you are very powerful indeed."

Sylvie relaxed a little. Maybe the man's hardness earlier was simply because she had not given any warning that she was coming. They were just not expecting her and didn't know who she was. She could understand that.

The man waved the two other instructors to him. "We will all take a personal responsibility in your training. We are the heads of the three disciplines of magic at the Wizard Conclave."

The other two with him didn't appear to be happy, and they now looked at Sylvie as if expecting something from her. But she couldn't imagine what.

"This is Master Wizard Jenessa Caron, wizard of the heart," he said, indicating the woman dressed in green robes. Then he pointed to the man wearing blue. "And this is Master Wizard Larue Vallette, wizard of the earth."

The man gave Sylvie a nervous smile and a nod of his head. Sylvie felt an immediate kinship for the man and smiled back. Maybe it wasn't going to be such a bad place after all.

The man who had been speaking pushed the hood back from off his face. His coloring was darker than the other two instructors, and his head was bald. A red birthmark appeared to pulse on the side of his forehead. He smiled broadly, but it was more predatory than cordial.

"And I am Master Wizard Gamal Turomi, wizard of the mind and currently High Wizard of the Wizard Conclave," said Gamal with a flourishing bow and tiny grin.

"Acting High Wizard," said Larue in a low voice.

Gamal shot him a dangerous look, and Sylvie wondered what she had walked into.

CHAPTER TWELVE

Sylvie and Jax were each escorted by first-year students to smaller buildings on either side of the main building. Jax appeared nervous, but he told Sylvie not to worry and that he would see her shortly at the next meal.

The building that housed the students was not very crowded, a point emphasized by the pleasant young girl, Malea, who showed her to her room.

"Summer is a great time to be here," Malea said with eyes both bright and full of excitement. "We all get our own rooms. You'll love it here, I'm sure."

Sylvie was glad for the privacy of her own room, but worried about the lack of friends or companions. She was not used to being alone.

"How long have you been here?" Sylvie asked. She felt lost and wanted to know something—anything—about the school.

"Only since the first of the year," Malea said.

"And have you enjoyed it? Are they helping you with your abilities?"

"Well, my abilities are new," Malea said with a small frown. "And most of what we do is sit in classes, listen to lectures, and read books. They don't let us practice much yet."

Sylvie didn't like that. She wanted to figure out what she could do. They arrived at a room and Malea led her inside. "And the teachers, are they nice?"

"Most of them yes, but…" Malea poked her head out the bedroom door and then back in again before continuing. "But…things have changed recently. You met Master Gamal?"

Sylvie nodded.

"Well, he makes everyone nervous," Malea said. "No one has seen High Wizard Danijela for days. He says she is very sick."

"But you don't believe him?" Sylvie asked.

Malea shook her head but didn't say anything out loud.

The young student carried one of Sylvie's packs over toward a table upon which a small washbasin sat. But right as she went to set it down, she tripped and the pack hit the table, knocking the porcelain washing bowl off of it.

Without thinking, Sylvie stretched her hand out and the bowl came to halt in the air about an inch above the floor. With another wave of her hand she brought it back to the table. How had she done that? This was one of the first times she had been able to perform magic intentionally.

Malea gasped. "You can't do that!"

"Do what?" Sylvie took her pack and laid it on a simple single bed. Besides the washbasin and the bed, a small wardrobe and a desk filled the room up. A window was above her bed and looked out on the rock garden they had passed on their way in.

"You can't do magic without permission," Malea explained. "That's the rule for first years."

"But it would have broken," Sylvie said.

Malea shook her head. "It doesn't matter. It's the first rule."

"Am I a first year, then?"

"Have you been here before?"

"I don't know," Sylvie answered honestly. She still couldn't remember her life before Elise and Eva had found her and nursed her back to health. But even after a few hours at the Wizard Conclave she felt a sense of connection. "I had an accident and can't remember anything."

"Oh," Malea said with a surprised look. A bell sounded off in the distance. "Oh, it's time for class. I guess you can come with me today, then after they test you, you'll get your own schedule for whatever discipline you are in." Her eyes took in the wash basin that Sylvie had saved from being broken. "But I surmise you're already ahead of me."

Sylvie followed her dutifully and met with the flow of others in the great building as everyone headed toward their classes. Sylvie felt out of place—she was the only one without a burgundy, green, or blue cloak. Entering her first classroom, Malea went to what Sylvie assumed was her assigned seat and Sylvie hung back in the rear of the classroom and took an empty chair there.

The teacher walked in, greeting each student, without noticing Sylvie in the back. Once she came to the front of the classroom she turned around and noticed Sylvie.

Her eyes bugged out behind her glasses and she appeared to take a few deep breaths to steady herself.

"We have a new student with us today," she said through tight lips. "Master Gamal has…"

"You mean High Wizard Gamal?" piped up a male voice from the far side of the room.

Sylvie looked over and saw a young man about the same age as Malea. She thought he looked at least four years younger than herself, even though she didn't have any idea how old she really was. The young man stood up. He had light brown hair, fair skin, and brown eyes, and wore a burgundy cloak over his clothes. His smug expression appeared to irk the teacher.

"*Acting* High Wizard Gamal," said the teacher, accentuating the first word, "has asked everyone to help our newest student, Sylvie, feel at home. It seems she has lost her memories."

A stream of whispers and gasps echoed around the room as all twelve students turned and looked in Sylvie's direction. She couldn't do anything to hide her reddening face, so she just smiled. She was glad that the teacher quickly got into the lesson of the day.

Sylvie found her first two classes that afternoon captivating. They discussed theory of the magic disciplines as well as general history of the kingdoms on the western continent. It was information that she didn't remember knowing. But what she heard didn't surprise her in the least.

Time for the evening meal came and she followed Malea once again, this time to the cafeteria. Seeing Jax sitting by himself she joined him with her plate piled with food from a buffet up front. It seemed everyone in the room was curious about the two of them and kept glancing in their direction. An older girl walked by the table and turned to Jax with a broad smile. Her hair was as blond as Sylvie's own, but ran in a long braid down her back. Her eyes were large and blue and her cheeks rosy as if she had been running just a short time before.

"Welcome to the Wizard Conclave. I'm Jocelyn. Will you be staying with us long?"

Jax had to force down a bite more quickly than he had planned, which resulted in a few hard coughs before he could speak.

"Jax," he said. "And I'm not sure of my plans yet." He glanced over at Sylvie before continuing. "But I would like to stay for a while and learn about your kingdom."

Jocelyn opened her mouth to say something but a loud voice called out from across the room.

"Apprentice Jocelyn. Please leave our new guests alone."

Sylvie turned to look. The speaker seemed more like a guard than anything else. His stance was firm and his dark eyes hard.

Jocelyn stiffened and her smile turned sour. As she began walking away, she briefly touched Sylvie's shoulder.

"I'm glad you're back, Sylvie," she said out of the side of her mouth. "Something's not right here. We need you."

The words surprised Sylvie and she stared at Jocelyn as she walked away. What did they expect her to do about it?

CHAPTER THIRTEEN

Late that evening Henry halted the horses and threatened Kyril and his friends with harm if they caused any trouble. He hired two men in the town to stand guard over them while he walked away with his wife and son. Both guards were broad-shouldered and carried at least a sword and a knife—and most likely had more weapons on their battle-readied bodies. Kyril was sure that Henry had offered them a portion of the pay he would receive for turning them in.

"What trouble can we cause at this point?" Kyril grumbled to Joelle and Hasani. During their midday meal they had once again been given the poison that kept their wizard powers at bay. "Still enjoying the adventure, Hasani?"

"Kyril!" Joelle slapped him on the arm. "Be nice."

"Sorry," Kyril said. But he just didn't *feel* like being nice. Regardless, he knew it was not right to take it out on Hasani—this was all his own fault. He was the leader of this group and he should have been more vigilant in keeping the medallions and his friends safe.

"Understandable, Kyril," Hasani said. "I would be interested to understand where they got the poison from. If I recollect correctly, too many doses could harm us permanently."

"But Bale will help us," Joelle said with concern. "I know he will."

Kyril hoped she was right.

"What about the mark on your hand?" Joelle pointed at it. "Anything there?"

Kyril nodded slowly and felt a bit of hope at the thought. "A little. The poison doesn't seem to control it as much as our wizard powers. I can still feel the medallion close by in Henry's pack."

Joelle turned in that direction and her focus lingered a bit longer.

"I need my staff back too," she said. Henry had tied it to the side of one of the spare horses along with some of their other gear. "There are only two guards. Even without our powers, we have a chance."

"I know you're talented with that staff and all, but I'm not so sure that Hasani or I have much ability to fight without our powers." Kyril had used a sword a few times, but even with his wizard powers he wasn't much of a fighter. "I wish Sylvie was here."

They all nodded in agreement. As a wizard of the earth, Sylvie had tremendous abilities in a fight. In many kingdoms of the western continent, the king, queen, or emperor had a wizard of the earth holding the title of battlemaster. Well, they could sure use a battlemaster right about now.

Soon Henry came back and grabbed the pack off his horse that held the medallions. Joelle and Hasani looked at him worriedly. Now would be a great time for Bale to show up and save them. Kyril looked around and thought he saw a shadow of a man move behind a nearby building. He braced for an attack and rescue, but none came.

Instead, Henry ordered the two guards to bring the three of them discreetly down the street and to the outskirts of the small village. They approached an old one-level home. It was run down and looked to have been in a fire years before. Grass grew tall around the blackened walls and a portion of the brick fireplace was crumbled on the ground. Torn curtains hung in small front windows, but around back, a new door stood shut and locked.

"Put them inside the back room and don't let them get away," Henry said, tossing one of the guards a key. "I won't have them ruining my future now. I'll be back soon."

Kyril found himself gulping hard. At least in prison on White Island there was some sense of decorum among the wizards; here they were no better than thieves and barbarians.

The guards dragged the three wizards up a few steps and in through the door. The inside was not much better than the outside. They were taken to a room in the back. It had only one high glassless window for ventilation that was not nearly big enough for any of them to escape out of. A few tattered blankets were thrown recklessly across a half-blackened wooden floor.

As Henry walked away Kyril heard him mumble, "I've been living under my father-in-law's shadow too long—now it's my turn to be somebody."

The guards locked the door to the room and they could hear something heavy being dragged in front of it.

"If anyone comes out," said one of the guards, "they will get a sword in their gut, no questions."

Joelle sank to the ground. Her face was pale and she appeared to be worse off than Kyril and Hasani.

"Joelle," Kyril asked. "What's wrong? Are you sick?"

"I don't know," she said, trying to be brave, but Kyril could see the beads of sweat forming on her forehead. It was warm, but not enough to warrant that at this time of evening.

"It's the poison," Hasani said. "I'm afraid that because she is a healer herself, her body is fighting even harder against the poison than ours."

"But that's good, right?" Kyril became excited. "Maybe she can fight it off and free us."

Hasani shook his head. "It doesn't work that way. The only thing that will make this poison lessen is time. But the longer her body fights it, the weaker she will get."

"I can't help it," Joelle said, joining back into the conversation. "But I fear Hasani is correct. I am getting weaker."

Kyril dropped to the floor next to Joelle and Hasani sat down opposite them. Their only hope now was that the mark on his palm and its connection to the medallion would grow stronger…or perhaps that Bale would get them out.

* * *

Kyril awoke sometime later, but in the pale light of the room he couldn't tell how much time had really passed. Joelle groaned, and Hasani, who was already awake, moved over closer to her.

"She needs help, Kyril," Hasani said, his eyes holding a fear that Kyril hadn't seen in them before.

Kyril went to the door and started pounding on it. "Help!" he called out. "Joelle is going to die if she doesn't get help!"

No one answered, and after a few minutes Kyril stopped.

"They'll have to bring us food soon," Kyril said.

Hasani gave him a questioning glance.

"They have to keep us poisoned," Kyril said. "It'll be time for our next dose soon, I would suppose. I wonder how long we've been in here."

"About nine hours if I had to guess," Hasani said, holding on to Joelle's hand.

Kyril blew out a breath of air. He wasn't sure how they would get out of this situation. He could imagine the harm that Gamal was doing every minute they were detained from finding him and the medallions.

"Kyril," Joelle said, "we'll be all right. You'll get the medallion back."

"I wish I shared your optimism."

The three sat in silence for some time in their own thoughts.

In the quiet, Kyril heard a small grunt toward the direction of the narrow window. He stood up and walked toward it wondering what it was.

Suddenly a small hand appeared on the ledge followed by a face.

"Remi!" Kyril called out.

"Remi?" Joelle whispered from the other side of the room.

"How did you get up there?" Kyril asked.

Remi appeared to struggle to stay hanging from the window ledge, then after a moment steadied himself.

"A few old crates," Remi whispered with a broad smile. Then before anything else was said, he thrust a hand through the empty opening.

"Take it," he said.

Hasani had joined Kyril by the window and reached his hand up and grabbed a small vial from Remi's outstretched hand.

"What's this?" Hasani appeared as perplexed as Kyril felt.

"The antidote," Remi said with a quick breath. "I stole it from my father." His face beamed brightly. "It's not much, but Joelle saved my life. I hope it's enough. What my father is doing is not right. He had the antidote all along. I know he means well and just wants to take care of my mother and I, but…"

"Where did your father get them—the poison and the antidote?" asked Kyril.

Remi screwed up his young face. "When we passed through here the other day, a man and a woman gathered the townspeople and told them that three dangerous wizards would be traveling through here. They said there was a great reward for the medallions they had. He gave out the poison and antidote to any that would be traveling the road between Arc and Gildan. My father saw it as an opportunity."

Kyril heard a floor board squeak in the house. "The guards are coming. Remi, what did this man look like? Was he older and bald with a red birthmark on his forehead?"

Remi laughed. Apparently the description was funny to him. "Oh no," he said as he started to disappear from the window. "There were two of them; both only a little older than you." He started to wobble and a crash ensued behind the house. Remi grabbed the window sill with one hand to keep from falling. "I gotta go before my father finds me."

The sound of boots scuffled outside of their door and they heard the jangle of keys.

"What else can you tell me, Remi?" Kyril needed to know who was after them.

Remi's hand slipped and his head dropped below the window ledge.

"Remi?" Kyril called out.

They heard a small grunt and the sound of Remi dropping to the ground. "The girl had skin like yours and was pretty and wore a lot of makeup." He called out his last words."

"Altia…and I bet Jordan was with her," Kyril said in a low voice.

The door opened and one of the guards stepped through with an outstretched sword.

Hasani dropped back to the ground, keeping the vial hidden behind him.

"What's going on in here?" said one of the guards looking around suspiciously.

Kyril only shrugged his shoulders feigning innocence.

The other guard gave him a strange look, then proceeded to walk in with three water skins—containing, Kyril was sure, more of the poison. But now at least they had the antidote.

The first guard held his sword at their throats as the other forced the drink to their lips. "Drink up."

CHAPTER FOURTEEN

Sylvie was enjoying her classes immensely. The knowledge she gained seemed to bring more control to her powers and abilities—even though she was told she could not use them without permission. But she found them responding to her needs more and more automatically as the day went on. It was as if a dam was slowly breaking loose.

She saw Jax at the midday meal and he appeared to be faring well also. He had been able to join weapons training and was already showing up the local wizards with his skill with the bow.

"They treat it like just another weapon," said Jax. Once again they were alone at a table, enduring the stares of others.

"Isn't that what it is?" Sylvie asked.

"Oh no, not you too!" Jax slapped the palm of his hand on his head. "A great archer makes the bow a part of him—another appendage. You must become one with it. The bow and arrow are not the weapons; they are just tools. The user is the weapon."

"I think I understand," Sylvie said. It was like the way she felt with the water and the earth. But to be as skillful as Jax she had a lot to learn. A male student sitting behind them whispered her name, and she started to turn toward the voice.

"No, don't turn around," he said.

Sylvie stopped and caught a look from the lone guard in the room. She had noticed they were stationed throughout the building. The school was more subdued than she thought a school should be. She'd been expecting more chatter, but everyone walked around nervously and tried not to pay Sylvie and Jax much attention—but she knew they did. Everyone did. Especially the guards.

Even the teachers were careful in the way they spoke to her, only doing so in class when necessary.

"Find her for us," the student said again.

"Find who?" Sylvie said in a low voice, only partially turning her head.

"Find the High Wizard for us," he said.

"Sylvie, what's going on?" asked Jax.

"Shhh," she said with a carefully placed finger on her lips. "Where is she?" Sylvie asked.

But before any answers came, an older servant approached her and Jax. "Master Wizard Larue has requested your presence," she said.

Sylvie and Jax stood and followed the woman out of the cafeteria. The guard put his hand out and stopped them.

"Where are you going?"

Fear crossed the servant's face. "Master Wizard Larue summoned them. It is time for her test."

The guard glared back and forth between the servant and Sylvie and Jax for a long moment, then nodded his head and stepped aside.

"No wandering off," he said.

The servant took them down a hallway, but instead of turning toward where Sylvie knew the offices were, they headed toward a back door. Sylvie glanced at Jax but he only shrugged his shoulders. The hallway was empty but bright. It was a narrow corridor with clear windows on each side. Paintings and tapestries of various wizards, battles, and magical creatures hung between the glass windows.

Sylvie took in each scenic portrayal in turn, but stopped abruptly to stare up at the painting next to her. Jax crashed into her from behind, almost knocking her down. The painting appeared to be of some type of battle. Men in armor brandished their swords and wizards on either side threw lightning from their fingertips. It was done in remarkable detail and the artist was truly talented—but it was a figure near the background of the painting that caught her attention.

It was a woman with long blond hair and blue eyes, wearing a blue cloak that fluttered around her in the air. Her expression was peaceful but purposeful at the same time. Hanging around the woman's neck was a silver medallion. It had three concentric circles with lines coming out from the center, three of them meeting the edge. Radiating out from the center was the beginning of a bright silver light.

Sylvie could imagine the power coming from that medallion and spreading across the field of battle, eventually bringing peace and balance. Her heart beat rapidly and she felt like she could reach out and touch the medallion and it would give her power. But before she could, the servant, now a dozen strides ahead, turned around.

"We must hurry," she said. "Come on."

With one last reluctant glance at the painting, she stepped away and followed the servant once again. But a thrumming of power still beat within her. It was as if she could still feel the medallion in the painting somehow calling to her.

"Where are we going?" Sylvie asked. "I thought Wizard Larue's office was the other direction."

The servant opened the door and with a quick glance back down the hallway, motioned Jax and Sylvie through. "He feels your test would be better suited to take place outdoors."

"Earth," she whispered quietly. Sylvie had learned enough already to know about the different disciplines. Maybe she was a wizard of the earth.

They continued down a stone walkway and then down a few wide steps to a lower portion of the grounds. There was a large hole in the ground, and many different sized and shaped rocks were scattered around. Wizard Larue joined them and then dismissed the servant.

Larue was an older man with gray in his hair at his temples. He was lean to the point of being skinny. His cheekbones were high and his nose long, but he carried a small smile on his lips—although it looked a tad contrived.

"Thank you for coming, Sylvonna Hickory," he said formally. "We're here again, it seems."

"Again?"

He sighed and looked around nervously. "You really don't remember?"

Sylvie shook her head. Why did everyone keep asking her that? Why would she pretend if she could?

"But your powers, your abilities, are still strong?" Larue said.

"I…I don't know," Sylvie said. "I can do some things, but I do not know how much I am supposed to know or do."

"I see," Larue said. "And you, Jax, what are you doing here? As an elf, you are a long way from home. What is your connection to Wizard Sylvie?"

Larue looked Jax up and down as if assessing him.

Jax smiled to try and dispel what was becoming a stressful situation. "I am her friend," he said simply. "I brought her here and will stay for a while to learn about the kingdom and to train more in weapons."

"And do you have abilities?" Larue's eyes bore into Jax and he took a step back.

Sylvie noticed a quick flicker of Jax's eyes to a pocket, where she knew he kept the SpeedStone. She had never wondered if he had other abilities or not.

"I did not grow up with many other elves," he said without giving away where he was from or really answering the question at all. "And most of them there did not like me so much."

Larue appeared to be thinking for a moment. "I trust you will keep Sylvie safe."

"Yes, sir," Jax said without hesitation. "I am her friend."

Larue seemed to relax a bit. "She will need it," he said under his breath.

Then he directed Sylvie forward to a small platform in front of the big hole and scattered rocks. "Close your eyes," he said.

She complied.

"Now tell me…what do you feel?" Larue said.

"I feel you and Jax by my side."

"Deeper and out farther."

"I feel the earth and the rocks," Sylvie said. And she really did. It came to her so naturally as if she had been there before. With the way everyone looked at her, maybe she had. She let her mind go deep inside the hole. "I can sense roots from old trees that used to stand here, the worms and the bugs."

As she went deeper she felt something else. Something more powerful. It made her think of the painting she had seen on the way out of the school. The silver medallion came to her mind. It was bright and shiny and full of strength.

"I feel the water in the earth," she said as she envisioned underwater streams running below the hot desert sand. She followed them for miles, back to the Saar River, the river she had seen from the bridge in the City of Arc. And once again, she felt a part of it. It permeated her and then she *was* the water, rolling over the rocks and pebbles.

Sylvie heard voices but ignored them. She was a river and didn't stop for mere voices.

The ground shook and she shifted her feet to regain her balance—but she lost her grip on the river and felt herself being washed away in it. Suddenly, she couldn't breathe.

Struggling to get back up over the water, the medallion she had seen in the painting came into her mind once again and she grabbed hold of it tightly. The ground shook again and then the screams became louder.

"Sylvie! Sylvie!" Somebody shook her. "Sylvie!"

She fought for a moment, trying to balance out the needs of the water, the medallion, and the person calling to her. The one calling out finally won her over and she opened her eyes.

Jax was standing in front of her with both hands on her shoulders. His eyes were round and afraid. Once he saw her alert again, he brought her in for an embrace—a warm embrace that felt strangely like the water she had been a part of. She took comfort and strength from him and let the tears stream from her eyes.

It had been sweet at first—all that power—but then so horrible. She hadn't been able to breathe. She'd thought she was going to die.

"What is the meaning of this?" came a booming voice behind them.

Sylvie jumped out of Jax's arms and turned around. Materializing in mid-air a few steps away from them was Gamal, his fists clenched and his eyes flashing a barely-controlled rage. His robes floated around him as if alive, even though there was no breeze.

A black medallion on a chain hung around his neck. It pulsed with waves of smoky black tendrils and Sylvie took a step back. After seeing and feeling the goodness of the silver medallion, this one reeked of evil.

"Master Larue, what have you done?"

Larue stepped forward and bowed low to Gamal, and with a quivering voice answered, "I was accessing and testing her abilities, sir."

"That's High Wizard," Gamal said.

Larue seemed to find more courage. "*Acting* High Wizard."

Gamal glared at Sylvie. "What are you hiding from me?" He reached a hand toward her, but Jax stepped between them.

With a flick of his wrist, Gamal threw Jax aside. He landed hard against a rock. Sylvie raced to his side.

"Jax," she said, leaning down to him.

"I'm all right," he said weakly. But he rubbed one of his shoulders.

Sylvie stood up and rounded on Gamal. "Why did you do that? He didn't do anything to you."

"He stood between me and you, that is enough," he said. "I am in charge here and I will have that medallion."

The silver medallion in the painting flashed through Sylvie's mind once again and she hesitated too long before answering.

"You know where it is?" Gamal's eyes lit up.

"No, no," Sylvie denied. And it was the truth. She didn't know where any medallion was. "I don't know where any medallion is. I still don't remember who I am."

"Are you sure?"

"Yes," Sylvie said, trying to tread carefully in front of this dangerous man. "I'm still learning here. I just…want to keep learning."

Gamal directed her attention toward the giant hole in the ground. She blinked a few times and shook her head. The hole was now full of water. Had…*she* done that?

"How?" she asked.

"How indeed?" Gamal said with another glare. "You are very powerful, Sylvonna Hickory, and I cannot allow someone in my school with your power unless you are honest with me."

Sylvie was afraid. How had she filled that hole with water? And judging by the way that Gamal had thrown Jax aside, he had to be more powerful than she was. And she didn't want to anger him anymore. She needed to learn who she was. And what better place to do that than in a Wizard Academy at the Conclave?

"I am being honest with you, High Wizard Gamal," she said, using the title she knew he preferred. "I want to learn who I am, and I will tell you about the medallion if I find it."

The words appeased Gamal and he smiled, though it wasn't the smile from a friend, but one from a man that Sylvie now knew—High Wizard or not—was very, very dangerous.

CHAPTER FIFTEEN

Over the next few days Sylvie settled in better to her classes. She had been moved to more advanced classes after her testing and, as she suspected, was assigned to be a wizard of the earth apprentice. She saw Jax at mealtimes and in the evening, but during the day most of her other classmates ignored her—well, they refused to talk to her, but constantly peeked in her direction.

"Apprentice Sylvonna," said Wizard Ingall, "are you paying attention?"

Sylvie was taken from her internal musings, and found all the other students staring in her direction. Her face heated up and she turned her attention back to the teacher. He was an older man in his fifties with blond hair that was speckled with silver. He wore the blue robes of a wizard of the earth—the same color that Sylvie now wore. His mouth was firm on his thin face and he didn't appear very happy.

"What was the question again?" she asked.

The classroom laughed.

"What happened to you, Sylvie?" came a taunting male voice from a few rows behind her. "Did those Gildanians take your mind away?"

The snickering class fell silent. Ingall sucked in a breath of air.

"That's enough, Wydel," Ingall stated firmly.

"But it's what we are all wondering, isn't it?" Wydel continued. "Sylvie left here over a year ago as a powerful wizard of the earth…and now she comes back and is an apprentice once again. At the same time, our High Wizard Danijela Anwar gets mysteriously sick and someone we never heard of takes over the leadership of the school. Do you think we don't see that?"

"Yeah, where is High Wizard Danijela?" A female voice spoke from Sylvie's left. It was Jocelyn, the girl that had spoken to her in the cafeteria the other day.

"Yes, where is she?" asked another boy in front of her.

The name *Danijela* echoed through the core of Sylvie's mind. Flashes of her past raced through so quickly that she couldn't grab onto them, but they gave her some hope. Just hearing that name seemed to bring greater clarity to her thoughts. She must have some connection to the woman.

Instructor Ingall began sweating and looking around nervously as more students began talking at once. He cleared his throat a few times to try and get their attention, but to no avail.

"That will be enough!" Ingall yelled loudly. The ground shook and a lamp fell over on his desk. He reached over and brought it back upright again, but oil was now spreading across some of his papers.

Sylvie's heart raced and she noticed everyone else had gone silent.

Ingall moved a few papers out of the way and then went back to his lectern and placed his hands on either side of it. He looked down for a moment and then peered back up at the class. Sweat dripped down the side of his face and his body shook, but whether in anger or fear Sylvie couldn't tell.

"You all have been instructed in the new rules. There is to be no mention of our past High Wizard and there is no questioning our new master. Please don't make me tell you again." He glanced toward the door before turning his attention back to the class. "Class is dismissed."

The students began to stir and gather their things.

"And there will be no mention of this," Ingall continued. "You will all prepare a paper for tomorrow on the underlying principles of the source of power for a wizard of the earth. All of you!"

The class groaned, a few of them darting looks of anger at Wydel, and more at Sylvie. But she hadn't done or said anything wrong!

She held back in gathering her items and let the other students pass in front of her. As she walked by the instructor, she stopped.

"I've been your student before?" It was so hard to not remember anything.

Ingall twitched as if surprised by the question. "Class is over, Apprentice Sylvonna."

"But…I…" Sylvie said, confused. Wydel had said that she had left the Wizard Conclave as a powerful wizard. If so, then the instructors she'd had would know about her past.

"Can you just tell me where I'm from?" Sylvie pleaded.

Ingall's face softened and he wiped the sweat off his forehead. Sylvie braced herself for the first news about her past.

But before Ingall could say anything, a voice came from the doorway. It was Gamal once again.

Ingall stiffened and his eyes darted back and forth between the new headmaster and Sylvie. Gamal strode into the room with a broad smile on his face—one that never reached his eyes. Eyes that were dark, beady, and cold. The black medallion hung around his neck and Sylvie instantly felt repulsed by it once again, but she kept her footing and stayed where she was.

"Instructor Ingall," Gamal said. "Your students are done early today." He turned his attention toward Sylvie. "Except, it seems, for one of our brightest and newest students, Sylvonna Hickory. Is there something I can be of assistance with?"

Ingall shook his head a few times. "No, no, everything is fine. The class was quite rambunctious today so I let them go early to work on a paper that I assigned for tomorrow."

"Ah, good, good," Gamal said. His hand—seemingly involuntarily—moved toward his medallion and grasped it tightly. He took a deep breath and continued. "What is it that Apprentice Sylvonna needs additional help with?"

Ingall wiped sweat from his forehead once again. His cheeks were flushed and his hands opened and closed at his sides with a nervous twitch.

"Since it is my first day in his class, I needed clarification on the assignment," Sylvie jumped in, after realizing that Ingall didn't know what to do or say. "I really don't understand what the rest of the students know, being new and all."

Sylvie's words were clear enough and she was sure that Gamal also understood her underlying meaning. If he knew about her past and knew that she had attended the school before, why were they all keeping it a secret from her? Obviously this was not her first class with Ingall, nor with any of the teachers here. If what Wydel had said was true and she had left there as a full and powerful wizard, she must have been living there at the Wizard Conclave for four or five years at least.

"Yes…yes…" Ingall stuttered before getting control of his thoughts. "I assigned the students to write about the sources of power of a wizard of the earth, and she was just asking a few questions."

"I see," Gamal said. "It must be so strange to not have power come from your minds."

"Like wizards of the mind, you mean?" Sylvie asked. She didn't completely understand how it all worked, but she feigned more ignorance than she felt. "I've heard some talk since I've been here about the three wizard disciplines, but it's all quite confusing."

Gamal took a step closer to her. "You'd better not be toying with me, young lady."

Ingall took a step back but Sylvie stayed in her place. She did not like this headmaster, but she surely wasn't going to cower at his bullying. He had no right to treat her like he did.

"Good, good," Gamal appeared to relax a little. "I'm glad to still see the fire in your eyes. That means you might find the medallion yet."

The medallion? Her thoughts moved back to what she had felt beneath the school during her testing. There was something of great power there.

"You're remembering something?" Gamal had a gleam in his eyes.

Sylvie shook her head and cleared her mind. She couldn't let Gamal know what she was thinking. She didn't know what a wizard of the mind could do, but she thought that he would dig through her mind if he could. She had to be more careful.

Gamal leaned in, his face only inches from hers. "You are running out of time. Soon, I will get what I want, with or without your help."

"I told you I don't remember," Sylvie said with a burning anger.

"That's what you say," Gamal said, straightening.

A shade of shadow lifted out of his dark medallion and power crackled from his fingertips. Without any more words he turned and headed toward the door. Just before exiting he turned his head swiftly.

"Ingall," Gamal said in a low voice. "I don't want to hear of any more incidents with your class. And I expect you will help our young apprentice here to remember what she has forgotten. If not, I suspect you are aware of what could happen."

Ingall nodded his head and Gamal smiled wickedly and left the room. Silence prevailed for a moment. When Sylvie opened her mouth to speak, Ingall interrupted.

"Class is over, apprentice," he said. "Along with the others, I expect your paper on my desk at the beginning of class tomorrow. Goodbye."

Sylvie stood there for another moment but realized that she wasn't going to get anything else from Ingall so she gave a brief smile, turned, and left the classroom.

CHAPTER SIXTEEN

Sylvie felt like everyone was staring at her as she walked the long hallway of the school toward the door that led to the practice yards outside. Opening the door, she let out a deep puff of air and breathed in a new one. She had not realized she had been holding it in most of the way there. The air outside was hot and dry but it felt right to her.

She walked on paving stones that were laid in a path that led straight from the school to the archery practice area. Palms lined the walkway, giving a brief respite from the direct sun. When she reached the end of the walkway, she turned around and looked up at the school. The light brown sandstone seemed to reflect the heat of the sun—or was it a trick of magic? Whatever the reason, it hadn't been warm at all inside the school. Recesses, balconies and windows dotted the back side of the building.

Starting at the top tower, she brought her eyes down one story at a time. *The High Wizard's rooms, the ballroom, the library, and the classrooms.* The words came to her mind as she peered at each level. She did know this place!

The level with the library seemed to hold her attention for some reason. She took a step toward it but then stopped, remembering she had come to talk to Jax. She walked over to a fence that enclosed the archery fields.

At one end of the field to her right stood targets of various sizes and distances from the shooters, a group of young men and women on her left. Jax stood out in front with his bow drawn and an arrow ready to launch. A moment later, the arrow sailed through the air and landed in the center of the farthest target, but when she turned back to Jax, there were already two arrows in the air. He pulled a fourth out of a quiver on his back and shot it before the second and third hit their targets. Soon, all four arrows stuck out of the centers of various targets.

Sylvie clapped her hands in delight, but the sound brought unwanted attention in her direction. Jax smiled and waved, and after brief words to his instructor, trotted over to her.

"That was amazing!" she said to him.

His smile was contagious and he laughed. It was good to see him happy. She had been afraid that pulling him away from the only home he had known would be difficult for him. But he seemed to relish the newness of everything, was making friends easily, and was quite relaxed about it all. She wished she felt as good.

"What's wrong?" Jax asked.

"Nothing," Sylvie lied. "You appear to be having fun. You'd better be careful. Some may get jealous of you."

"Jealous of me?" Jax said. "No way. You wizards have all the abilities."

"You have yours, too," Sylvie said with a smile. "The control you have with archery and ..." she left the left of the sentence unsaid, but her eyes flicked to the pocket where she knew Jax kept the SpeedStone.

Jax lost his smile and glanced nervously around. "No one can know I have that, Sylvie. If anyone else found out, it could be dangerous for both of us."

Sylvie nodded her agreement then changed the subject away from the SpeedStone. "Speaking of abilities, I think I've been here before…and already graduated."

"That wouldn't surprise me," Jax said. "I've seen the things you can do, remember?"

"But I *don't* remember," Sylvie said, stomping her foot on the ground. "It's so frustrating."

Jax took her by the elbow and led her back toward the school. "Tell me what happened."

With a deep sigh, Sylvie repeated what had happened in the classroom and with Gamal. As she finished, they walked back into the school, and Sylvie headed toward a sturdy staircase off to their left.

"I think the library may have some answers for me," Sylvie said.

Jax shrugged. "I've never been to a library before. What is it?"

Sylvie laughed out loud. "I actually don't remember being inside one either, but I know what it is. It has books."

"Books?" Jax said. "You mean a whole room full of books?"

When they finished climbing the stairs, they headed toward a set of double doors. Jax pulled one out toward them and entered right behind Sylvie. She stopped short and he ran into the back of her.

"Sylvie!" Jax said.

"Sorry."

When she didn't move, Jax came up beside her and gazed around. "I didn't know there were this many books in the whole world."

A small chuckle to their side had them turning their heads. Behind a counter stood a short man with oversized glasses. Sylvie couldn't imagine anyone being older—he had to be in his nineties at least—but his blue eyes held an intelligent sparkle to them.

"Welcome, Wizard Sylvonna and Sir Jax," he said. "I am Wizard Nathanael, the head librarian here at the Wizard Conclave. You may call me Nathanael…or just 'Librarian.'"

"You know us?"

The librarian's eyes softened and he pointed with short fingers. "I know you, Sylvonna Hickory, and Jax's reputation has preceded him. We don't get many elves out here in the desert."

"There are so many books here," Jax said. "I've only seen three in my entire life."

The librarian scanned the area around them and then lowered his voice before speaking to Sylvie. "And you, my dear…is it true you do not remember being here before?"

Sylvie shook her head. "I don't remember much at all. I was found at sea and saved by…" Sylvie didn't know how to explain about Eva and Elise and their village.

"She was saved and nursed back to health by some relatives of mine," Jax jumped in. "We thought it best to come to a wizard school to get answers."

Two students walked by, leaving the library, and Nathanael waited until they were gone to resume talking.

"There are many answers here," he said a bit cryptically. "But are you ready for what you find?"

"What do you mean?" Sylvie asked.

Instead of answering, Nathanael only smiled. "I'm glad you are back, Sylvie. The school needs you. The Kingdom of Arc needs you."

Before Sylvie could ask what the old librarian meant, a woman came up beside him. Her demeanor was not as friendly. Her hair was dirty blond and hung down to the middle of her back. She was at least twice Sylvie's age.

"Nathanael, return to sorting the new books," she said. "I'll take care of these two."

"Yes, Anne," Nathanael said, but before he turned back around he winked at Sylvie and mouthed the word "Welcome."

"You will excuse Nathanael, as you can see he is quite old and forgets what he is doing much of the time." Anne appeared annoyed. "But High Wizard Gamal said to keep him around. He might be useful yet."

"You mean Acting High Wizard," Sylvie said, although not knowing why. "I hear the old High Wizard Danijela is sick, but not dead."

A scowl flitted across Anne's face. "What are you two doing here?" she snapped at them.

"I have a paper due tomorrow on the basic power of earth wizards and needed some information," Sylvie said, not really knowing for sure why she had been drawn there.

"Aisle ten on the left you will find everything about wizards of the earth and their power," Anne said with an annoyed look. "It's right past the section on magic artifacts."

Mention of artifacts made Sylvie's heart skip a beat. With a quick thanks to Anne, she dragged Jax down the aisles and stopped at aisle nine.

"This isn't aisle ten," Jax said.

"I know," Sylvie said, and instead stepped into aisle nine and began running her fingers over the titles of the books there, whispering some of the names out loud. "Dragon Artifacts, Magical Items, Artifacts of the South, Magic and Medallions…" She stopped at the last one and pulled it out.

"What's that?"

"I'm not sure," Sylvie said. "But it feels important."

She flipped through the pages carefully. There were drawings of various medallions of different sizes with brief explanations of their magical properties, if known. Something jogged her memory as she glanced through the pages.

"I've seen a book like this before," she said, looking up at Jax with a grin. "I know I have."

Jax peered over her shoulder. "Anything interesting?"

Sylvie continued to turn the pages—until she stopped on one, and felt something inside her begin to rumble. She closed her eyes to try and prevent any uncontrolled use of her power. She didn't want to call more attention to herself.

"Sylvie, are you all right?" Jax took her arm in his. "What's wrong?"

Sylvie pointed down at the page where a very precise colored drawing of a golden medallion sat directly in the middle. It drew her attention like nothing else she had seen since waking up from the accident.

"I recognize this," she whispered as she moved her hand up the page. As she touched the center of the medallion, a bright light flared up in her mind. For a brief moment she saw a set of stone stairs leading down underground and into a dark room. A bed and small washbasin sat against a back wall, and there was a woman sitting on a worn bed. But it was too dark in the dim candlelight to see anything else. She tried to look harder.

The shelves around her in the library began to shake and she heard a few screams close by. Jax grabbed her hand and the book fell from it to the ground. She tried to reach for it but he pulled her away and started toward the main aisle. They were almost there when the shelf began to teeter and books began to fall off.

Without thinking, Sylvie stuck her hands out in front of her and willed the shelf back in place. Almost immediately the shelf stopped rocking. Then, with a quick flourish of her hands, the books that were on the ground flew back onto the shelves…though with some embarrassment Sylvie realized she didn't know in which order they should be. Soon, all appeared normal once again.

A gasp sounded behind them and Sylvie and Jax turned around. Standing there with an open mouth was Jocelyn, and beside her stood Wydel.

Before they said anything, Librarian Anne came around the corner.

"What's going on over here?" she said accusingly. "I heard a bunch of shaking. You're not doing magic in here, are you?"

She said the last while looking directly at Sylvie. Her heart pounded, not knowing what to do.

Wydel stepped forward. "Thanks for checking on us," he said with mock kindness. "I tripped and fell against a shelf. A few books fell off. Nothing to worry about."

Anne glared at Wydel and then the others. "Figures it's you," she mumbled. "If you're not going to study then leave my library." She pivoted and went back in the direction from which she had come.

"Have a nice day!" Wydel called out.

Jocelyn gave him a light punch in the shoulder. "Don't push it. She's a mean one."

The two then turned their attention back to Sylvie and Jax. Wydel motioned them back into aisle nine and after making sure there was no one else listening, dropped his voice lower.

"We need to talk," he said to Sylvie. "You're our only hope."

Sylvie gave them a confused look. What did they expect from her?

"We think we know where High Wizard Danijela is and you might be the only one that can get to her," Jocelyn said.

"Why me?" Sylvie said. "Where is she?"

"In the basement," said Wydel.

With those words, images flashed again through Sylvie's mind of a woman on a bed in a dark room. She had blond hair, the color of Sylvie's own, but shorter. Was it really the High Wizard?

CHAPTER SEVENTEEN

Wydel put a finger to his lips, motioning the others to follow him. He walked past all the shelves of books to a table sitting in a small alcove at the back of the library. All four sat down and peered around nervously.

"Sylvie, you and the High Wizard Danijela were very close," Wydel said quietly, leaning forward. "She was your mentor and we all supposed you would follow in her footsteps someday."

"Me?" Sylvie gasped, her voice louder than she intended. After making sure that no one had heard her she continued. "A High Wizard?"

Jocelyn put a hand on her arm and smiled. "You will. I'm sure. But things are not right here at the school. I don't trust Gamal. He's up to something."

Sylvie nodded. "I agree. He keeps asking me about a medallion."

"A medallion?" asked Wydel. "Yes, I've heard Master Gamal speak of that."

"He says I know about it and that he'll force the information out of me soon if I don't tell him," Sylvie said. "Just now I saw one in a book…and…and…it did look familiar to me." She pounded a fist on her forehead. "But I just can't seem to remember what it means."

"You will in time, Sylvie," Jax said. "Don't worry about it for now."

Sylvie smiled at Jax. He was always so positive. But she didn't think she had the luxury of not thinking about it anymore. Gamal was getting desperate, and she didn't know how much longer she had to remember before he did something terrible to her.

"You need to talk to High Wizard Danijela," said Wydel. "She'll know what to do and where you can find…this medallion."

"But how do we get to her?" Sylvie asked. "I'm sure she is guarded."

Wydel pulled a piece of paper out from the inside of his cloak, unfolded it, and placed it on the table in between the four of them.

"What's this?" Jax peered down.

"A map of the lower levels," Wydel said with a broad grin.

"Where did you get that?" Jocelyn asked.

Wydel waved a hand in the air. "Don't worry about it. All that matters is I have it."

They all stood and looked at it for a moment trying to orient themselves to where they were.

"But how can we tell where to go?" Sylvie asked.

"I've heard she's being held under the school somewhere," Wydel said.

Jocelyn covered her mouth to stifle a laugh. "Oh, Wydel, you do have a way of finding out things don't you?"

Wydel grinned and then pointed to what appeared to be a hallway with markings for doors. "There are plenty of rooms down here. I'm sure she is guarded, but I have a plan to minimize the number of people around."

"Of course you do," Jocelyn said, then turned to the others. "Wydel is known as a bit of a trickster around the Wizard Conclave. I would just blast my way in there if I was brave enough, but as a wizard of the mind, I'm sure that Wydel has a better plan." She rolled her eyes. "At least he always thinks he does."

Wydel chuckled. "You wizards of the heart, always want to jump into things. We have to plan it out. And yes, I do have a plan."

Jocelyn harrumphed but let Wydel continue.

"I was thinking of more of a diversion outside on the grounds, giving Sylvie a few minutes to sneak downstairs and try to contact the High Wizard." Wydel stated his plan with a broad stroke of his hand over the map.

"I'll go with Sylvie," Jax said. "I don't want her to go alone."

"What about the guards or Gamal and the other teachers?" Sylvie asked. "He's always watching me."

"That's where my plan comes in," Wydel said, his eyes sparkling with mirth. "Ever heard of the midnight rivalry?"

Sylvie and Jax shook their heads and Jocelyn started to join in, but then her eyes widened.

"Gamal doesn't know much about our school," Jocelyn said. "I think Wydel is proposing a mock show of competition between the three wizard factions at midnight. It would provide enough distraction that eventually even Gamal would have to come outside to see what was going on."

"And to think that mind of yours is being wasted as a wizard of the heart," Wydel said to Jocelyn.

"We can think on our own, Wydel," Jocelyn said, her eyes flashing in anger. "I've taken the same strategy classes you have."

"I was just joking," Wydel said, putting his hands in the air in surrender. "We all need to work together on this one. All three disciplines."

"What about the teachers?" asked Jax.

"Don't worry about them," Wydel said. "Most of them, except for the few that Gamal brought along with him, want the High Wizard back again. They are just too afraid to do anything about it. The new High Wizard scares them all."

"*Acting* High Wizard, you mean," Sylvie automatically repeated what she had heard from Wizard Larue.

Wydel waved his hand, dismissing her clarification.

"So when does this happen?" Jocelyn said. "We need time to set it up."

"Tonight," Sylvie said without thinking, but she knew it was right. "I might not have much longer before Gamal gets more drastic."

"But…" Jocelyn started.

"She's right," Wydel said. "It must be quick. We just needed Sylvie here to get it done. She's the most powerful earth wizard here I suppose…well, except for Danijela."

"But I don't remember everything," Sylvie said with a frown. "What if I mess it up?"

"You won't," Jax said in a soothing voice. "Anyway, you'll have me there with you." He cracked a smile.

Even though Sylvie knew he was only trying to comfort her, his presence actually would help. Jax was the only stability in her life right then.

Wydel stood up and the other three followed suit. He turned to go when a sound came from the other side of the bookshelf, and Head Librarian Nathanael walked around the shelf.

The four students stopped in their tracks. He looked each of them in the eyes. Finally, Wydel and Jocelyn turned to leave, but Nathanael grabbed Sylvie's hand. Jax stiffened next to her and appeared ready to jump in if the librarian did anything to hurt her. Instead, he placed his hand on hers, dropped something into her palm, then leaned in and whispered in her ear.

"Give it to the High Wizard," Nathanael said in a low voice.

Sylvie opened her mouth to ask a question, but she was interrupted as two other wizard of the heart apprentices came around the corner.

"Ah," Jocelyn said to the two younger apprentices as she walked toward them, "want to have a bit of fun tonight?"

She spoke to the two in hushed tones, but Sylvie could see their eyes light up and their heads nod eagerly. Once Jocelyn had finished telling them the plan and they'd left, she turned back around to finish her conversation with Nathanael, but he was nowhere to be seen.

Jax took a few steps and looked down the side aisle toward the center of the library. He shook his head when he turned back around. "He's gone."

Sylvie closed her fist around the object without showing it to the others. She didn't know if they had seen it or not.

"Crazy old librarian," Wydel muttered as he pointed to a spot on the hand drawn map. "Inside the kitchen, there is a little used access door leading down to the next level. That should get you past all but the last two guards. Hopefully, the ruckus we cause outside will pull at least one of them—if not both—in our direction for a few minutes. If not, you might have to take care of them yourself."

Sylvie's eyes went wide with wonder. What did he mean?

"I'm not saying kill them," Wydel said with a grin, "You'll be fine, I'm sure. My plans always work."

Jocelyn almost choked on a laugh.

"Well most of the time, they do," Wydel appended his statement.

Sylvie nodded, hoping that she would indeed think of something. "Midnight tonight," Wydel said once again to Sylvie and Jax. "Go then."

The four split up, Jax and Sylvie heading in the opposite direction from the other two, who went back to their studies.

"I always wondered what a school would be like," Jax said with a shake of his head. "But I didn't imagine this."

"I don't think this is normal, Jax," Sylvie said. "But then, what do I know?"

They both laughed and headed toward the door of the library.

"Find what you were looking for?" Anne asked just before they reached the door.

"Yes…" Sylvie paused. She hadn't known what she wanted coming into the library, but she did get something. "Yes, I did."

Tarrying outside of the door, she opened her hand and showed Jax what Nathanael had given her. It was a small clear vial with a pink-tinted liquid inside. Jax raised his eyebrows at her and she shrugged.

"He only said to give it to the High Wizard," Sylvie said. "I don't know how he knew we were talking about her."

"Now what?" Jax hunched up his shoulders.

"Now we take advantage of Wydel's midnight competition and try and find the High Wizard." She hoped that after their midnight escapade, the High Wizard would help Sylvie remember who she was.

CHAPTER EIGHTEEN

Joelle was shivering and cold, though at the same time she knew she burned with fever. As a healer, she knew the signs of poison all too well. She would have rather had a broken bone or a flu. Poison was difficult to heal in the best of times, and their situation now was certainly not getting any better.

Kyril opened the vial and brought it to her lips, but she moved her head to the side.

"No, you and Hasani need to take it," she said. "I'm not sure if there is enough for all of us."

"I'll manage," Kyril said. "But you need it more than we do."

"You're wrong," she insisted. "There is a better chance that you will be cured and can access your powers to get us out of here than me. I'm too weak."

"No, I won't let you die, Joelle," Kyril said, tears rimming his eyes. "We'll find a way to get out of here without our magic if we need to, but you need more strength."

Joelle didn't have enough strength to argue anymore, but again she turned her head away.

"Kyril, she's right," Hasani said, his voice barely audible.

"How can you say that?" Kyril cried out. "She's our friend."

The room grew quiet and Joelle turned her head back toward the other two. Kyril was still holding the vial in his hand.

Hasani glanced at Joelle and his eyes softened toward her.

"We need to think clearly here," he said, turning back to Kyril. "You are our best hope for getting us out of here. You need to take more of the antidote."

Kyril ground his teeth in frustration. Then he stood up and walked to the door and pounded on it again. "Let us out of here!"

But there was no response.

"Where is Bale?" he yelled. "Why hasn't he rescued us?"

Joelle just shook her head. She had no idea. "For all we know, he was captured too."

"Kyril," Hasani said. "Please take some of the antidote. Even a little will begin to counteract the poison. It doesn't take a lot."

Kyril flopped back onto the floor between Joelle and Hasani. He pulled the stopper out of the vial, tilted his head back, and poured a few drops on his tongue.

"I'm not taking it all," he said before handing it to Hasani, who did the same.

He then brought it over to Joelle, but once again she shook her head. With frustration he put the stopper back on the vial. Almost half of the small bottle was already gone.

"We should get some sleep and reserve our strength," Hasani said. "The antidote will work in us while we rest."

Joelle watched Hasani and Kyril lean their heads back against the wall while she pulled a tattered blanket up over her on the floor. She knew she wouldn't have much energy left by the time she woke up, but hopefully the antidote would begin working in the other two and that Kyril might get some of the powers of the medallion back. She turned her eyes up and looked at him. As if sensing her, he opened his own eyes, and they softened when he gave her a slight smile.

She wished she had the power of the medallion with her right then to discern his thoughts. What was he thinking? She knew he would put her and even Hasani's health and well-being over his own; that's the way he was. He didn't see himself as others did. He still thought of himself as a weak, timid wizard, but he had grown so much in the last month since stopping the attack on Emperor Alrishitar. He took the charge to find the medallions and stop Gamal very seriously. And Joelle knew his mind was still ticking trying to figure out how to get everything done.

The situation appeared somewhat hopeless—not a feeling that Joelle was used to. As a child and even during her training at the Wizard School at White Island, she had been happy and excited to learn and try new things. Healing others brought her such joy and satisfaction…something she wasn't sure now she would ever be able to do again.

She let tears roll from her eyes as she closed them and tried to sleep. At least in sleeping, she wouldn't have to think of what might happen. Her last thoughts were of Sylvie. Hoping that her friend was still alive had kept her going all this time, but now…now, she might never see her friend again.

* * *

Joelle was jolted awake by her own gagging and coughing. Swallowing hard, she felt a cool liquid roll down her throat. She opened her eyes to find Kyril hovering over her, the empty vial in his fingers.

Joelle swallowed again and realized what had happened.

"Kyril!" she said, coughing again. "What have you done?"

Hasani woke up and joined the conversation. He looked from Kyril's empty vial and then to Joelle.

"I'm saving your life, Joelle," Kyril said, his eyes hard, but holding back tears. "That's what friends do. You think I care about Gamal and the medallions if I lose my friends? We already lost Sylvie. I can't…"

Tears fell from his eyes and he was unable to say any more. Joelle had been prepared to yell at him, to tell him he was foolish and short-sighted, but she couldn't do it. Not like this.

Hasani reached out and clutched Kyril's shoulder in a warm gesture. "Good friends are hard to come by." He smiled and nodded his head in acceptance of what Kyril had done.

"Oh, Kyril!" Joelle cried out, and leaning on one elbow she tried to bring herself to a sitting position.

Both Hasani and Kyril rushed to her aid. She then leaned forward and embraced Kyril. He stiffened at first but then wrapped his arms around her.

Joelle began to cry. She had been so strong through all this. The attacks in Gildan, their time on White Island with the imposter there and…Kaldar…Thoughts of him brought a small smile to her lips. But then she thought of Sylvie and how much she missed her and she began to cry again.

And through it all Kyril had been there—the hero that didn't see himself as such. The kindhearted young man that, with the acceptance of the powers of the medallion, had taken the peace and balance of their entire continent on his shoulders. And through it all he had put up with her insistent chattering and questions, her infatuation with Kaldar, and her sometimes silly emotional whims.

And now, now, he had used up the rest of the antidote on her. She was blessed to have such friends as him, and Sylvie, and Hasani. People that cared for her and loved her.

Love.

She felt it grow inside her. Despite how she felt physically right now, she still did feel love. Love for her parents, who loved her so much even though they had adopted her, love for her instructors that had taught her so much, love for the opportunities she'd had to heal and serve others, and love most of all for her close friends.

Kyril gasped in her arms, and she opened her eyes and leaned back out of his embrace.

"Your hands, Joelle," Hasani explained. "They're glowing."

Joelle looked down and laughed, though tears still streamed from her eyes. She could feel the antidote working within her. Her powers were returning. She reached her hands toward her two friends and placed them on their shoulders.

Their eyes widened and tears came to their own eyes.

Kyril laughed. "It's amazing."

Hasani bowed his head slightly to her. "Joelle El'San, I have never felt so much love and joy in my entire life. My heart is lifted and somehow—you are healing us even with the small amount of antidote we had. You truly are a mighty and powerful wizard of the heart."

Joelle felt her power waning, but she kept her hands on their shoulders as long as she could. The mark on Kyril's hand began to glow. She continued to draw the poison out and infuse them with healing and joy for as long as she could. But suddenly, she grew faint and dropped her hands.

Hasani reached out and helped her lean back against the wall. She closed her eyes briefly and tried to keep from passing out.

"Joelle," Kyril's voice called out to her.

"I'm fine," she whispered, lying only slightly.

"Are you sure?"

She nodded her head but couldn't make herself think.

"It looks like you made the right choice, Kyril," Hasani said. "Now we all have our powers back. Can you transport us out of here?"

Kyril shook his head. "My powers are not strong enough yet, and I'm not sure if I can do it anymore without the medallion."

With eyes closed, Joelle felt Kyril kneel down beside her and touch her arm.

"Are you really going to be all right?"

Joelle opened one eye and caught Kyril's worried expression. She smiled at him and opened her other eye.

"I will be, Kyril," she said. And she knew she would be. She just needed a bit of rest to restore her powers. "Thank you."

Kyril's mouth grew into a broad smile. "Oh no, Joelle, thank you. Because of you, we are going to get out of here and get the medallions back."

"And do you have a plan?" she asked with a smile of her own. She really did have great friends. "Are we going to fight our way out of here? If so, I need my staff back from Henry."

Kyril shook his head. "No, I have a better idea. What if Henry doesn't know we have our powers back?"

"You're talking about going along with his plan," Hasani said with a smile, quickly catching on, "and surprising them."

"I'm really glad you are here, Hasani," said Kyril. "It's nice having another wizard of the mind around."

"Hey, what about me?" Joelle said with a laugh. She sat up a little straighter. "I did just heal you. Now, what do you mean about going on with their plan? Isn't that dangerous? How will we get the medallions back? When…"

"She is definitely feeling better," Kyril said to Hasani with a wink.

They all laughed and enjoyed a moment of respite from their precarious situation. Joelle knew that, despite Kyril's optimism, getting out of town with the medallions would still be difficult.

CHAPTER NINETEEN

Sylvie lay in bed waiting for midnight to come. She was restless, her heart pounded and she couldn't sleep. Her mind raced with possibilities of what could happen in the next hour. Would Gamal find her? Would she find the true High Wizard, Danijela Anwar? Would the High Wizard really know who she was? The issues were growing, with no apparent end in sight.

The growing list of questions in her mind pricked her memory. It seemed there was someone she used to know that asked a lot of questions. A friend, maybe?

Sylvie wondered how many friends she had and if they missed her. She had been told she had been in Gildan for the past year, but she couldn't remember any definite details about being there. Surviving a storm in the sea was hazy at best, and nothing was completely clear in her mind until she had woken up on the island with Elise and Eva tending to her.

She knew she must have a family. Did they know where she was? Did they miss her?

Growling in frustration, she got up off the bed and strode to the small window. The summer night was clear of clouds, but only a sliver of the moon hung low on the horizon, making the grounds of the school hardly discernible in the dark.

Off in the distance she began hearing footsteps and muted voices. The students were leaving their rooms and going off to the practice grounds for the *tournament*. Would they all go? Would any stay behind and wonder what Sylvie was doing? More questions, all unanswerable once again.

Already dressed in dark brown riding pants and a dark shirt, she wrapped a black hooded cloak around her shoulders—much darker than the usual blue she wore during the day to her classes. Tucking her blond hair inside the hood, she pulled it up and over her head.

She grabbed her small knife and hid it under the cloak in the waistband of her pants, placed the vial of liquid that the librarian had given her into a small pocket, took a deep breath, and headed toward the door. She pulled it open a few inches and peered down the hallway. Voices echoed in the distance but no one else appeared to be close by.

She quietly closed the door and with soft boots on her feet, padded carefully and quietly to the outside door. With a quick look around, she opened it and slid outside. Keeping to the darkest shadows, she slid around the back of the main building.

"Sylvie," came a quiet voice.

She froze for a moment and then looked around. Jax emerged from behind a statue. He was dressed similarly to her but had his bow strapped across his chest and a quiver of arrows hanging over his shoulder.

"Isn't that a bit much?" Sylvie whispered.

"I'm prepared," he said seriously. "What if we meet Gamal or one of his cronies?"

Sylvie nodded in understanding, and together the two of them snuck toward a rear servant door. It was on the side of the building nearest the servants' quarters. Jax reached the door first and pulled on it, but it didn't move.

"It's locked," he said with surprise. "Why would it need to be locked?"

Sylvie didn't know, and she wondered if somehow Gamal had found out what they were doing. Off to the back of the school she saw a few lights and torches flicker through the trees and bushes. It seemed that Wydel had gathered enough people to stage a tournament.

Placing her hand on the lock below the doorknob, Sylvie felt her power and the metal lock mechanism responded to her touch. They heard a *click*.

Jax raised an eyebrow but said nothing as he tried the door again. This time it opened, and he ushered Sylvie in before him. They found themselves in some type of small mudroom. Stray cloaks hung on pegs, and boxes lined one wall. They reached the other side in a few steps and strode into the back of the kitchen.

A light flickered in the corner and, without warning, a woman poked her head up from behind a counter only a few feet away from Sylvie and Jax. She gasped and took a step backwards; her arm hit the handle of a pan and knocked it to the floor. The echo of the copper bouncing on the hard stone floor filled the room.

"Oh, my," the woman said pushing a lock of gray curls out of her face. She was shorter than Sylvie and much more plump. Her cheeks were red and her blue eyes sparkled with surprise. "You startled me."

Besides being caught by surprise, she didn't seem afraid, but for a moment Sylvie didn't know what to do.

"How did you get inside?" She picked up the pot while speaking. "The doors are usually locked in the evening."

Jax tensed beside her and took a step forward. The woman squinted at her.

"Sylvonna Hickory, is that you?" the woman said with a friendly smile.

"You know me?" Sylvie asked with trepidation.

"Of course I know you," she said. "I've been working here long before you attended. I heard you were back. Come for one of your late-night snacks again?"

"I...I..." Sylvie didn't know what to say, but they needed to get moving.

"Oh, yes, my dear," said the woman. "I've heard you lost your memory. Terrible thing that is. My name is Marcie. I thought I left something out and so I came back to check on it."

"I used to come here at night?" Sylvie knew they needed to hurry, but she was hungry for anything that she could learn about her past.

Marcie smiled and two dimples appeared on her cheeks. "Oh yes, you labored hard after dinner in the practice yard every night—even that last summer after you had become a wizard—and you worked up an awful appetite. If I remember, it was apple tarts that you sought out most of the time." Marcie started rummaging around. "I'm sure I have one or two left somewhere here from a few days ago. Should still be good."

"We really need to hurry," Jax whispered.

Marcie stood up straight and peered at Jax. "Oh, you must be the handsome elf I've heard so much about."

Jax stuttered a moment and turned red. Sylvie giggled.

"I know you're not supposed to be here, but your secret is safe with me," Marcie said in a conspiratorial tone. "Young people do get hungry at night."

"Yes, that's what we came for—some food," Jax rambled on. "No other reason for us to be out late at night."

Marcie gave him a strange look but shrugged and turned back to the counter. She returned with two hand-sized apple tarts.

"They aren't warm, but…"

"Oh, I'm sure they are fine," said Sylvie, taking one from her, while Jax took the second one. She brought it up to her mouth and the scent of it brought up a familiar sensation to her. And she took a small bite.

It was cinnamon-y and sweet and her taste buds jumped with delight. But then—new memories raced through her mind. She looked around, and she was suddenly seeing the room as it had been in the past. Pots and pans were in slightly different places and the room was brighter. Food filled the counters, including apple tarts. It was slightly disorienting so she shook her head to clear it…and then felt a pull from beneath the school once again—as she had felt during her testing. Something powerful and magical was there.

"Are you all right, my dear?" asked Marcie.

"Yes, yes, I'm fine," said Sylvie. "It's just that I remembered being here before."

A noise outside the kitchen door caught their attention and Jax gave her a nervous look.

"Now, what could be all that racket at this time of night?" Marcie moved toward the door.

Jax and Sylvie went in the opposite direction as Marcie opened the door a few inches. Footsteps could be heard running down the hallway, and a loud voice caught their attention.

"What are those students doing now?" Gamal said, his voice booming from somewhere farther down the hallway.

A few lights flashed, evidence of wizards gathering on the main floor.

"Let's go!" Sylvie motioned to Jax.

He nodded his head and the two moved quietly toward the other side of the kitchen. A door—just as Wydel had said was tucked back behind some shelves. The sounds from Gamal grew louder and as they reached the door they heard Marcie close the kitchen door on the other side of the room.

"I don't like that man," Marcie said.

It brought a smile to Sylvie's lips. They slipped through the side door and into a darkened area where Marcie couldn't see them.

"Sylvie, Jax, where did you two go now?" Marcie's voice faded as the door closed behind them. She laughed and Sylvie hoped that she wouldn't give them away—but she didn't think she would.

Sylvie brought up a dim light in the palm of her hand and they found they were now standing in a short hallway lined with shelves of bottled food. The narrow door opposite them wasn't locked, and they went through it to find themselves looking down a flight of stone steps.

Jax took the lead and headed down, with Sylvie close behind. The door opened into another small room. Wooden shelves once again lined the stone walls, but they were dusty and clearly hadn't been used for anything in quite some time. After going through another door, they now stood in a hallway that was much wider.

Hearing a few dim voices they froze in place. Sylvie cupped her other hand over the light, making sure it wouldn't be seen from very far away.

The sounds from above in the school grew louder and they stood for a moment trying to figure out what to do. They crept forward slowly, and after passing a few doors, came to a corner.

"What do you think is going on up there, Cabe?" asked a man's voice from around the corner.

"Who knows with wizards," said a man in a higher voice. "Why don't you go up and see?"

"But orders are to stay here and guard the High Wizard."

"Come on, Roald," said Cabe. "The lady is sick and isn't going anywhere. Go see what's going on—and get us some food from the kitchen while you're at it."

Roald snickered. "Always hungry, Cabe. Don't you eat enough at mealtime?"

"No, I never get full," Cabe said.

Roald laughed again. "Oh, to be young. All right, I'll go and check things out. You keep the lady safe here."

Sylvie and Jax heard Roald's footsteps fade into the distance and then peered around the corner. Lit by a torch on the wall, the guard that was left behind—Cabe— appeared to be in his twenties, tall and thin. He had a tuft of hair on his chin and was currently walking around and rubbing it. There were multiple doors in the hallway, but the two guards had mentioned the High Wizard, so she must be behind one of them.

Cabe sauntered down the hallway, muttering to himself. "Need to stretch my legs a bit." But before he left he walked to one of the doors, and, with cupped hands called out. "Everything all right in there?"

After no answer he smiled and continued. "I hope she gets better soon. I always liked her," Cabe said to himself as he walked farther away from where Sylvie and Jax stood around the corner. "Now the new guy, Gamal, he's not so agreeable with everything…but he pays me well."

Jax motioned forward and Sylvie couldn't believe their luck. Moving as carefully as they could, hoping the muttering guard wouldn't turn around until he got to the end of the hallway, the two of them scurried to the door that Cabe had talked into. Putting her hand on the doorknob Sylvie tried to lift the latch, but it wouldn't budge. Looking closer, she noticed it was locked. She was going to use her magic once again, but Jax brought out a set of keys.

"Where did you get those?" Sylvie whispered.

Jax pointed to a peg on the far wall and she smiled. Grabbing the key ring down, she placed the key in the lock, opened the door and quickly moved inside. Jax closed the door behind them.

The room was lit by a dim candle. It was smaller than her own was and consisted of a bed, a small washbasin on a short table, and a chamber pot in the corner—just like she had seen in her short vision earlier. A few books were scattered on the floor. A form on the bed squirmed and moved to sit up. She had blond hair like Sylvie's, but shorter, and a full face with enough wrinkles to give her character, but not enough to look old. Her eyes were blue and currently were opened very wide looking at the two people who now stood in front of her.

"High Wizard?" Sylvie asked, not knowing for sure if it was her.

"My heavens, is that you, Sylvonna Hickory?" said the woman. "Of course it's me. Don't you know your own mentor? Have I aged so much this past year?"

"I…" Sylvie didn't quite know what to say. Something was familiar, but more so in her heart than her mind. She instantly felt a kinship and closeness to this woman that was unlike anything she could remember or describe. Her throat caught for a moment before she could continue. "I…feel like I know you, but I have lost all my memories."

The High Wizard frowned for a moment, but then she just patted the bed next to her. "Come sit down and tell me about it. I'm sure we can figure this all out."

Sylvie took a step forward, but then stopped and looked back at Jax.

"And who is your friend here?" the High Wizard asked. "We don't get many of the Elvyn kind here in our desert kingdom."

"This is Jax," Sylvie said.

"Jax, I am Danijela Anwar," said the High Wizard. "Now, why don't you both tell me what's going on?"

"It's kind of a long story," said Sylvie, "but we don't have a lot of time right now. We're here to rescue you."

CHAPTER TWENTY

"Everything all right in there, High Wizard?" Cabe's voice called out from outside the room.

"We need to be quieter," Sylvie whispered. "We snuck in here, and we don't think we have much time before the other guard comes back."

"I'm fine," said the High Wizard, loud enough for the guard to hear.

"This is for you." Sylvie thrust the vial toward the High Wizard. "Librarian Nathanael said to give it to you."

"Such a sweet man," the High Wizard said. "But I'm afraid that this room is warded against magic even if I had my own back."

Jax gave Sylvie a worried look.

"Gamal has taken over the Wizard Conclave and keeps threatening me to come up with a medallion that I know nothing about." Sylvie said, keeping her voice low. She and Jax were now sitting on the bed close to the High Wizard, all three of them as far from the door as possible. "We need to get you out of here so that you can help the school, find the medallion, and get rid of Gamal. All…well, most of the students are on your side—at least that is what I'm told. They don't really speak to me much."

Danijela smiled broadly. "Don't worry about that Sylvie, they are not as strong as you are and are only being careful around Gamal I am sure." She paused for a moment before continuing. "But Sylvie, it is you that needs to find the medallion, not me."

"But…" Sylvie started, but was interrupted with a finger on her lips.

"As you said, we don't have much time. Now you must listen to me."

Sylvie nodded, but stayed quiet.

"After graduating early, you've been in Gildan for a year as a guest instructor of the Wizard Academy there," the High Wizard began. "From what I heard from my friend Mezar, the Emperor of Gildan, you have been extremely helpful lately in securing the kingdom from a group of usurpers. However, one man, Gamal, got away."

"You knew that?" Sylvie asked. "Then why…"

"Not now," the High Wizard said, quieting Sylvie once again. Her face turned more serious. "I underestimated him. But you cannot do that. A friend of yours in Gildan: Kyril. He obtained the first medallion, a golden one. Besides augmenting his own wizard abilities it gives him the ability to transport. You left Gildan to come here…"

"You were on your way here when you crashed on Vorwyth," Jax whispered beside Sylvie. "That's what happened."

His words surprised her. Even though her path hadn't gone the way she'd expected, she'd still made it to where she was supposed to go.

The High Wizard's eyes grew bigger, and she looked from Jax to Sylvie. "It appears I've missed a few things this past week while being in here. If you've been to Vorwyth, I'd love to hear that story sometime. Now, after you left Gildan, Kyril and Joelle—another friend of yours from the Realm—returned with another medallion. That's the last I heard before Gamal took control of the Wizard Conclave."

Sylvie tried to follow but there were so many names and places in the story that she had a hard time keeping up. What was she involved in?

"Now you must find the third one," Danijela continued. "All three together will bring balance back to magic and be what is needed to force Gamal and his evil shadow magic away for good. He is a danger to all our lands." The High Wizard stopped for a moment and her mouth went taut and her eyes narrowed. "That man subverts all that is good in magic and is wreaking havoc on all our lands. It's taken a lot of work over the years to get everyone comfortable with the power of wizards in their midst."

In the silence, they heard conversation outside the door once again.

"Roald is back," Jax hissed.

"We need to get you out of here," Sylvie said to the High Wizard.

She shook her head. "Not yet. You need to find the medallion first, Sylvie. That is the only way we can defeat Gamal and get the world to accept the good in magic once again. It's why you are here. I will escape when the time is right."

"But how?" Sylvie sighed. Her mind was spinning with the story that the High Wizard had told them. She could hardly keep the events and names straight. She was sure that the High Wizard was telling the truth, but she had no idea what to do about any of it.

The High Wizard placed the vial on the bed next to her, grabbed both of Sylvie's hands in her own, and peered into her eyes. Sylvie could see so much power there that it almost made her pull away, but the High Wizard hung on. But there was something else in her blue eyes also—caring and love. And even though Sylvie couldn't feel the woman's magic in the room, or her own for that matter, she did perceive the compassion in her demeanor and it brought tears to her eyes.

"Sylvie, you are the greatest wizard to graduate from the Wizard Conclave in years, perhaps even since I was here as a student eighteen years ago. You have the potential to be one of the most powerful wizards that has ever walked the western continent. Before I was locked away I had communicated with King Darius of the Realm, Mezar, Emperor of Gildan, Bakari, the Dragon King, and even that foolish but once powerful High Wizard Roland Tyre from Alaris. They were all worried about Gamal and his forces. From what I understand, uniting the three medallions is the only way to defeat him, but it seems the medallions choose their own recipients, each from three of our kingdoms, the Realm, Gildan, and now hopefully you, from the Kingdom of Arc."

Yelling was now heard outside of the door. It was Roald.

"What did you do with the key, Cabe?"

"Key?" Cabe questioned back. "I never did anything with the keys. They were right there on the wall."

"Well they aren't anymore," Roald said. "He's going to kill us, you know. Once he is done with the students outside, Gamal is going to kill us if we have lost the keys. Now, what did you do?"

"All I did was take a walk down the hall," Cabe said. "That's all—just to stretch my legs. No one came down here, I'm sure of it."

"Well we'll have to make sure that the High Wizard hasn't escaped," Roald said.

"They're coming back," Danijela said. "Now listen to me, Sylvonna Hickory." With those words she grabbed Sylvie's face with both hands.

Sylvie's mind went blank for a moment and she felt like she was falling. She tried to pull away but she couldn't. All of a sudden she found herself in a dark cave and the High Wizard stood next to her.

"How?" She gasped as she looked around. She could see, but there was no source of light.

"We are in the magic stream," the High Wizard explained briefly, "but I can't hold it for long. It's a place where powerful wizards can go to communicate across vast distances, or to even travel if necessary. The room I am in blocks my ability to practice magic in the physical world, but I've stored enough energy for a few moments in this realm."

Sylvie tried to take a deep breath and take it all in. But it was difficult to understand.

"The medallion you seek is here in the school somewhere," Danijela said, "but even I do not know for sure where. I was studying all the books I could last week before

Gamal came. Ask the head librarian for help, he can help you, but you must hurry. Gamal will move soon, with or without the medallion. Before night falls once again, you must find the medallion."

"But I can't even remember who I am!" Sylvie cried out, and tears came to her eyes. "I can't do this! Why can't you? You're a powerful wizard with lots of friends, and I'm all alone."

"I told you that the medallion chooses, and it has not chosen me; I'm hoping it will choose you. Jax and the other students will help you, and I would guess your other friends will be here soon. All three medallions must be together to defeat him. You are the last hope we have, Sylvie."

"But what about you? Why won't you come out with us and help us?"

Danijela began to fade. "I will be out soon. The time needs to be right. But until then, Gamal would just put me back. Without your powers and the medallion, we are not strong enough for him."

She wanted to ask more—more about her life, about who she was. More about the mission and the medallion…but the walls of the spirit realm shimmered around her and once again she found herself back in the room on the bed next to the High Wizard. Her hands dropped away from Sylvie's head and Jax stood up.

"They're not here yet?" Sylvie was confused. They had talked for minutes.

"Time moves slower there. It's only been a second here," the High Wizard said. "That's why I needed to take you there to speak."

Jax appeared confused, but the turning of the door handle brought their attention back to the task at hand. "But how do we escape the room without my powers or being seen?"

Jax smiled and held his hand out in front of them. The SpeedStone pulsed orange in his hand.

The High Wizard gasped. "A gemstone!"

The door opened and Jax grabbed Sylvie's hand, and suddenly they were speeding out the door. They tried to squeeze past the guards, but there wasn't enough room and they knocked down Roald.

"What the…?" Roald mumbled, looking around, but not being able to see them since they moved too fast.

Jax placed the keys back on the peg and then proceeded to speed down the short hallway, through the door, up the stairs, through the kitchen, out the back door of the school, and around back before they came to a brisk halt.

Sylvie stumbled and Jax grabbed her, but they both fell behind a bush. Trying to untangle themselves, they noticed a long line of students coming up from the practice yard. Gamal, along with Jenessa and Larue, the heads of each wizard discipline at the school, walked behind them and corralled them back toward their bedrooms.

Jax and Sylvie stayed hidden while they walked by, dangerously close.

Gamal had a hold of Wydel's shoulder. "Is this your doing?"

Wydel tried to pull away, but couldn't. He sought the attention of the other headmasters and said loudly, "It's a tradition here, sir. Don't you want to keep tradition?"

Gamal lowered his voice and said something Sylvie couldn't hear, then grunted and shoved Wydel out of the way.

Gamal glanced around. "Where are you, Sylvonna Hickory?" he taunted. "I know you are around somewhere."

Sylvie froze and tried to still her beating heart.

Gamal grinned then turned to Headmaster Jenessa and three guards. "I'm not sure what Wydel was thinking, I'm going down to the dungeons to check on the old High Wizard. Make sure to check Sylvonna Hickory's room. If she is not there, let me know immediately."

"Go!" Jax whispered to Sylvie. "I'll create a diversion. Hurry, you can't be caught." With that he raced out of the bushes and then fell to the ground feigning a hurt ankle.

Sylvie's heart was racing even before she took off running. She'd always been fast—the thought made her smile. Where had that come from? Maybe she was finally remembering a few things. She sprinted across a garden, around some benches, and jumped over a small wall, not caring if she stayed in the shadows, just needing to get back to her room as soon as possible.

She felt like she could hardly breathe, partially from the physical exertion, but mostly from what she had heard from the High Wizard. She felt she was playing catch-up on her own life. Why did others know more about her than she did herself?

But as she ran, a firm resolve began to settle somewhere deep inside her. Danijela had said she might one day be the most powerful wizard on the continent. If she was so powerful, why was she running from Gamal? She was tired of being afraid. Well, no more!

The ground beneath her feet shook and she could hear cries out in the distance—others must have felt it too. Water gushed out of the fountains, spraying a hundred feet up in the air. And still she ran. She pulled it all in to herself—the power in the ground, the rocks, the water, the trees, the very earth itself. Lightning crackled from the sky and hit a corner of the school building. Ancient rocks blackened and a few tumbled to the ground. And she soaked it all in. The power was intoxicating. She became the power around her and her speed increased, the ground lending its strength to her. She pulled open the door to her dorm building so hard that the hinges broke off and the door crashed to the ground and slid ten feet across the floor.

Sylvie slowed down when she reached her own room. Students from her building were coming in the other entrance and she knew Gamal's headmasters and guards would soon be following. She closed the door behind her and took a few seconds to try and calm her beating heart. She tore off her clothes and pulled a nightshirt on, and then jumped in her bed and pulled up the covers just as her door crashed open.

Sylvie sat up in bed, pretending to be awakened and surprised at the interruption. She was still breathing hard from the run and absorption of power, but she hoped they took it for the sudden late night interruption.

"Where have you been?" asked Jenessa, the wizard of the heart headmaster.

Sylvie tried to appear surprised at the question. "What do you mean? I've been sleeping. Is something wrong?"

A guard stepped forward and looked around the room, then turned back to Jenessa. "Seems like she's been here the whole time."

"What about the shaking and lightning?" Jenessa looked suspicious.

"I'm not sure what you are talking about," Sylvie said, her heart thumping but trying to appear outwardly calm. "Is there something I can help with? Is there a problem?"

"No, no, Wizard Sylvonna, no problem here," Jenessa said. "A problem with some students. High Wizard Gamal only wanted to make sure you were safe."

"And so you busted into my room for that?" Sylvie feigned anger—well, in reality it wasn't so feigned after all. "I am a student here, not a prisoner. I am allowed my privacy."

The guards backed up, but Jenessa scowled around the room once more. With a nod of satisfaction, she finally backed out of the room and motioned for a guard to close the door.

Sylvie fell back on her pillow and breathed deeply. She closed her eyes and tried to sleep. But all she could think of was the medallion that she had to find. And she had less than a day to do it.

CHAPTER TWENTY-ONE

Early the next morning the two guards unlocked the room where Kyril, Joelle, and Hasani were being kept. They had been given a small ration of food the night before, but luckily no more poison—Kyril didn't think that Joelle could have handled another dose. She had recovered somewhat after healing Kyril and Hasani, but she was still weaker than they were.

Their hands were retied and then led outside by the guards. Kyril had to shield his eyes from the bright sunlight. The morning was already warm and he definitely noticed the lack of humidity in the air. Three other rough looking men joined the guards that had brought them. All five had swords or knives drawn and didn't seem like they were taking any chances with the three wizards.

"I don't want any trouble until I get my money," said Henry from the back of the group. He walked forward and glared at the three of them.

"You don't have to do this, sir," Joelle pleaded, her voice soft and still weak. "We are on an errand from the Emperor of Gildan and can give you whatever you need to take care of your family."

Henry growled and pulled in Remi, his son, closer to him. Remi's eyes turned fearful, but he didn't say anything. "My son deserves more than I have. I've been promised enough money for all of us to live comfortably."

"And you trust those you are dealing with?" Kyril added. He could see that Joelle was trying to distract and anger Henry so that he might make a mistake. He obviously didn't realize their powers were back.

"I trust them more than you," Henry said. "You're only a bunch of thieves."

"Thieves?" Kyril asked. "Is that what you were told? Those medallions are ours. *You* are the thief, and by giving them to Jordan you are giving them to Gamal—a man intent on wreaking havoc."

"Who said anything about Jordan?" Henry squinted and walked closer to Kyril. Reaching a hand forward, he slapped Kyril hard across the face.

It was good that Kyril's hands were tied behind his back because he was sure that the mark in his palm had just flared to life in response to Henry's actions. It was all he could do to not break the ropes and strike him down. But he took a deep breath and maintained control—if only barely. He wanted to make sure that Jordan and Altia were caught as well.

"A name we heard, that is all," Joelle said, trying to help Kyril out. "He was among Gamal's followers in Gildan. We surmised he might be behind this."

Henry now walked over to Joelle and lifted his hand.

"No," said Hasani softly, but with a firmness backed by his power—and Henry's arm stopped still in the air.

Kyril hadn't realized that Hasani had such control over his power. His friend rarely used anything but his ability to remember things. He shot Hasani a look, begging him to be careful, but Henry himself could not feel Hasani's power—however the effect was as intended and he didn't slap Joelle.

"Let's get along with this, if this is what you mean to do, sir," Hasani said.

Henry grunted but turned around and yelled at his men. "Let's go!"

The five guards formed a perimeter around the three wizards as Henry, with his son and wife in tow, led them through town. The streets were quiet, although Kyril noticed people peeking out of their homes and shops, only to disappear again just as quickly.

Suddenly, a familiar face popped up in one of the windows.

"Bale," he whispered to Joelle. "I just saw him hiding."

"He'll help us," Joelle said.

"We'll see," Kyril mumbled, not sure of anything anymore. He had learned recently not to trust very many people. Those, he could only count on one hand—Joelle, Hasani, Sylvie, the emperor, and his son Zaidan. At the moment—based on the amount of time they had been kept prisoners—Bale was a toss-up on his list.

They soon arrived at an inn which by the looks of it, was most likely the nicest one in town. It stood three floors high and was composed of newly-painted stone with only a bit of wood for the door and around the windows. A sizable porch with rocking chairs jutted out from the front. Inside, oil lamps lined the common room, and various chandeliers hung throughout. The floor was stone as were many of the tables, although the chairs were wood. It was clean and nice and empty…well, except for six people standing on the far side of the room. Three rough-looking men stood with Jordan and Altia with another older-looking man beside them.

"Fenton," Kyril said. He remembered the man from the vision he'd had of Gamal while on White Island. He had light brown hair with edges of gray and light skin—he was most likely from the Realm. He had a dangerous—though excited—gleam in his eye.

"I asked for the medallions, not these meddling wizards," said Jordan to Henry.

Henry paused for a moment but then puffed out his chest and said loudly, "I want double the money for the medallions. These three should be enough compensation for that. I'm sure your master would like to have them as well."

Jordan was about to speak again but Fenton stepped forward instead. Jordan's eyes went dark and Kyril realized that the young wizard didn't like others taking precedence over him.

"Very forward thinking of you, sir," said Fenton, his voice soft but dangerous.

"And who are you?" Henry said, shuffling backwards a few inches.

"That is no concern to you," Fenton said, and with a wave of his hand the door behind them closed.

Kyril hadn't realized that Fenton was a wizard, but it made sense. Gamal surrounded himself with them. But that would make it even that much harder for their escape. Maybe they should have left when they could have, as soon as they'd taken the antidote.

"Do you have the money?" Henry asked.

"Do you have the medallions?" Jordan said, trying to regain control.

Fenton shot him a dark look and Jordan cowered back.

Henry nodded toward one of his men who brought a small pouch over to him. Reaching inside he pulled out Kyril's golden medallion. It was all Kyril could do to not jump forward and grab it. It called to him so intensely he could hardly stand it. His hand was growing warmer and the guard behind him yelled out.

"His hand!"

Everyone in the room turned toward Kyril. The guards with Joelle and Hasani moved in closer and put knives against their throats. Jordan leaped and grabbed at the medallion, but somehow Henry turned just in time and Jordan ran into one of the other guards instead. But the medallion flew from Henry's hand and landed on the floor closer to Fenton.

"Jordan!" Fenton called out, leaning down to pick up the medallion. "That is not for you. It is for the Shadow Master."

The mark on Kyril's palm burned even brighter, and with his magic fully restored now, he busted through the ropes holding him.

"I thought you said they were poisoned," Jordan said to Henry.

"They were," Henry said with surprise. "I…I…"

Remi slumped back farther in the crowd. His father caught his movement and must have realized what had happened.

"Remi, what did you do?"

"It wasn't right, Father," he said. "She healed me and they were nice to us. I just wanted to help them."

"Help them?" Henry roared and reached over toward the boy.

"No!" Kyril yelled and Henry stopped in his tracks.

With his hand outstretched, Kyril's palm burned brightly with a blue light, and he called the medallion to him. Fenton roared in pain as it ripped from his hand and flew through the air to Kyril. He grabbed it and spun around toward Henry. With one forceful push of air, he threw the man away from his son.

"Oh no you don't," Jordan yelled, and he and Altia moved in toward Kyril. They both proceeded to bombard Kyril with wizards' fire, but Kyril used his own ability now to transport away, so the fire hit the guards instead.

They screamed and yelled and tried to put out the fire. The one with the knife at Joelle's throat moved away just enough and with a roar that was uncommon for her, Joelle called out loudly with her hand outstretched. A front window burst, glass flying everywhere, as her wooden staff came flying through the air and landed in her hand. She instantly spun around and swept the guards off their feet, knocking them to the ground.

Kyril now stood against Fenton, Altia, and Jordan, all three raising their hands toward him and trying to throw him down. Jordan got in close and tried to grab the medallion from him, but as he did so, Kyril transported again across the room—but Jordan came with him. They both tumbled to the floor.

Jordan kicked out and caught Kyril in the side of the head. Stars gathered and he shook his head to clear it. Altia stood over him with a sneer on her face. How could Kyril have ever thought her attractive? It seemed like so long ago now—but in reality it had been just about a month since his adventures with the medallion started.

Wizards were meant to help and serve others, not to fight and gain power. Men like Gamal twisted their powers to serve their evil intents, and now greed, lust for power, and revenge were growing among the ranks of wizards in people like Altia, Jordan, and Fenton. Gamal had a lot to answer for.

Coming up behind Altia was Joelle. She brought her staff up and was just about to smack her on the head when a guard tackled her from behind. Kyril used the distraction to roll away from Jordan. He stood for a moment to catch his breath.

"Kyril!" Hasani called out from across the room.

Kyril turned and Hasani threw a cloth bag in the air toward him. Kyril jumped and caught it, pouring the contents on the ground in front of him. Joelle's silver medallion rolled out and he reached toward it. But Jordan's foot found it first.

"This one is mine," Jordan said and moved to pick it up.

"I don't think so," came a new voice, and suddenly Jordan's body collapsed onto the ground.

Kyril looked up into Bale's dark eyes.

"About time," Kyril mumbled.

Bale smiled. "I guess you wizards do need my help after all." He picked up the medallion and studied it for a moment. He cocked his head to the side as if considering how he might use it.

"Bale!" Joelle called out and stuck her hand toward him.

Altia tried to grab at it first, but Joelle clawed her way in front of her. Bale handed her the medallion and she slipped the chain over her head. Suddenly, she started yelling out orders to Kyril, Hasani, Bale, and anyone else that would listen.

Each time their adversaries would try to come in toward them, or shoot fire or air, or draw a sword, Joelle was able to thwart them. Her medallion continued to give her the ability to see the intention—and sometimes even the thoughts of others, ahead of time. Kyril used the power of the medallion to transport around the room, while Joelle swung her staff in a blur. Bale took out the remaining guards with his sword work and instructions from Joelle, and soon the non-wizards were out cold and the three remaining wizards were standing together and breathing hard.

"Now what?" Hasani asked. He had somehow stayed away from the fighting foray as much as possible, and only assisted where he could. His strength was not in fighting.

"Now we leave and continue on our way," Bale said.

"But we can't leave them here," Kyril said. "They will run back to Gamal."

"They're not going anywhere," Bale said.

And as he spoke, the door opened and at least twenty men and women entered. They appeared to be breathing hard as if they just arrived. Half were dressed like guards from Arc and half wore wizard cloaks of various colors. They came inside and stood still for a moment. One took a step forward and, with perspiration dripping down his face, saluted Bale.

"Sir, we are prepared to escort the prisoners to wherever you would like."

Kyril was dumbfounded. He didn't know what to make of it.

"Close your mouth, Kyril," Bale said.

Kyril did as he was told; not realizing it had been opened.

"Commander," Bale spoke to the leader of the group and pointed to Fenton, Jordan, and Altia. "Take these three back to Gildan. They will stand trial for sedition and rebellion."

Henry groaned on the ground and Remi moved over to his father.

"What about them?" Kyril asked Bale, still not believing that the young spymaster had now actually put himself in charge.

"That's up to you," Bale said. "They could be charged with kidnapping and the man could go to prison."

From the ground, Henry looked up at Kyril. "Please…I didn't have a choice. I…I…just wanted a better life for my family. I didn't mean for anyone to get hurt. I don't know anything about this Gamal or his plans. I'm just a poor man trying to make it in life."

Remi turned his tearful eyes up and Kyril's heart softened for the young boy. He glanced at Joelle and Hasani for any advice or help, but the two of them stayed silent and appeared comfortable deferring to Kyril.

Approaching Henry, Kyril spoke to him. "Even after we helped you, you kidnapped us, kept us in a room, and poisoned us—almost killing Joelle. If it hadn't been for your son, she might have died—all for your own greed."

Henry slowly stood up. There was a red scrape on the side of his face and he stood as if one leg was injured. Bale turned to Kyril, awaiting an answer.

"But we didn't die and we did get the medallions back," Kyril said. "And we appear to be back to normal with the poison purged from our systems." He paused. He pulled upon the power of the medallion and felt a rush in his mind, helping him to see steps ahead of where they now were. "You will stay in the Kingdom of Arc and be assigned a year of duty and service to your kingdom in whatever way the local authorities see fit."

"How will my family survive?" Henry said, eyes dropping to the ground. "This is all my fault. I got greedy."

"Because your son bravely helped us I will award him a plot of land inside Gildan with enough money for him and your wife to live on and get a farm started while you are away. Once you get back, the land should be enough that you can make a living and support your family on your own."

Bale gasped. Henry nodded with tears in his eyes, and Joelle came up behind Kyril and put a hand on his shoulder.

"Very well done, Kyril," she said with a soft voice in his ear. "You dispensed justice and mercy like a true ruler."

Kyril stiffened for a moment. He was not anyone's ruler. But a renewed sense of purpose thrummed through his mind from the medallion. The medallions brought balance and peace to the world—to both those with magic and without.

Bale nodded at Kyril with respect in his eyes and soon everyone was rounded up and marched away, leaving only the original travelers together once again.

"Thank you, Bale," Joelle said to him as they walked back outside. Their horses already stood packed and ready to go. "You must have been busy. How did you get so much help so fast?"

"Being in the spymaster's office does have some advantages," he said with a grin. "Someone has to watch out for you wizards."

Kyril rolled his eyes but laughed in spite of himself. The man could be frustrating, but he did really help them turn the tide in the fight and give them a way to continue on their journey. Maybe he was one more person Kyril could really trust.

"You are quite a remarkable man, Bale Nabhani," Hasani said. "I wouldn't be surprised if tales or songs were told of your heroics."

"Oh great," Kyril mumbled. "That'll go to his head now."

But instead of smiling and accepting the accolades, Bale's countenance fell and all grew quiet for a moment.

"My one failure will always outweigh any good deed I do," Bale said. "I failed Sylvie."

Kyril was surprised at Bale's sentiments and it suddenly put everything back into perspective.

"It's not a failure if we find her and destroy Gamal," Kyril said, turning toward their horses. "Let's get to the Wizard Conclave and find the third medallion."

Bale nodded his head to Kyril, jumped up on his horse, and took off.

The others followed suit and soon they were on their way again.

CHAPTER TWENTY-TWO

Sylvie woke up early the next morning and wrote her paper on the foundation of where a wizard of the earth received their powers. Even though she couldn't remember learning about it before, she'd *lived* it. She didn't need a book to tell her about earth powers or how one accessed them. She had felt it a few times already the night before—and it was more incredible than she could ever imagine.

Reminiscing on the previous evening she remembered how she had raced across the schoolyard and gardens. Each time her foot hit the ground she felt a new surge of energy. She had opened herself up to it all and it was amazing. She realized there was energy in everything that existed, whether those things were living like the trees around her or were inanimate objects like the rocks beneath the earth or the moisture in the air. As a wizard of the earth she was able to harness this into her own body, and could enhance her abilities multiple times over. As she ran, each breath brought new clarity and new potential to what she could accomplish.

At least that was how she had felt at midnight. Now, early the next morning, she didn't feel so powerful. She was tired, anxious, and worried about what the day might bring. Would she be powerful enough to defeat Gamal? It frightened her that he had somehow tricked and trapped her old mentor and that Danijela herself admitted that she may not be as powerful as

Gamal—at least not with the dark medallion that he wore around his neck at all times.

A soft knock sounded on her door and she jumped. Opening it carefully, she was relieved to see Jocelyn standing there. She invited her in and closed the door.

"Well?" Jocelyn asked. "Did you find the High Wizard?"

"Yes, we did," Sylvie said, nodding her head, "but we weren't able to rescue her quite yet. Well, I should say she wasn't ready to leave yet. She'll help us when the time it right."

Jocelyn's face fell. "Wizard Gamal was very angry last night. I'm afraid the school will be on tighter controls today."

Sylvie grimaced. "That'll make it hard. The High Wizard told me I needed to find the medallion soon or she was afraid that Gamal would either force me or move forward with his plans regardless of having the medallions."

"We'll all do what we can to help you, Sylvie."

"All?"

"The school isn't crowded during the summer, and most of those here know you…or knew you…oh well, you know what I mean."

Sylvie understood. As hard as it was for her to not remember anyone, it must be difficult for others to know her and things about her without herself being aware of it.

"But I'm afraid there are some who are siding with Gamal and want more influence for wizards," Jocelyn said. "They say that Gamal preaches that wizards should rule the world— especially wizards of the mind."

Sylvie understood. There would be some looking to take advantage of this precarious situation. But she knew what needed to be done.

"I need to go back down under the school to the magical artifact storage rooms today. The High Wizard said I needed to be the one to find the medallion and that's the only place I can think of where it could be." She hadn't yet told anyone about the pull that she felt to the medallion. It had already called to her many times. It had to be someplace near, but she couldn't figure it out. She hoped that meant that Gamal couldn't either.

"That's wonderful," Jocelyn said, clapping her hands together. "Soon, this will all be over."

"We'll see about that," Sylvie said. "It's hard operating without knowing what I know. The High Wizard said I am very powerful."

"You are," Jocelyn said. "But what about Gamal? He is powerful too. Did you feel the earth quaking and see the lightning last night? He must have been really mad. I wouldn't have thought it from a wizard of the mind."

Sylvie nervously reached for her paper, and turned back to Jocelyn with what she was sure was a red face. "That wasn't Gamal."

"What? You mean…?"

"Yes, it was me," Sylvie said. "I was running back to my room before the headmasters came and…it finally all came together for me. The feel of the earth under my feet and air around me. I felt it all…all the energy of the earth."

"Wow," Jocelyn said. "That must be amazing. As a wizard of the heart, when I feel things the most, my abilities and powers grow, but it's hard to maintain for too long. I can't imagine feeling all the power in the world around me." Jocelyn grew more serious. "But you must be careful. Wizards of the earth can burn themselves out."

"So I've heard," Sylvie said. "Since I can't remember what I already know, it's hard to know how much is too much."

"Well, if you are bringing lightning down from the sky and shaking the earth, that's getting close, I would imagine."

"I've stopped the waves of the sea before," Sylvie said matter-of-factly.

Jocelyn laughed out loud. "You might be one of the most powerful wizards in a long time, Sylvie. I'm so glad you are here."

The two walked out of Sylvie's room and made their way toward the main building where breakfast would be served and classes held.

Just before arriving at the cafeteria, Jax and Wydel approached from the other end of the hallway.

"Was that you last night, shaking the earth?" Jax asked, falling into step beside Sylvie as they entered the cafeteria.

Suddenly all the conversations stopped and the room became totally still. From a far corner three guards—two more than usual—glared in Sylvie's direction almost daring her to say or do something wrong.

Sylvie ignored them and tried to disregard the look of the others as she and Jax, Wydel, and Jocelyn moved to the line of food.

"Wydel, nice competition last night," bantered a friendly male voice from somewhere in the room. "When's the next one? You're next on my list."

A smattering of laughter filled the room and the guards stiffened.

"Anytime, Marquis, anytime," Wydel said back. This time the entire room laughed and the chatter picked back up.

After getting her food, Sylvie shoved it into her mouth and then excused herself to run to the library before class started. She needed to ask Librarian Nathanael about any information he had about artifacts stored there at the Conclave. She needed to narrow down where to look.

She turned a corner without looking and ran into someone, almost knocking them over. When she turned to apologize she found Gamal glaring at her. His face held nothing but barely-controlled rage.

"You!" he said.

"I…I'm sorry," Sylvie said. This was the last person she wanted to see right now.

"Did you have anything to do with that so-called competition outside last night?"

Sylvie looked him in the eye. "No. I heard about it this morning. I guess they didn't think I was strong enough to participate."

Gamal's black medallion pulsed with a dull throbbing of light. Sylvie could feel its influence and took a step backward.

"Where are you going in such a hurry?"

"To the library," Sylvie said. She was glad to be able to tell the truth. "I had a question for the head librarian about magic artifacts."

Gamal appeared surprised for a moment but covered it quickly.

"You did want me to find a medallion," Sylvie continued, "and so I'm doing research to figure out where it might be. I think it may be close."

She was worried she had said too much. But the information had the desired effect on him. Gamal actually smiled, although it was not friendly by any means.

"Here, close by?" he asked, his eyes greedy. "Where?"

"I don't know," Sylvie said. "That's why I need to see the head librarian."

"Anne can help you with that," Gamal said as he crooked his finger and guided her down the hall toward the library. "I'm afraid Nathanael is not feeling well today."

Sylvie stopped for a moment just before the library door. "What happened?"

Gamal waved an impatient hand in the air. "I'm sure it's just old age. Did you know he is over 110 years old? Quite remarkable, isn't it?"

Sylvie was sure that Gamal had done something to him because Nathanael had talked to Sylvie just the other day, and he looked fine. His actual age surprised her also. She hoped Gamal didn't know about the vial he had passed on to her for the High Wizard.

Gamal opened the door to the library and summoned Anne. Sylvie didn't want to speak to her, but she had no choice now. She surmised this librarian was one of Gamal's followers. She bowed to Gamal as he entered.

"Master," Anne said, while giving a disapproving look to Sylvie, "what can I do for you today?"

"Our new apprentice, Sylvonna Hickory here would like some information on magic artifacts," Gamal said. "Please give her any help that she needs."

Anne smiled wickedly. "Of course, come, my dear."

Sylvie obediently followed Anne down the aisles of books. She turned for a moment and caught Gamal's eyes. They bore into her own but he said nothing before turning around and leaving the room.

"What interest do you have in magic artifacts?" Anne raised her eyebrows.

"I'm looking for information on magical objects that may be stored here at the Wizard Conclave," Sylvie said, trying to stay as close to the truth as possible. She didn't relish the thought of being caught in any lies.

"I'm afraid that information is off-limits to young students," Anne said condescendingly. "Now, stop wasting my time with…"

"Your *master* did say to help me with anything I needed, did he not?" Sylvie said, emphasizing the word master.

Anne stiffened, and appeared to think for a moment as if conflicted.

"And both you and I know that I am not really a student here," Sylvie pushed, trying to throw the librarian off even more. "I'm most likely more powerful than you…"

The librarian turned pale at those words and a brief flicker of fear crossed her face.

"…at least that's what I've been told." She shrugged it off as if it had been an innocent declaration. "As you know, I can't remember anything."

"Of course, of course," Anne said while trying to regain her composure.

Anne turned down a small aisle that led to a door on the wall of the library. She hesitated for a moment and fumbled with some keys that she removed from her pocket before looking over at Sylvie again.

Sylvie smiled and nodded her head toward the door. "As the master said."

Anne tried to insert the key into the lock of the door but her hands were shaking. Eventually, however, she got it in and turned it. A small *click* sounded and she pushed the door open. With a wave of her hand, a few candles ignited. Sylvie took a step in and scanned the room. It was a small room with shelves on three sides. Old books and scrolls sat neatly on the wooden shelves, and a small table with two chairs sat in the middle of the room.

Walking over to one wall the librarian pointed to a shelf. "These books are catalogs of magic artifacts throughout the Kingdom of Arc and possibly the other nearby kingdoms, with notations on what is stored here at the Conclave."

Sylvie walked toward the books Anne had originally pointed out. She grabbed one randomly and sat down with it.

"Thank you," Sylvie said sweetly. "I may be here awhile."

"But I cannot leave you in here alone," Anne said, waving her arms around. "These books are too valuable."

"I promise I won't steal anything," Sylvie said, looking the librarian directly in the eyes.

Just then, a voice called from out of the room. "Librarian Wizard Anne?"

She turned around to speak to someone. "Yes?" Anne asked, clearly disturbed by the interruption.

"It seems there is a line of students waiting for information at the front desk," a male student said. "Are you the only one here today?"

"Yes, it appears that Nathanael is sick," Anne snapped at the apprentice. "I'll be there in a moment when I'm done here."

Another student walked up. "Librarian, I need to find a book for a report on…"

"Oh, for heaven's sake," Anne said, clearly not happy. "Can't you students find anything on your own?"

She glanced at Sylvie and sneered. "You'd better not leave this room." Then she turned and headed toward the front desk.

That left Sylvie all alone for at least thirty minutes until class started. She was sure Wydel was behind distracting the librarian. She was glad that she had befriended him. She went to the shelves once again and ran her fingers over a few books. All had titles on their spines…except for one, which she thought was strange.

She pulled the light brown leather-bound book down off the shelf and wiped off the dust. It appeared to be a homemade journal. She opened it up and thumbed through its pages. They were filled with neat handwriting, listing artifacts on the left hand side of the page and their uses on the right. Many of the lines did not list uses. Most had a small number and letter combination scribbled on the left, starting with either A, B, or C.

Running her finger down each page she looked for anything that could be helpful. The minutes ticked by and she knew she didn't have much time before either Anne returned or Sylvie had to go to class. Nothing so far had stood out to her. How would she even know what she was looking for? Flipping back and forth through the pages she thought she spied a pattern. Some of the artifacts didn't have a letter or number by them and, upon second look, none of those had a known use listed either.

Sylvie heard footsteps coming closer and raced through the book as quickly as she could once again. This time she only read un-coded entries. About three-fourths of the way through, she found the words she had been looking for: *Silver Medallion.* A brief description ensued—it had three circles with six lines coming from its center, but under known uses, the word *none* was hastily scribbled.

She closed the book and pushed it back onto the shelf. She was just moving away from it when Anne appeared in the doorway. The librarian looked suspiciously around the room and then back at Sylvie, who had now stepped closer to the door.

"All done for today," Sylvie said with a smile.

"Did you find what you were looking for?" Anne asked as they left the room, and she locked the door behind them.

Sylvie smiled at the idea of a locked room in an academy full of wizards. They must trust the students a lot—it would only take her a moment to get in again upon her return.

"Yes, I found some interesting things," Sylvie said. She knew anything she said to the librarian would get back to Gamal, so she used that to her advantage. She needed to continue to string along Gamal so that he thought there was some hope for her to find it before he did anything rash. And so she flat-out lied. "I think I may be starting to remember something about a silver medallion." Sylvie put on her best perplexed look. "But it might not be anything. I need to do some more research before I report back to Gamal. You know how demanding he can be."

By that time, the two were back by the front door of the library and Sylvie saw the last of the students leaving ahead of her. A few turned around and gave her a wink. She smiled back. With everything going on, it was nice to know she had friends.

Sylvie surmised that the Wizard Conclave must have been a fun school to attend. She just wished—for the hundredth time at least—that she could remember something about her years there!

CHAPTER TWENTY-THREE

Like all the other students, Sylvie handed in her paper to Wizard Instructor Ingall as she walked into the class. Then while he scanned through them, he—to Sylvie's surprise and interest—assigned the class a reading on magic artifacts. A small, worn around the edges pamphlet on the subject was handed around to everyone. Sylvie ran her fingers over the cover, imagining that she might have read the very same one when she had attended this class the first time.

Sylvie heard Ingall grunt partway through the session, so she glanced up at him. He was staring back at her; his nose twitched over his small mustache, but his eyes appeared thoughtful. He opened his mouth as if to say something but glanced at the door to the hallway first and thought better of it, instead returning to his papers.

Soon, something caught Sylvie's eye on the page she was reading. It had mentioned that some artifacts were so powerful or suspected of being powerful that they had to be shielded in a special room that didn't allow other magic to be used in the room. She instantly thought about the room where Danijela was being held.

If her room was shielded that way, then others in the basement might be also; more evidence that she would find the medallion there. The question was how could she get down there undetected once again? Soon class was over and she headed out of the room with the rest of her classmates.

"Miss Hickory," said Professor Ingall in a small voice as she walked past. "May I have a quick word with you?"

She held back and let the other students leave. It was quiet for a moment, then Ingall cleared his voice.

"Your theories on the source of power of a wizard of the earth are interesting, especially the part on the power of water. I've never heard of an earth wizard with much affinity for water; I'm not sure if that is something I would include."

Sylvie was anxious to get out of class and figure out a way to get downstairs. She wasn't interested in a scholarly discussion at the moment. So she just shrugged.

"I could be wrong," she said.

Ingall furrowed his brows at her and lowered his voice. "I know you are powerful, Sylvie. All of us do, but you must be careful. Theories like this could get you in trouble. Gamal looks through all our work. He is paranoid that we are trying to undermine him."

"And are you?" Sylvie stood with one hand on her hip.

"I...I...no..." Ingall's gaze flickered toward the door.

"Well you should be," Sylvie said angrily. "Rather than let all of this fall on a sixteen-year-old girl with no memories." She spun around and headed toward the door, not letting Ingall say anything else. She meant what she said. There were dozens of powerful wizards in the school. They could get rid of Gamal if they would band together. So why didn't they? What did he hold over them?

The answer was chaos. She realized she had seen very little magic used since she had been at the Wizard Conclave—a place that supposedly taught magic. A sudden thought occurred to her. Maybe they couldn't. Had Gamal somehow interrupted magic at the school? As she reached the doorway, she sent out her senses all around her. Since the previous night, she had felt more in tune with the power around her. Now, however, something didn't feel right. There was a darkness to it. It felt unbalanced.

She turned around and watched the professor. His shoulders sagged and his face dropped. His eyes said he wanted to do more, but he was afraid.

With a deep breath, Sylvie waved a hand in front of her and drew the water out of a cup on his desk. She spun it around in the air—like a big blob of water. Even though the air was dry in the Kingdom of Arc, there was still some moisture in it, and she pulled it out, making the blob of water grow larger in front of Professor Ingall. She then split the water into three portions and spun them around in the air. Twirling her hand around in a circle, she pushed the water toward the window, opening it with her abilities, and let the water go outside.

Ingall moved to the window and watched as the three blobs of water formed together once again and then flew over the top of a fountain. Digging deeper inside of herself, Sylvie pulled the fountain stream higher, and it engulfed the water that she had taken from his cup. Then Sylvie dropped her hand and the fountain returned to normal.

A few students walking outside stopped and stared at the spectacle.

Ingall turned around, and now fear covered his face and his lips trembled.

"There is a way to stop Gamal," Sylvie said. "And I will find it."

Sylvie left Ingall standing in silence and walked to her next class. It felt good to use her magic. It should not be something she hid. She slid into her seat a bit late. The professor gave her a stern expression then began his daily lecture.

"Sylvie, are you listening?" Wydel's whisper came from two seats behind her a few minutes later.

She turned to look at him. His words had startled her out of her thoughts. He pointed her attention back to the front of the room. The professor stood staring at the class, apparently waiting for an answer. In the stillness Sylvie's stomach rumbled and those around her stifled their giggles. Why was she suddenly so hungry?

"Miss Hickory," the professor said. "Maybe you could answer for us?"

"What was the question again?" Sylvie asked. Now the entire class laughed. But with it came smiles and winks—it was a good-natured teasing.

The professor sighed. "I asked the class for one thing that helps a wizard recover after using their powers."

And that's when Sylvie got the joke. Her stomach rumbling had been in reaction to the powers she had just used in Professor Ingall's room.

"Food." The words rolled off her tongue without her thinking about it. "Food provides needed energy back to the body and helps us to recover quicker."

The professor nodded his head, but Sylvie's mind was already elsewhere once again. She suddenly had an idea of how to get downstairs. As soon as class was over she pulled Jocelyn aside. Wydel joined them.

"You're a wizard of the heart and can heal, right?" Sylvie asked Jocelyn.

The wizard shrugged. "Technically yes, but I've only done it only under strict supervision. Next year, I'll be allowed to do more on my own."

"Can you make someone fall asleep?" Sylvie asked as she pulled the two of them down the hall and toward the kitchen. The plan was now racing through her mind.

"Why would I do that?" Jocelyn was clearly intrigued.

"Can you?"

"Sure, I guess I could. But I haven't done it before. I'm not allowed to do things like that on my own. But I've read about it before.

Sylvie opened the door to the kitchen and with a quick smile back at the other two, said, "Just follow my lead."

They appeared confused but nodded their heads anyway. Sylvie found Marcie working toward the back. She approached, got her attention, and then made sure no one else could hear them.

"Has food gone down yet to the High Wizard?" Sylvie asked.

Marcie gave a baffled expression and tried to tend to her duties.

"Marcie, I know where she is and I know that she at least has to eat, and this is the only place her food could come from." Sylvie looked Marcie directly in the eyes. "Has she had her midday meal yet?"

With a quick glance around the room first, Marcie shook her head.

"Then we would like to take it to her," Sylvie said.

"What?" Wydel whispered. "We'll be caught. I thought you were trying to find the medallion."

Sylvie shushed him and turned back to Marcie and lowered her voice even more. "I know you Marcie." She didn't really remember the woman, but the previous night the cook had acted very kindly toward Sylvie and Jax. "What if I told you I intend to help free the High Wizard and get rid of Gamal?"

A younger woman began approaching them as if to gather up some plates.

"I'll get them, Lysa," Marcie snapped at the girl. "Go help in the dining room."

Lysa almost tripped over herself moving away. Marcie then stared back at Sylvie for a moment before speaking.

"I won't even venture to ask how," she said, then let out a quick breath. "But if anyone can save her, it's you." She nodded her head toward a nearby counter. "There's her food. Grab an apron from the closet and I'll give you space to leave without the others seeing."

Sylvie, Wydel and Jocelyn each grabbed aprons. Sylvie and Jocelyn donned theirs, but Wydel stood looking down at his.

"Put it on, Wydel," Jocelyn said, her lips twitching trying to hold back a smile.

"But…" Wydel said.

"Do it," Sylvie said, more commanding than she intended. Wydel stiffened but did as she asked.

"I look stupid," Wydel said. He had removed his robe and now wore a white apron over his shirt and pants. It was too tight across the chest.

"Yes, you do," Jocelyn laughed, not being able to hold it in any longer.

Sylvie grabbed a plate of food, then a few additional biscuits that were freshly baked and just out of the oven. She gave them to Wydel who juggled them between his hands and blew on them to stifle the heat.

"Everyone gather in," Marcie called out to the rest of the kitchen staff away from where the three young wizards stood and around a corner. "I need to talk about cleanliness in our kitchen."

A few moans ensued and Sylvie motioned for Jocelyn and Wydel to follow her into the small pantry.

CHAPTER TWENTY-FOUR

Sylvie remembered her route from the night before—through a narrow door and the pantry, out the other door, and began walking down the stairs. Reaching the end, she noticed that there were torches on the wall every few feet lighting the way. They quickly reached three guards.

Sylvie had Wydel give Jocelyn the biscuits, then took in a deep breath and let it out again while motioning Wydel to stay hidden behind them. He did look ridiculous, and she let a small giggle leave her lips. The noise caught the attention of the guards.

"Food for the High Wizard," Sylvie called out.

"It's a bit early, isn't it?" said Cabe, the younger guard from the night before.

Sylvie shrugged. "Just following orders." She then had Jocelyn move in front with the freshly-made biscuits in her hand. "But we brought a treat for you men. Fresh out of the oven."

Their eyes lit up, and Cabe was the first to walk toward Jocelyn.

"When you touch them, make them get tired," Sylvie whispered to Jocelyn's back.

She stiffened but continued forward and handed Cabe one of the biscuits, holding his hand for a moment and smiling up at him. He returned the smile, then turned away, rubbing his eyes once before devouring the biscuit. Next, Jocelyn handed one to Roald, the guard from the previous night that had gone upstairs before Sylvie and Jax had arrived.

"How long have you been a guard?" Jocelyn held on to his hands a little longer. She looked up into his eyes as he answered.

"Twenty years, miss," the man said, but soon stifled a yawn. "Maybe too long. Seems I'm getting tired early in the day now."

The other man laughed but moved over to get his biscuit. He had darker hair and skin than most in the Kingdom of Arc, and he held his head high like he was better than them. He was maybe five years older than Sylvie. Before grabbing his biscuit, he smiled at Sylvie and walked toward her. He ran a finger through a spoonful of mashed potatoes on her plate.

"Mmmm, good," he said, putting the finger in his mouth.

Sylvie grabbed the plate away from the man, but he snaked his hand out and grabbed Sylvie. A spark flew from his fingertips as he held her tight.

"I know who you are, Sylvonna Hickory," the man said. "The Shadow Master would not be pleased that you were down here to visit the former High Wizard."

Sylvie's heart skipped a beat. She glanced past Jocelyn's shoulder and saw the first two men were already slumped against the wall with their eyes closed. Jocelyn had indeed made them fall asleep.

"Shadow Master," Jocelyn said. "What is that?"

The man turned toward Jocelyn for a moment, but it was enough for Sylvie. She took the plate of food and smashed it over the man's head. He wobbled for a moment but didn't fall. With a punch of air, Sylvie knocked him down the rest of the way.

"What did you do?" Wydel came forward.

"Big help you were," Sylvie said, annoyed that she hadn't planned for a wizard to be guarding her former mentor.

Wydel opened his mouth to answer, but Sylvie softened her voice. "Sorry, I'm not sure how long they'll all be out," she said. "We need to hurry." She grabbed the keys from the hook and moved to open the High Wizard's door. She slipped inside while the other two hung back at the doorway. The High Wizard jumped a bit from where she sat on the bed reading a book.

"Sylvie!" she exclaimed. "Have you found the medallion?"

"No, but I think it's in one of the storage rooms down here," Sylvie said. "We're here to look."

"We?" she asked.

Sylvie moved to the side and motioned the other two to come in.

"Ah, Jocelyn," the High Wizard said. "I always did think you had a lot of sense. Seems you're helping Sylvie defeat Gamal."

"One of the guards called him a Shadow Master," Jocelyn said after a brief bow to the High Wizard. "What does that mean?"

The High Wizard's face dropped and she shook her head. "Nothing good at all." Before she could explain further her eyes caught the third person and her lips curved back up into a smile.

"Wydel!" she said. "Not how I expected…you to be dressed. What are you doing here? Usually you're out causing trouble with a trick or two."

Wydel blushed and pulled the apron off over his head. "I told them I looked stupid."

Sylvie smiled but got back to business. "Do you know where the magic artifacts storage rooms are?"

"There are three down this hallway." The High Wizard started to move, but a chain held her foot back.

Sylvie put her hands on it to break it, but nothing happened.

"The room blocks magic," the High Wizard reminded her.

Then she remembered the keychain she was holding and brought it out. "But I have a key."

After fumbling for a few moments, she found the right key, unlocked the High Wizard, and they snuck out into the hallway. The High Wizard eyed the three men on the ground and raised her eyebrows, but said nothing. The small group moved instead down the hallway. There were three doors, marked A, B, and C.

"Where's the other room?" Sylvie wondered aloud.

"What other room?" the High Wizard said. "There are only three rooms where we keep the magic artifacts. They are sorted from the most powerful to the least. Do you know which room the medallion is in?"

Sylvie shook her head. "None of them. I looked in the journal and a medallion was listed, but its use wasn't known and so it had no room letter or number assigned to it."

"I see," the High Wizard said more seriously. "That makes things more difficult."

"Why?" Sylvie asked. "Where is it?"

"Why do we need the medallion?" Jocelyn asked.

Sylvie brushed the question away and watched the High Wizard for her answer. The woman pursed her lips as if deep in thought, then let out a sigh. She looked at all three of them in turn as if deciding something. "There is another room."

"Another room?" Wydel stepped forward. "Where is it?"

Danijela glanced at him as if measuring him up, then with apologies, pulled Sylvie away from the other two.

"What is it?" Sylvie asked.

Danijela lowered her voice. "It's in the records room in the library."

"I didn't see anything there," Sylvie said with a shake of her head. "I was in there."

Danijela smiled. "Do you think artifacts with unknown powers are kept out in the open? This is a secret that only a few people know about—and Gamal is certainly not one of them. There is a hidden room behind the back shelf."

Sylvie breathed a sigh of relief. She had finally found out where it was. "I can get back in there. That should be easy."

"No, not so easy," the High Wizard said. "You need two people to open up the secret room—two specific people."

Sylvie watched Wydel and Jocelyn for a moment where they stood patiently waiting. Wydel appeared on edge and perturbed to be left out.

When the High Wizard spoke, it was very quietly. "To open the secret room, you need the High Wizard and the head librarian."

All of Sylvie's previous excitement left her in a rush and she hung her head. "But you are in prison down here and Head Librarian Nathanael is said to be sick and I don't know where he is."

"I do," the High Wizard spoke as she turned and walked back toward her cell. But she stopped and put her hand on another unmarked door. "He's in here."

"Who's in here?" Jocelyn asked, joining Sylvie and Danijela at the door.

"What's going on?" Wydel asked. "We don't have much time. Where is the medallion, Sylvie? Isn't that what we came for?"

The wizard guard they had knocked out began to stir on the ground.

"Are you ready to get out?" Sylvie said to the High Wizard. "Did you take the vial of liquid?

The High Wizard nodded her head. "Yes, I did. Even though I was in a room that disallowed magic, they weren't taking any chances. They put some concoction in my food that would poison my abilities also. The vial that Nathanael gave you had the antidote. Now that I'm out of that room, I can already feel my powers returning." She flexed her arms, and just as the man on the floor raised his head she slammed a minuscule amount of magic into him, putting him back to sleep.

"That was much needed," the High Wizard said, smiling.

Sylvie raced over to the man and signaled Wydel to help. They lifted him up and put him in the room that the High Wizard had been held in, and then locked the door.

"What about them?" Jocelyn said, pointing at the two still sleeping on the ground.

"You put them to sleep?" The High Wizard held her lips tight.

Jocelyn lowered her head and mumbled. "I'm sorry. I know I'm not supposed to use magic unattended yet."

Danijela's lips held firm, but her bright blue eyes twinkled with amusement.

"Seems like the current circumstances must allow for the breaking of some rules," she said. "Heaven knows I did my share at your age." The High Wizard laughed. "My mentor was constantly on me for not doing things right."

Jocelyn and Wydel seemed stunned and at a loss for words. Sylvie, however, didn't remember enough to know what to be surprised at.

"I wasn't always old," the High Wizard said with another laugh. "Now, let's get our head librarian out. After all these years of service he certainly doesn't deserve such treatment."

"What do we need him for?" asked Wydel. "I thought we were going to get the medallion."

Sylvie was getting a bit frustrated at Wydel's sudden questioning everything. "We are," she answered, "but we need the Head Librarian to help."

"You mean you know where it is?" Jocelyn asked. "That's wonderful."

Sylvie used her keys to unlock the door. Nathanael sat up from his bed and blinked his eyes a few times to adjust to the light streaming into the room.

"Aaah, I see our young wizard has freed us both," the head librarian said.

"It's good to see you again, old friend." Danijela moved into the room and gave the man a hug. He stood an inch or two taller than her.

Leaving the room, they all looked again at the two guards.

"Let them be," the High Wizard said. "They were only following orders. They were always kind to me. They won't know until it's too late that we aren't in our rooms anymore. But we must hurry."

"So you have a plan?" Nathanael asked the High Wizard.

She looked at Sylvie, then back to Nathanael.

"It seems…Sylvie needs us to open the room."

"The room?" Nathanael appeared confused for a moment, but then his eyes opened wide as he looked at each person around him. "That room is dangerous. It's been years…you remember what happened last time, Danijela."

"I do remember, Nathanael," Danijela said. "But it may be our only chance to defeat Gamal. He has called himself the Shadow Master."

Nathanael stumbled and Wydel helped him from hitting the floor.

"That is bad news indeed."

CHAPTER TWENTY-FIVE

"We need another plan," Wydel said. "Now, where is the medallion?"

Sylvie let Danijela answer. She had obviously been concerned about who she shared the information with—though she didn't think there was any harm telling Wydel. So far he had been very helpful to her. Nathanael looked about to protest, but Danijela spoke first.

"In the library," she said with a long sigh. Sylvie noticed she didn't say where in the library—she was still protecting the information. It would be a dangerous thing for too many people to know the whereabouts of powerful objects without defined uses. She bet Gamal would love to get his hands on that stash.

"But we need to get you two up there without anyone else seeing and alerting Gamal," Sylvie said.

"Time for another distraction?" Wydel's lips curled up into a devious, but excited, smile.

"You always were one for tricks," the High Wizard said.

"If you only knew half…" Jocelyn mumbled, then blushed when she realized that the High Wizard had overheard her. "I mean…well…"

"I think you'd be surprised by what I know," she said.

Now it was time for Wydel to look nervous.

"Don't worry, apprentice Wydel," the High Wizard said. "It's good for young ones to have fun. So about this idea of yours?"

"Well, it's got to be something big enough to evacuate the building," Wydel said. "Maybe another contest? No…" He answered himself with a shake of his head. "An attack? No, that would take too long to orchestrate."

"Wydel!" Sylvie said. "Do you have an idea or not?" She stomped her foot hard on the ground and the floor shook a bit more than she intended. She really needed to learn to control her magic better.

"That's it!" Wydel's face lit up. "An earthquake."

The others were getting impatient with Wydel, but Sylvie understood. "I would bet that between the High Wizard and me, we could create quite the quake. The difficulty will be to get everyone to take it seriously enough to leave the building."

"A hard shaking on the upper floor should help," added Jocelyn.

"You've been hanging around with Wydel too much," Danijela said, but her smile showed she was only teasing. "But I think that might work."

"We need to keep ourselves protected," Nathanael said. "We can't be having a block of stone fall on our heads before we get to the library."

They all agreed and spent a few more minutes discussing the details. Then headed to the pantry room.

Nathanael appeared tired from the climb and the High Wizard held his arm tightly.

He patted it. "Thank you. You've always been such a sweetie to me, Danijela. I remember you at fifteen coming here with the last High Wizard Sallir. By the time you had traveled with him from your father's summer house in the mountains, his patience with you was wearing thin."

The High Wizard blushed and pushed back a strand of blond hair behind her ears. Then let out a nervous laugh before her face grew more serious. "It's times like these I really miss that man."

Nathanael nodded.

"We need to work quickly," Danijela said.

"Marcie!" Sylvie said suddenly.

"The cook?" Jocelyn asked. "I don't get it."

"Who has access to the entire building and all the rooms?" Sylvie asked.

"Servants!" Wydel grew excited. "Yes. Yes. If they start yelling about the earthquake right away, word will spread fast. We need to make sure that wherever Gamal is, he knows for sure he has to leave."

"I'll go," Jocelyn volunteered.

The rest of the room turned to her and she appeared nervous. Sylvie hadn't taken her for one to go jumping in like this—she didn't know if she had the nerve.

"I can do it!" Jocelyn said more firmly. Then she smiled innocently and put her hands on her cheeks.

They all laughed.

"I'll personally warn him and lead him out of the building and to safety," Jocelyn said.

"Fine," Sylvie said, then turned to Nathanael and the High Wizard. "Stay here for a moment while I talk to Marcie."

The group grew quiet and Wydel and Jocelyn gave her an intense look. She realized that she had just ordered the High Wizard.

"I'm sorry," Sylvie said. "I didn't mean to imply that I was in charge. It's just that…"

The High Wizard put her arm on Sylvie's own. "Don't worry, my dear. You are the one that has to retrieve the medallion, and someday…someday…" She hesitated for a moment as if deep in thought.

"Not now, Danijela," Nathanael said from her other side.

The High Wizard blinked a few times. "Yes, you are right, of course, old friend." Then turning to Sylvie, Wydel, and Jocelyn, she continued. "Go and get things set up. We'll wait here for your return. But we must hurry before it's noticed that we are not locked away anymore. By the time the next meal comes around, we'll be found out."

Sylvie nodded her agreement and, with Wydel and Jocelyn in tow, went back out into the kitchen. There were only a few helpers there at the time, but she spied Marcie talking to one of them in a far corner. She shooed the other girl away as they approached.

"Master Wizard Jenessa is not feeling well," Marcie said. "Glenda's bringing some food to her office on the top floor."

"Stop her," Jocelyn said.

Marcie opened her mouth—and then for some reason looked at Sylvie for confirmation.

"It's my way upstairs," Jocelyn explained to Sylvie.

Sylvie understood and nodded her head to Marcie and she called the serving girl back. Jocelyn held out her hands to take the tray from her. "I'll take it for you. I'm going that way."

The servant looked confused but did as she was asked, and soon Jocelyn was heading toward the door to the main hallway. She stopped with one hand on the doorway and looked back.

"You'll be fine," Sylvie assured her. "You'll know when."

She nodded and left.

Marcie crinkled her eyebrows in confusion and set the serving girl off on another errand. "What are you up to?" She looked from Sylvie to Wydel.

"We need your help," Sylvie said. "How quickly can you get word of something to all of the servants?"

"Well…" Marcie appeared surprised at the question. "I…I guess fairly quickly. I can send a few of the younger boys to run around and tell them all something. What do you have in mind?"

"I can't explain it all, but can you trust me?" Sylvie pleaded.

Marcie nodded. "I hope so."

Wydel frowned but stayed quiet.

"You do want the High Wizard back and Gamal gone, don't you?" Sylvie asked.

"Of course," Marcie said. "Of course."

"Soon there will be an earthquake…" Sylvie began.

"How do you know that?" Marcie asked.

"Don't ask," Wydel said with a shake of his head.

Marcie gave him a look of scolding, but Sylvie reached out, took hold of Marcie's arm, and drew her attention back to her.

"Please just believe us for now. There will be an earthquake. When it happens, we need the servants to…uh…overreact a bit; you know, scream and yell for everyone to leave the building. We need everyone outside."

Marcie nodded her head but didn't say anything.

Sylvie continued to explain for another minute, and then Marcie called some boys over to them with explicit instructions to deliver to the servants.

"How much time do we have?" Wydel asked.

Marcie smiled. "Ten or fifteen minutes; they're quick, but we don't always know where everyone will be."

"I'm going ahead to the library," Wydel informed Sylvie. "I'll make sure Anne and any other students are out of there before you and…" He caught himself before giving away their plan. "Well…before you do whatever you need to do in there, and then I'll come back to help you."

Sylvie shook her head, knowing that the less people who knew about the secret place the better. "We'll be fine. You just make sure that everyone stays outside."

"But what if you need help," Wydel pushed his point.

"No, Wydel, not this time," Sylvie said firmly. "We don't have time to argue about this."

Marcie put her hand on her forehead. "Are we all going to be all right?"

"Yes, of course," Sylvie said with a smile. "But, for your safety Marcie, you run outside with the others, all right? Get people as far away from the building as possible for as long as you can."

Wydel moved to go. "Good luck, Sylvie" he said a bit sarcastically. Sylvie realized he must still be sore at her for not letting him be with them in the library. "We all hope you find what you are looking for."

"Thanks, Wydel," she said with a soft touch to his arm. She really didn't want him mad at her. She had few friends as it was. "Thanks for all you've done. I know I don't remember you, but I hope we were friends before."

Wydel's grin grew about as wide as it could. "Well, you were a little too intense in your studies for us to hang out much, but we did know each other and I respect your power, even if you aren't a wizard of the mind."

Sylvie's face dropped. She had hoped that she'd had friends here at the Wizard Conclave, but…

"But this has been fun," Wydel said with an impish grin as he left the room. "More than you know. I have a feeling things are about to get real exciting around here."

"That boy!" Marcie shook her head with a laugh as Wydel walked away from them. "He's going to be a troublesome wizard someday."

"But hopefully a good one," Sylvie added.

Marcie nodded her agreement. "Now, I'm off to the dining room. The midday meal will just be finishing up and so there'll be a lot of people there. Just be careful, Sylvie."

"I will," Sylvie said out loud, but inside she didn't know how this was all going to end. Something was going to happen soon and she didn't know if she would survive it or not. But in the end, she hoped she would at least remember who she was.

CHAPTER TWENTY-SIX

Sylvie returned to the small pantry where the High Wizard and Nathanael waited for her.

"Are you ready for this?" the High Wizard asked Sylvie tenderly.

For some reason, Sylvie's eyes filled with tears. She brushed them away, but she knew they had been noticed.

"It's all right to be afraid," the High Wizard said. "I've been afraid plenty of times in my life."

"You have?"

"Of course. Fear is not a weakness. The real test is how you respond to that fear. Do you let it control and cripple you? Or do you rise above it and take control of it?"

"You make it sound so easy," Sylvie laughed.

"Oh no, it's not easy," the High Wizard said. "But fear can be a great motivator in achieving greatness."

"I don't want greatness," Sylvie said with a shake of her head. "I just want to remember who I am."

"But what if you never do?" The High Wizard peered at her intently.

"What do you mean?" Sylvie felt like the High Wizard had punched her in the gut. What did she mean by that? She would remember...wouldn't she? She *had* to.

"Would you still be doing what you are doing right now if you knew you would never remember who you are? Would you still be helping a wizard school that you don't have any recollection of attending? Would you still have helped me regain my powers and free me?"

As she spoke, Danijela's voice grew louder and more intense. Her blue eyes flashed brighter and power crackled around her now. "Would you still be trying to get rid of the Shadow Master even though you have no idea of the kind of power he might use against you?"

When Sylvie didn't answer right away, the High Wizard grabbed hold of Sylvie's arm and shook her—a grip hard and full of wizard power. Power that now flared up in Sylvie herself.

"Yes," she said. What she was doing was the right thing to do. "Of course I would."

The High Wizard smiled and let go of Sylvie's arm, but her power still grew around her. "And that's why you are the one chosen for the medallion, my young wizard. That's why you are here."

Sylvie nodded but didn't know what to say. She felt as if she'd heard all of this before from the High Wizard.

"Are you ready?" the High Wizard asked.

Sylvie steeled her heart and drew up the power inside of her. She felt the strength from the stones around her, and then reached outside of the building and felt the brush of the wind, the strength of the trees, the flow of the water fountains, and the rising heat of the sand. And became one with it.

"Then let's do it!"

With a flourish of his wrinkled hands, Nathanael brought up a protective bubble over their heads. A split second before

Sylvie let her own power loose, the building rocked as the High Wizard released her own incredible power. It blew the door off the hinges in front of them and she walked out of the pantry and into the kitchen. Sylvie and Nathanael followed.

The three of them moved to a window and focused on the grounds outside of the building. Danijela pushed her hands out and the grounds shook again. Off to the side, Sylvie saw a piece of stone fall from higher up on the building.

People screamed off in the distance, and voices grew louder out in the hallways. Sylvie hoped they wouldn't hurt anyone with the shaking of the building. They waited another minute before shaking it again. Sylvie drew up water deep from the hot earth, and in rolled a wave, with stone pavers buckling up under the pressure. She sent her mind deeper and soon became one with the water under the ground. It moved under the building, shaking it on its foundation. Soon, spurts of water blasted up from the ground below.

The High Wizard studied Sylvie for a moment. "Incredible," was all she said.

"She's using water," Nathanael mumbled from the other side of the High Wizard. "Not many can do that these days. In Wizard Jantzen's treatise on…"

"It's not the time for one of your history lessons, Nathanael," Danijela said with a smile.

The head librarian's eyes furrowed for a moment, then he shrugged and continued to maintain the bubble of protection over them.

Groups of wizards and instructors began to pour out of the back of the school and head out toward the practice fields.

Sylvie could see Marcie guiding people as far away from the building as she could, but there was no sign of Wydel, Jocelyn, or Gamal.

"Where is he?" Sylvie mumbled as she sent a harder shock to the floors above them. "That should get his attention."

A chunk of stone dropped from the ceiling above them, but Nathanael's protection held "Be careful," Nathanael said. "I haven't lived all these years to be killed by wild magic in the kitchen."

"Sorry," Sylvie mumbled. "But I don't see Gamal."

"He might be out the other side," the High Wizard offered with a shrug. "We'll give it another good shake, and then we need to get to the library."

After a few more minutes they slowly ventured out of the kitchen. The hallway was eerily quiet, aside from the few faint yells outside in the distance. Going to the staircase they looked up; all appeared empty.

A side door flew open, and both Sylvie and Danijela took on a defensive posture. Down the hallway toward them came a thin man, carrying a bow in one hand and a quiver of arrows in the other.

"Jax!" Sylvie called out, and both she and Danijela relaxed their battle stances. "What are you doing here? You need to get outside with the others. It's not safe in here for you."

"I saw the building shaking and knew it was you." He smiled as he spoke, and Sylvie—for some reason—thought about how handsome he was. A silly thing to think about at a time like this. "I mean, who else could do something so grand? But I didn't know if you were in trouble."

"I'm fine," Sylvie said more harshly than she intended. It came mostly from the distraction he was to her right now. "Did you see Wydel or Jocelyn?"

"I think I saw Wydel in front with a small group of wizards, but I'm not sure. Most were running out of the building and heading out back."

"We need to go!" Nathanael directed them up the stairs. "If this boy figured out the earthquake wasn't real, then Gamal might also."

Sylvie couldn't stay mad at Jax for long. He had been her longest friend—that she could remember, at least. Sylvie and the High Wizard followed Nathanael up the stairs, and Jax moved up next to Sylvie.

"So you didn't see Gamal or Jocelyn out there?" Sylvie asked again.

"No," Jax shook his head. "Why?"

Sylvie felt worry growing deep in her gut. She shouldn't have allowed Jocelyn to go by herself.

"You need to find her, Jax," Sylvie said as they neared the top of the steps.

"No, Sylvie," Jax said. "I need to help you."

"Jocelyn went to lead Gamal out…alone." Sylvie turned with the others toward the library.

"Oh, no," Jax mumbled. "Stupid girl. That man is trouble for sure."

Stopping at the doorway, Sylvie said, "Please, Jax. I need to go with the High Wizard and Nathanael to retrieve the medallion."

"You found it?" Jax said with excitement in his voice.

"I don't know for sure," Sylvie admitted. "But I think so. Please—go and find Jocelyn."

Jax stood for a moment as if deciding what to do. He glanced at the library and then looked up toward the highest rooms in the building. Then he turned to the High Wizard.

"Make sure Sylvie doesn't get hurt," Jax said.

The High Wizard nodded and Jax bounded toward another set of stairs that would take him to the upper floors.

"Be careful Jax," Sylvie called out, then turned and entered the library with Nathanael and Sylvie.

"That boy cares about you," the High Wizard said.

Nathanael chuckled, but Sylvie tried to ignore the blush she knew was creeping up her cheeks.

True to his word, Wydel had made sure that everyone had left the library. They hurried past rows of books to the locked research room. But then, Nathanael stopped.

"We need the keys," he said, turning back toward the desk.

Sylvie reached her hand toward the keyhole, and picturing the locking mechanism inside, drew upon the power of the earth around her in the wood and stone. *Click.*

"I've always wondered why we locked it anyway with all these wizards around," Nathanael mumbled. "We've become too trusting, perhaps."

The three wizards entered the room, and Nathanael waved his hand to make two candles on the table flare to life. When Sylvie gave him a surprised look he shrugged.

"I may be old, but I am still a wizard."

Danijela chuckled as she moved toward the back of the room. She stretched up for a book on an upper shelf but couldn't reach it, so Sylvie retrieved it for her.

"Is this what you want?" she said.

The High Wizard rolled her eyes but only responded by taking the book and opening it. Inside was a hidden compartment with a key. She took it out and then nodded toward Nathanael.

"Head Librarian," she said. "It's your turn now."

Nathanael reached both of his hands out and touched two different books. After a few seconds both began to glow. There was a quiet grinding sound behind the shelf as it began to move to the side. A tall, narrow doorway stood behind the shelf. Nathanael pulled out a cord from under his shirt, the end of which held a key similar to the one the High Wizard had taken from the book.

"There are multiple safeguards to keep outsiders from getting into this room," the High Wizard said.

The two wizards took their keys to the door, but there was no keyhole or door handle on it. Instead, they traced patterns on the door with their fingers. Soon, two holes appeared in the middle. Both of them took their keys, placed them into the holes at the same time, and turned.

The entire outside of the door began to glow, but it didn't open. Suddenly a light flashed so brightly that Sylvie had to shut her eyes.

When she opened them again the light was gone and the door still stood closed, with the keys once again sitting in the hands of the two older wizards.

"It didn't work," Sylvie moaned in defeat. All of this and they couldn't get into the room after all.

"Sure it did," the High Wizard said with a smile and a wave of her arms around the room.

Sylvie turned around and jumped in shock. The small reading room had disappeared and in its place was a room full of artifacts sitting neatly on shelves. A small lectern was in one corner with an ancient looking book sitting on it.

"How?" Sylvie couldn't understand what had happened. "Where are we?"

"We are in a room downstairs," Nathanael explained. "With the turn of the two keys, the rooms changed places."

"But what if someone comes in?" Sylvie looked at the door that had, at least before, led to the library.

"They would only step into the other room," Nathanael said. "But it only lasts ten to fifteen minutes at most, or we may be stuck in here for a while."

When Sylvie gave him a questioning look, he only shrugged.

"More safeguards set a long time ago. Now, we must hurry."

The High Wizard picked up the old book and began to flip through its pages. She stopped and put her finger on a certain spot and then looked around the room. She then proceeded to walk toward a cupboard, the only one in the room. Sylvie wondered why she hadn't noticed that before.

Sylvie joined the High Wizard in front of the cupboard as she used a bit of magic to open it. Peering inside she could see three objects. A small black obelisk, a statue of a small dragon, and a silver medallion on a chain.

"It's there," Sylvie gasped. She had hoped, but she hadn't really known for sure. She reached her hand forward.

"Be careful," said Nathanael's from behind. "Some of these unknown artifacts can be quite nasty. Just last year, I spent a few days as a man only three inches tall, and once I even…"

"Just be careful, my dear," repeated Danijela with a glance back at Nathanael that quieted him. "And don't touch the other two artifacts. Nathanael is correct; we don't know what might happen. Once Emperor Mezar told me that Kyril had found a medallion and was told there were two more, I had an inkling it was here somewhere, but before I could figure it out, Gamal had imprisoned me."

Sylvie moved her hand forward and images of everything she could remember since her accident flickered through her mind. Waking up on Vorwyth, Jax helping her escape, discovering she had magic, her wizard test, and the connection she had felt with the High Wizard. Her friends, Wydel and Jocelyn, had believed in her and trusted her. And now was the moment of truth.

Before she reached the medallion, a new feeling began to grow inside of her. It was powerful, but different from her own magic. It was stronger, but simpler and quieter.

Do not fear, came whispered words to her mind. *Bring balance to the magic. Bring balance back to the kingdoms of men and wizards. Bring me to you.*

Her fingers touched the edge of the medallion and she felt a surge of power inside of her. Power that she was sure others throughout the grounds of the Wizard Conclave could feel. She brought it up closer to her and suddenly a blackness ran through her mind.

"Nooooo!" came Gamal's voice from nowhere, and a swirl of blackness cut off the room she was in. Instead, a vision formed in front of her.

Sylvie could see Jocelyn lying still on the ground. A lump formed in her throat and she tried to concentrate on the medallion in her hand and the meaning of what she was now seeing in her mind.

"This is the last time an elf meddles in my business," she somehow heard Gamal say.

As he turned, Sylvie saw Jax standing at attention against a wooden door opposite Gamal. He appeared unable to move. Gamal moved closer to him and came within inches of his face, but Jax's expression didn't change. Jax began to hum a tune and Gamal appeared to struggle to keep a hold on him. Jax turned his eyes slightly and seemed to catch Sylvie's own eyes. There was a calmness in them that surprised her. It seemed as if he gave her a slight grin, and then he blinked. His strength in front of Gamal was astounding.

If Jax could do that, she could do this. Taking a deep breath, she banished thoughts of Gamal from her mind and swung the silver medallion over her head. But before the chain even touched her neck, she saw Gamal plunge a knife into Jax's stomach. Sylvie faltered in her concentration as a cry caught in her throat.

For a moment she could see the High Wizard and Nathanael standing next to her once again, but then the room flashed so brightly that she had to shut her eyes. But in that light came clarity and power and knowledge. And with that knowledge came the awareness of two other medallions.

One gold and one bronze.

CHAPTER TWENTY-SEVEN

The rest of the trip riding north toward the city of Arc had been uneventful for Kyril, Joelle, Hasani, and Bale. They'd come across many small towns, so they were able to stay in an inn the night before. Joelle's strength was returning and she was almost fully healed.

Kyril shielded his eyes in the morning sun and had to blink often to keep sand from flying into his eyes.

"See how the land changes from grasslands to desert here?" Hasani pointed. "It's caused by a unique wind pattern that gets caught between the western Blue Sea and the Superstition Mountains. It swirls around here and takes all the moisture out of the air, leaving it dry and hot."

"Our walking library," mumbled Bale. "Is there anything you don't know, Wizard Hasani?"

"Don't tease him, Bale," Joelle shot back.

Hasani only shrugged, not offended by Bale's words. "Well, Bale, I do have a gift of remembering most everything I read, and I've read a lot! It's very exciting. I've studied the politics and geography of the Kingdom of Arc before, but this is my first time here. Isn't it wonderful?"

Kyril wiped his forehead. "I'm not sure how wonderful it is, but it's going to get hot today."

"For once I agree with Kyril," Bale said with a light laugh. "It's only morning. How hot is it going to get?"

"Well, at this time of year," started Hasani, appearing to do calculations in his head, "and as close as we are to the City of Arc, I would determine…"

"It was a rhetorical question, Hasani," Bale said with an eye roll toward Kyril.

Kyril himself tried to hide a snicker, but it came out as a snort instead.

"Both of you should be nicer to Hasani!" Joelle rode up between Bale and Kyril. "He knows more than all of us put together. I bet he could tell us about every plant or town we pass. I'd love to have that much knowledge, but I can't seem to keep that much information in my head. But somehow I do remember all the ways to heal someone. I wonder why that is…"

Kyril leaned up and glanced over at Bale on the other side and grinned. The young spymaster nodded his head toward Joelle and then moved his mouth open and closed many times as if mimicking her never-ending talking. Kyril laughed and Joelle turned to him with eyebrows furrowed.

"Are you making fun of me?" Joelle's green eyes flashed.

Kyril didn't know what to say so he turned his face forward.

"You know with the medallion I can discern some of your thoughts and intentions, Kyril," she said.

"That's not fair," Kyril said. "Anyway, it was Bale!"

"Me?" Bale said. "I would never…"

Before he could finish, Joelle screamed loudly and Kyril's heart jumped up through his throat. He looked around for any sign of danger. Bale's sword rang out as it left its scabbard and he joined Kyril in looking for the reason behind Joelle's scream.

Then Joelle laughed, and the fear left Kyril, replaced with a lifting of his heart.

"Joelle," Hasani said in a serious voice. "You shouldn't play with our emotions that way. That's not very polite of you."

Joelle huffed. "I'm sorry you got trapped in the bubble of my magic, Hasani, but these two…" She waved her hands at Bale and Kyril. "They deserved a little fear."

"You mean there wasn't any danger?" Kyril asked.

"No," Joelle said with her head held high. "Just me." And with that, she picked up the pace and jumped ahead of the three young men. "Catch me if you can. I'll race you to the city."

Bale actually laughed. "I can't say it's ever boring riding with wizards." He jumped out behind Joelle, leaving Kyril and Hasani behind.

Big grins spread across their faces. With a yell they pushed their horses forward, and soon all four were racing down the desert road toward the City of Arc.

Kyril could see the outlines of the city walls a few hours later. They were tall, thick, and tan—made of some sort of sandstone. So opposite of the domes in Gildan and even the architecture he had seen in the Realm.

"Let's stop for a break," Kyril said, pointing toward a small copse of palm trees up ahead. "I could use a drink."

The other three agreed and they pulled off to the side of the road and toward the small oasis. A pair of travelers were leaving just as they got there.

"How much farther to the Wizard Conclave, good sirs?" asked Joelle.

One trotted closer. He had blond hair and fair skin like the other, but had a linen over his head to protect him from the heat.

"I'm not sure you want to go there right now," he said. "I assume you are students?"

"We need to do some research in their library," Hasani said. "It's a matter of grave importance."

"Well, we've heard rumors," the man continued. "Something's not quite right there."

"What do you mean?" Bale asked, bringing his horse up in front.

"Seems to be someone new in charge."

Bale turned and looked at Kyril and Joelle.

"Do you know his name?" Bale asked.

The two men just shrugged. "No, just that he's got things on lockdown and seems to be looking for someone or something. Just be careful. If you take the road around the city instead of going through it, you could be there in an hour of hard riding."

The two men turned their horses back to the road, leaving the four travelers silent for a moment as they dismounted their horses and let them graze on a few tufts of grass. Kyril joined the others in drinking a bit of clear water from a small spring under the shade of six tall palm trees.

Kyril sat down under one of the trees and leaned his head back against the trunk.

"Do you think it's him?" Joelle asked no one in particular, but they all knew who she meant. "Has he infiltrated the Wizard Conclave now?"

"He'd have had time to get here from when I last saw him in Cyrene," Bale said matter-of-factly, then after a few seconds of silence his voice dropped lower. "Do you think she is there too?"

They all knew who he meant.

"We'll find her, Bale," Joelle said. "I'm sure Sylvie is fine. She's one of the strongest wizards I know."

"But so is Gamal," Bale said. "You said he calls himself the Shadow Master now; that sounds bad for sure."

"Until he has all three medallions," Hasani added, "he can't beat us. And we know at least two of them are here."

In response to Bale's words, Kyril watched Joelle's hand mirror his own as it moved up to grab hold of her medallion. All of a sudden his mind was whisked away from the oasis—just like it had been when they had found the other two medallions.

This time he stood in the back of a forge. Next to him stood Joelle on one side and…

"Sylvie!" Kyril almost fell over as Sylvie materialized on his other side.

"You're alive!" Joelle cried out, and Kyril watched as tears ran down her face. "Where have you been? Where are you now? I see you found the third medallion."

She was right. Sylvie was wearing the third medallion—a silver one whose pattern mirrored his own. However, Sylvie had not yet said a word. She glanced around worriedly, and she barely seemed to notice Kyril and Joelle. She looked well to Kyril, but her eyes held more fear than surprise in them. Her blond hair bounced around her shoulders as she continued turning around.

An older man wearing a thick black apron stood a few feet away from the burning forge. He had just used tongs to set something aside. Before Kyril could tell what it was, a man entered.

"King Anikari," Kyril whispered. He had seen him twice before—both times when the other medallions had been found.

"Where are we?" Sylvie finally said.

"It's over 400 years ago," Kyril tried to explain. "They can't see or hear us. We're only witnessing what happened somehow. That's King Anikari. It looks like the metalsmith is making our medallions."

"Our medallions?" Sylvie asked as if suddenly realizing that Kyril and Joelle had a medallion like hers—only of a different color and material. "Who are you? Are you with Gamal?" She took a defensive posture as if preparing for battle.

"Sylvie," Joelle pleaded. "It's us, Joelle and Kyril. Can you see us? Where are you right now?"

Sylvie's face grew dark. "I'm in the library at the Wizard Conclave—at least I was. Now, why did you bring me here? I need to help Jocelyn and Jax. They're in Gamal's room."

"Gamal is there with you?" Kyril asked.

Before she could answer, King Anikari spoke. "Are they ready?"

The metalsmith nodded and proceeded to hold up three medallions. King Anikari pulled out three chains and handed them to the man.

"Each chain has been imbued with one of the magic disciplines—earth, mind, and heart," King Anikari spoke. "Put them through the medallions carefully, Allyn."

After the man did as he was asked, he handed them to Anikari. The king took a few moments to align them together. They sat identically on top of each other. A loud noise outside took his attention for a moment.

"I need to hurry," Anikari said. "It appears we have won the war, but I'm afraid the evil has not been vanquished. My old friend has turned against us and has delved into the dark arts."

Allyn nodded his head solemnly. "Are you sure you can do this alone, my lord? You really should have all wizard disciplines present."

"I do what I must," Anikari said. "There must be a way in the future to rein in chaos and bring balance back to the world of magic and men. I tried to peacefully bring the cities of my new Realm together, but others got greedy and almost destroyed it all."

Anikari closed his eyes and wrapped his hands around all three medallions. A dim light surrounded them, and then grew brighter and brighter until Kyril had to turn away. He watched as Joelle and Sylvie did the same.

"They can't see us or hear us?" said Sylvie.

"No," Kyril said. "Remember when I told you about my first vision on the hill when Anikari gave the three medallions to wizards of different kingdoms—the Realm, Arc, and Gildan? Then when Joelle found her medallion we went back even further in time and saw a man steal the powers of his friend and call himself the Shadow Master."

"That's what Gamal calls himself," Sylvie says.

"Yes," Kyril said. "And you said he is there with you?"

"We can finally defeat him then?" Joelle asked Kyril.

Suddenly the bright light dimmed and Anikari stood once again with all three medallions.

"Did it work?" Allyn took a step closer.

King Anikari peered down at each of them, turning them over in his hand. "They *must* work. I cannot stand the thought of someone else being betrayed so. Greed is one of our worst enemies—especially the greed of a wizard. As wizards, we are supposed to help and guide others, not destroy them. I'm afraid that someday, people will not tolerate us if too many wizards turn to the dark."

"The metals will last for as long as their powers do, my lord," Allyn said. "Their ores came from deep in the Superstition Mountains in old magical caves—where dragons are said to have lived. I used all my skill and magic in making each one identical except for the material—brass, gold, and silver.

The king nodded his head. "It is done then. It's all I can do to help those after I am gone. But all of the medallion holders must work together. Only together can balance be established once again and evil eradicated."

"How will they find them when they are needed?" asked Allyn as he began to clean up and fire down the forge.

Anikari had already begun walking toward the door. He turned his head around and smiled. "One does not find the medallions; they will find wizards who are worthy."

"Then it's time for us to defeat Gamal once and for all," Joelle said. "Sylvie, we're only an hour away from you. Hold on!."

Sylvie stood stiffly for a moment then tilted her head. "And who are you?"

Kyril didn't know what to say and Joelle's mouth hung open silently. He knew it wouldn't be long until they left the vision. They never lasted much longer than five minutes or so. The air around him started to change.

"We're your best friends, Sylvie," Joelle cried out, clearly hurt and perplexed. "Why don't you remember us?" The air around them started to swirl, and Sylvie's outline became fainter.

"I don't remember anything before the shipwreck," Sylvie whispered. "I'm trying, but I still can't." Tears came to her eyes and she angrily wiped them away. "I thought finding the medallion would bring back my memories, but it obviously didn't."

The scene finished changing around them and Joelle screamed and reached toward Sylvie, but she was no longer there.

"Joelle, Joelle!" Hasani came rushing over to her, with Bale close behind. "What's wrong?"

They were back now at the oasis. Kyril could still hear the echoes of Joelle's scream. Her face was pale and haunted. One of the horses nickered behind them and Kyril stood up and glanced around. Off in the distance, the two men they'd spoken to were still heading down the road away from the City of Arc.

"How long were we gone?" Kyril asked.

"Gone?" Bale said. "What do you mean? You both sat down against a tree while we were talking about Gamal and the medallions, and then a moment later Joelle began yelling ."

Kyril shook his head. The vision had only lasted a few seconds in the real world. He didn't know how it worked, but this was the third time he'd experienced it.

"She's there," Joelle whispered, wiping tears from her eyes.

"Who's where?" Bale looked confused. "What is going on?"

"Sylvie's at the Wizard Conclave," Kyril said.

"That's great," Hasani said, beaming.

"Then why is Joelle crying and you are looking so distressed?" Bale asked, pacing back and forth between the two. "What aren't you telling us?"

"Gamal is there too, it seems," Kyril said.

Bale stopped pacing and his face went pale. "But she's all right? Sylvie's alive?"

"Yes, she's alive and has the third medallion, but…" Joelle hesitated, but started crying again.

"Yes? But what?" Hasani tried to comfort Joelle. "Why are you crying?"

"We'll be there soon." Bale ran toward his horse. "Come on. They said an hour if we hurry. You'll have all three medallions, and with everything we know we can defeat Gamal. I'll tear him apart if he hurts Sylvie."

All four jumped on their horses and began riding.

"Wait!" Bale said, riding up to Kyril. "You never answered me! Is Sylvie all right?"

With pursed lips, Kyril shook his head from side to side. Finally, he let out a puff of air and, with it, the dreaded answer to Bale's question.

"Sylvie is there and like Joelle said, has the medallion," Kyril said, then took in Joelle's face. Her tears had stopped, but her eyes were still red and swollen. "But she doesn't remember who she is or who we are."

With a low grunt of frustration, Bale picked up speed and all four travelers pushed the horses as hard as they could toward the Wizard Conclave.

CHAPTER TWENTY-EIGHT

Sylvie took a deep breath and the room in the library came into view around her once again. She found both the High Wizard and head librarian watching the glowing silver medallion that now hung from her neck. She didn't know what to think of what she had just seen.

Kyril and Joelle, as they had referred to themselves, seemed legitimately concerned for her and knew about the medallion. She wanted to trust them…but it was hard without her memories.

"What's wrong?" the High Wizard asked. "You look sad."

"I was hoping my memories would come back," Sylvie said, wiping a tear from one of her eyes. "But they didn't."

Sylvie put her hand against the stone wall and the medallion flared to life once more. Her mind came back into focus and she saw another brief glimpse of Gamal in his room, and she remembered what she had seen before. She turned to the others.

"Gamal is still in his room with Jax and Jocelyn," Sylvie said, rushing out the door. "We have to help them."

"How do you know that?" the High Wizard asked, following closely behind.

"I just do," Sylvie said. She didn't know how the medallion worked, but twice now since touching it, she had seen Gamal in his room.

"I'll stay here," Nathanael said from behind. "I'll only slow you down."

"Be careful, old friend," the High Wizard said, turning her head but not slowing down. "Keep the others out until we take care of Gamal."

Sylvie reached the stairs and placed her hand on the banister. The wood called to her and images flashed repeatedly through her mind. It was all very overwhelming, and she stumbled and fell. Danijela helped her back up.

"Are you all right?" she asked.

Sylvie shook her head a few times. "I'm not sure. Every time I touch something, I see images."

Without touching the banister again, she ran up the stairs with Danijela at her side.

"What kind of images?" Danijela asked as they reached the second landing and rounded the stairs for the next level.

"People, events…" Sylvie said. It was all so confusing. "I'm not sure. I saw Gamal in his room with Jocelyn on the floor, and he was hurting Jax."

"You're seeing reminiscences of old memories and events," Danijela said. "That must be part of the power of your medallion."

Out of breath, they ceased talking as they ran up the rest of the flights of stairs. Coming to the top floor, they stopped for a moment, and Sylvie looked around. She'd never been there before, but she tried to visualize what she had seen and where the medallion was now leading her.

"He better not have taken my rooms!" The High Wizard glanced to her right and the building shook again with her anger.

A flash of light at the end of a hallway caught their attention, and a moment later something rammed into both Sylvie and Danijela, and they collapsed on the floor. Hearing a sound, Sylvie sat back up.

"Jax!"

Jax moaned and untangled himself from them. His right side was soaked in blood and his face was pale.

"You used the stone to get away," Sylvie realized. "Is Gamal still in his room?"

Jax nodded weakly. "Go, Sylvie. I'll be fine."

Jax grimaced, and Sylvie knew he was putting on a front. He was hurt.

"I'll watch him," the High Wizard said to Sylvie. "Go."

Sylvie could use Danijela in confronting Gamal, but was torn between helping Jax and getting to Gamal. But Jax weakly put his hand on her arm.

"Please, I'll be fine," Jax said, begging her once more. "Help Jocelyn and get Gamal before he gets away."

"Watch over him for me," Sylvie said. Going in alone may not be the smartest thing, but she needed to make sure that Jax would be all right. She couldn't lose him.

Danijela nodded and turned to tend to Jax.

Sylvie gritted her teeth, stood up, and began walking toward where Jax had come from. She cautiously approached the door and pushed it open gently. She spotted Jocelyn lying on the floor, unmoving, so she rushed toward her—but then was hit from behind. It was all Sylvie could do to put her hands out in front of her and break her fall against the back of a large cushioned chair.

"I'll take that medallion," Gamal said from behind her.

She felt fingers try to pry the chain off her neck. But she launched her body backwards and the back of her head slammed into Gamal's forehead. He grunted and released his grip on her medallion.

Sylvie now spun around, her back against the chair. Gamal's own black medallion let off a whisper of black smoke and Sylvie thought back to the vision of King Anikari making the three medallions.

"That's not one of them," Sylvie said.

Gamal's forehead was already swelling with a bruise. He appeared confused for a moment but continued to move closer. Sylvie lifted her hands in front of her and felt the power of the medallion augmenting her own powers. She sidestepped off of the small carpet and onto the stone floor. The stone connected to the earth deep down in the foundations of the building; it almost sang to her with power.

"The other two should be here soon," Gamal said. "They've been captured and should be on their way here by now."

Sylvie thought about the two medallion-holding wizards in her vision—they hadn't looked like they had been captured. But they *had* said they would be here soon.

Before Gamal could say anything more Sylvie lashed out at him with a burst of silver fire. As it came to him, it split and went around him, while his own black medallion pulsed with fire. Suddenly, he disappeared and Sylvie heard his footsteps behind her. She spun around and was knocked down by a blast of black-infused air. After rolling instinctively on the ground, she jumped back up to her feet, and by sheer will threw Gamal back against a nearby wall.

"You are stronger now than before."

"Before?" Sylvie paused. "You knew me before?"

Gamal laughed loudly. "Oh, this is so wonderful. You still don't remember, do you? I was your mentor, Sylvie. I taught you all you know."

"But the High Wizard…" Sylvie had felt such a connection to her.

Gamal shook his head. "Oh yes, you were her pupil once, but your real powers came after I taught you. We were planning great things together in Gildan. Then you left me in in Cyrene. You were caught in a great storm. I thought you had died, until you showed up here at the Wizard Conclave. I've been trying to help you."

Sylvie didn't know what to think. It was all so confusing. What if he was right? She couldn't deny what she didn't know.

"I don't believe you," she said without thinking.

"Everything I've done has been to help you remember Sylvie," Gamal said, trying to smile, but to Sylvie it came out as a sneer and weak attempt to sway her. "You don't really know who you are."

He was right. She didn't know who she was, but she knew the type of man Gamal was. He had terrorized the entire school, had usurped Danijela's authority, and had treated her with nothing but disdain since the moment she had met him.

She doubted his claims of them working together. But whether she had been that type of person before wasn't important; she wasn't that type of person *now*. But she had to be careful. He was very powerful.

Gamal reached into his pocket and pulled out a small statue. Sylvie felt the room around her darken in its presence.

"We don't even really need the medallions anymore, Sylvonna," Gamal said with a gleam in his eye. "I have enough other artifacts to enter the magic stream."

Sylvie was confused once again by words she didn't understand. But she put on a false smile and took a step forward. "Can you really help me remember?"

Gamal's eyes went wide with surprise and he held his hands out to his sides. "Of course, my dear. It's what we have been working for all this time. I, a wizard of the mind, you, a wizard of the earth—all we need is a wizard of the heart…" He turned his attention back to Jocelyn's still body for a brief second.

Sylvie realized he had been trying to turn Jocelyn into one of his followers. She took another step forward. "And then we will have all the power, master—Shadow Master isn't it?"

"Yes. Yes!" Gamal's red birthmark pulsed on the side of his forehead with excitement. "The plan is already in motion. We will soon rule the nations with the power of a God."

"And your black medallion, where did you get that?" Sylvie was now trying to stall him until she could attack him unawares.

His eyes went wide and dark as he handled his medallion. "My last master, Targon, had inherited it from his father. It had been passed down for many generations from the original shadow master. It is his power. It grows more powerful with every killing. And now it's mine."

"What about the other medallions?" Sylvie asked. "What if you had them all?"

Gamal thought for a moment, surely contemplating the power all the medallions would bring him. She had distracted him with her questions.

"With them I could rule more than just this world," Gamal said. "With their power together, along with my black medallion and the other artifacts…I will be unstoppable. Kingdoms and worlds will bow before me. I will then truly be the Shadow Master."

His voice rose as he spoke and his eyes took on a glassy look. Sylvie felt fear down to her toes, but also great strength at the same time. She realized he had gone from saying *we* to *I,* and she fully knew then it was all a lie. He'd never been her mentor. Summoning all the power she could, she flicked her hand out toward him with one blurred motion and grabbed at his black medallion.

Pain shot through her hand and into her body, but she held on, willing her own silver medallion to fight against the Shadow Master's evil powers. Gamal lifted his head and screamed. Gold and black fire and smoke swirled around the two of them.

Sylvie gritted her teeth and called on more power. The school shook with her desire and she dove down deep into the earth, but still the black medallion shot its eerie tendrils into her. She wouldn't be able to do much more alone.

"Give it to me!" Gamal bellowed, reaching toward her medallion. "You little wretch!"

Out of the corner of her eye, Sylvie saw the High Wizard creep into the room. She grabbed a metal candlestick off a table by the door and snuck forward behind Gamal. He was too obsessed with Sylvie's medallion to notice.

Sylvie threw all she had at Gamal—fire, wind, and air—but he held his own and deflected each attack. Scorch marks blackened the walls and furniture cracked and broke. The High Wizard stood behind him on tiptoes, raised the candlestick as high as she could, and brought it down hard on the back of his skull.

Immediately, his powers ceased and Sylvie fell forward on the floor. Out of the corner of her eye she watched as Gamal's body slumped to the floor next to her, blood gushing from the back of his head.

"Sylvie, are you all right?" Danijela came and knelt down by her side. "I've never felt so much power from one person."

Sylvie took a few deep breaths before answering. Stars swam in her vision and she tried to keep from passing out. Her own powers had receded somewhat, but the medallion still glowed around her neck. She looked at the concern written across the High Wizard's face, and thought about what Gamal had been telling her about herself. She didn't believe any of it. She *couldn't* believe it.

Nodding, she sat up, "Why didn't you use your powers against him?"

"Everything you threw at him held him at bay," Danijela said. "His magic is strong. I figured magic or not, a good knock to the head would put him out."

"I'm glad you came along when you did, but what about Jax?" Sylvie asked.

But before Danijela could answer back Jocelyn groaned and her hand twitched. Both Sylvie and Danijela rushed to her side.

"Jocelyn." Sylvie placed her hand on her forehead. "I'm here."

Jocelyn's eyes fluttered open and a low moan escaped her lips. "He knew, Sylvie," she said. "He knew it was a distraction. He was waiting here for you and the medallion. He knew you would come for him."

Sylvie frowned. How could he have known? No one else knew about their plans—plans that had only just been made.

"She needs a healer," the High Wizard said, taking Sylvie from her thoughts. "But I'm afraid to move her."

"I'll get someone," a voice said weakly from the doorway.

"Jax," Sylvie said. "You should not be up."

His entire side was now soaked in blood and he slumped against the doorframe before sliding down to the floor. "Maybe you're right," Jax said with a slight grin. "I just didn't want to miss any of the action."

Sylvie glanced over at Gamal lying on the floor, then back to Jax and Jocelyn. "What a mess," she hissed. "All for the sake of greed and power."

Danijela stood up. "You stay here with them, and I'll go get more help."

Sylvie nodded and tried to decide whether Jax or Jocelyn needed her more. She didn't have any healing powers—at least that she knew of—but she could at least try to make them more comfortable. Sylvie grabbed a small pillow from a nearby couch and propped Jocelyn's head up with it. She glanced over at Jax, his hand held tightly to his side. He nodded that he was fine—but he didn't look good at all.

She hurriedly wrapped Jocelyn in a blanket from the bed to keep her from going into shock, then turned back to Jax. His eyes were now closed and his face was gray and sagging.

"No, no." Sylvie rushed to his side. "Jax, Jax, wake up."

She heard shuffling behind her and figured it was only Jocelyn moving around. But then she heard a deep groan.

"Sylvie!" Jocelyn called out weakly.

Sylvie turned around and looked up, only to watch Gamal's thick hand slap her across the face. Her head snapped painfully to the side. Gamal stumbled and reached his fingers toward the chain of the medallion once again.

Sylvie's head was in a fog, but she shook it off and as Gamal's hand came closer her medallion flared to life on its own. Golden tendrils of fire leaped out and stung his fingertips.

Bellowing in pain, he stumbled backwards toward a window, and Sylvie pushed out a blast of air toward him. She missed. He edged closer to the window.

"This isn't over yet," Gamal growled. "You've made a big mistake. I don't need your medallions to rule the world. You won't stop me now!"

Before Sylvie could understand what was happening he turned around, put his hands on the window frame, and jumped out the window. Jocelyn cried out and Sylvie ran toward the window and looked down.

Among shards of glass, Gamal fell quickly at first but then grabbed his medallion with both hands and black smoke engulfed him. By the time he should have hit the ground, the smoke had dissipated and Gamal was nowhere to be seen.

Sylvie leaned out the window farther and was just about to follow him. She figured she might be able to summon air to float, or use water to get safely to the ground. But either option was only theoretical at this point. Stepping up on the windowsill, she prepared herself to do something. She couldn't let him get away.

But then Jax coughed and Sylvie turned her head.

"Sylvie," he whispered her name, his eyes hardly open. "It hurts so much."

After one last look outside—out of the corner of her eyes she saw Gamal speaking to someone, she let out a frustrated grunt, changed her plan and ran over to Jax. His skin burned and his eyes were swollen. He weakly held out the orange garnet SpeedStone to her.

"It's yours now, Sylvie," he croaked. "Thank you for letting me see the world."

"No," Sylvie cried out, tears pouring down her face. "No, Jax. You'll be fine. We'll find a healer."

"I think it was a poisoned blade," Jax whispered. He closed his eyes and the orange gemstone dropped from his hand and hit the floor with a loud clunk.

CHAPTER TWENTY-NINE

A short time later Sylvie was sitting next to Jocelyn in the healers' room. They waited silently, both watching two experienced healers work on Jax. So far he had stayed unconscious. Spidery tentacles of blackness had begun spreading out across his skin from the wound in his side; so far the healers hadn't been able to stop them.

Jocelyn had recovered for the most part, but she was still weak. The background din of students and teachers returning to the school from being outside reached the far corners of Sylvie's mind, but not enough to take her attention away from Jax.

With the lapses in her memory, Jax had been her longest friend. He had saved her from the island at his own peril and although he had never ventured out into the world before, had done remarkably well—and even seemed to bask in his newfound freedom.

"I'm sure he'll be fine," said Jocelyn. She had offered to help in the healing, but she was still weak from her confrontation with Gamal.

Sylvie only nodded her head. She wanted to believe her words, but her heart feared Jax dying.

"He saved me, you know," Jocelyn said, smiling at Sylvie. "If he hadn't arrived when he did, Gamal would have killed me,

I'm sure. When I wouldn't turn to his side, he threatened to kill me. "

Sylvie lifted her head toward Jocelyn. "It was dangerous to let you go there. I shouldn't have done it. I'm sorry."

"No," Jocelyn said. "It would have worked if he hadn't known. Once the rumbling started, the servants began running around and yelling—just like you had asked. I was going to run in and offer to escort Gamal to safety. But…" She scrunched up her face as if trying to remember something.

"But what?" Sylvie moved closer to the edge of the hard wooden chair.

"Well…" Jocelyn paused again and gathered her thoughts. "While everyone else was moving toward the stairs to get out of the building, I was hiding in a closet waiting to go in. I kept the door opened a bit so I could see what was happening. A man came running by, heading toward Gamal's room. I didn't think much about it in the chaos of things. But a few moments later, he came back out. He appeared nervous and stayed mixed in with a group of servants who made their way downstairs. Do you think he could have warned Gamal before I got there?"

"Did you get a look at him?" Sylvie asked.

"Not really. It was all so crazy. He had a burgundy cloak on—but so do most of the wizards of the mind apprentices. The cowl was pulled up over his head…but I didn't see anything else. I'm sorry." Jocelyn's eyes grew worried.

"But no one else knew," Sylvie said, slightly too loudly. The healers threw her a stern look for breaking their concentration. "Only the High Wizard, Nathanael, Marcie, you, and…" She paused for a moment, not wanting to believe what had just flashed through her mind.

"And Wydel," Jocelyn finished for her, but didn't seem to notice Sylvie's pause and worry. "When I first got to Gamal's room, he immediately rounded on me. He didn't even pretend to not know what was happening. He knew that you were working with the High Wizard to get the medallion and that I was part of the plan. Jax came in soon after and…Sylvie are you listening?"

Sylvie jerked a bit in her chair. "What?"

"What are you thinking about?"

Sylvie couldn't bring herself to tell Jocelyn what she had been thinking about and tried to act interested, but instead, she began to feel sick to her stomach. She wiped the tears from her eyes.

"Sylvie, are you all right?" Jocelyn asked. "You look like you've seen a ghost. I'll get one of the healers to look at you."

"No," Sylvie said firmly. "They need to help Jax. I'm fine. I just need some air." With that she stood up and walked out of the room.

Where was Wydel? She hadn't seen him since he had left the kitchen. She looked at the faces of the students cautiously reentering the school, but he was not among them. When she reached the outside doors, she walked down the steps and over to one of the fountains.

Sitting on the edge, she dragged her fingers in the water and all of a sudden scenes from the past—things she had never seen—flashed through her mind. She saw glimpses of men and women meeting at the fountain late at night, caught echoes of passing wizards talking together around it…and then something dark and black raced by in her mind.

Sylvie stuck her hand deeper into the water and called upon the power of her medallion, hanging now around her neck. She tried to concentrate on what she could see in her mind and what she felt. It was a brief encounter between two people. Sylvie could see Gamal, right after he had jumped from the window and disappeared, along with a younger man who wore a burgundy cloak like the one Joelle had described. He spoke a few words to him that Sylvie couldn't hear. She willed the man to turn around, but she couldn't see his face or hear his voice clearly enough to make out who it was.

Suddenly they disappeared and Sylvie opened her eyes again. She was just beginning to learn about the powers her medallion gave her—apparently, as the High Wizard had guessed, she now had the power to discern past activities by touching where they had been. But it was all very confusing and jumbled.

A loud commotion and the sounds of reckless horse hooves brought Sylvie to her feet. Riding with wild abandon into the grounds of the Wizard Conclave came the two people she had seen in the vision of the medallions being made—the ones that seemed to know who she was. The man and woman were accompanied by two other men, one dark skin and long hair braids, and the other not quite as dark, but broad-shouldered with short hair. The bigger man passed the other three and rode wildly toward Sylvie.

"Sylvie," he yelled out and before his horse even stopped, jumped from its saddle—almost tumbling to the ground—and ran toward her.

Sylvie tensed and brought her hands out in front of her body to defend herself. But something in the man's haunted brown eyes stopped her. Tears ran down his face as he stumbled into her and grabbed her in a big, tight hug.

"I'm so sorry, Sylvie, I'm so sorry," the man cried as he held her tightly.

She stiffened at first and tried to push away, but the man wouldn't let her.

"Bale," called out the redhead from her horse—in the vision, she had said her name was Joelle. "You're going to squeeze her to death. Let her breathe."

Bale pulled back and looked into Sylvie's eyes as if he knew much more about her than she could remember.

"I…I'm sorry," he mumbled, "It's just that I thought you were dead. I didn't want to believe it, but…I failed to protect you. Please forgive me."

Sylvie watched the other three dismount their horses and approach her. All of them had broad smiles across their faces. They were all about her age and although they appeared tired, had an excitement in their eyes.

She looked at each in turn and then brought her attention back to Bale. He had wiped his eyes and stood a little embarrassed, but awaiting an answer.

"I…" Sylvie began. How could she forgive someone she couldn't remember? But the look on his face was so expectant. She knew he had carried some kind of burden with him that he was ready to unload. She scanned the group once again. "I have no memory of who any of you are, and I certainly can't hold any grudges for what you may or may not have done that I can't remember. So consider any offense forgiven."

Bale took a deep breath and a new sparkle entered his eyes. Before she knew what was happening, the other three circled around her and gave her hugs.

"Sylvonna," said the dark braided-haired man, "It is wonderful to see you again. I see you found the third medallion."

"That's Hasani," said Joelle, "he's the brains of the bunch and a wizard of the mind. Kyril is a wizard of the mind too, but not so powerful…well, he is with the medallion. And Bale, well, he isn't a wizard, but he saved us. You still don't remember us?"

Sylvie's heart felt heavy looking at the four people who appeared to know her quite well. She wondered what type of wizard Joelle was—the woman appeared pleasant, but was certainly quite a chatterbox. Kyril stood behind and scanned the gardens as if looking for something. Joelle's bright green eyes were on the verge of tears, but then she smiled and continued talking again.

"Oh yes, yes, you were wondering what kind of wizard I am," Joelle said, to Sylvie's surprise. "I'm a wizard of the heart."

"And a very powerful healer," added Kyril, taking a step forward. "What happened? You said Gamal was here?"

"Yes," Sylvie said to Kyril, but then turned back to Joelle, realizing what she had said. She grabbed the woman's hand and pulled her back toward the main building. "You really can heal?"

"Yes, I suppose, but…" Joelle began.

"Joelle, no more questions," Kyril said, but softened the words with a smile. "Can't you see that Sylvie is overwhelmed right now?"

Sylvie nodded her thanks to Kyril. Her eyes lingered on his medallion for a moment and she felt a glimmer of recognition. Her own medallion seemed to glow in response.

"Jax, my friend…" Sylvie tried to explain as they hurried toward the building. But he was more than a friend. She couldn't let anything happen to him. She spoke to Joelle. "Gamal stabbed him and there's some sort of poison spreading. If there is anything you can do for him—please, try."

They had just reached the door to the building when a voice called Sylvie's name.

She turned and her stomach dropped again. "I can't deal with you right now," she said to Wydel. She knew it sounded harsh, but if her instincts were correct, he had betrayed them to Gamal for some purpose she couldn't fathom.

"But…" Wydel stopped a short distance from them. His face fell with disappointment.

Kyril, Joelle, and Hasani entered the building, but Bale hung back and took a step between Sylvie and Wydel. His hand went to a sword at his side. Wydel glanced from Sylvie to him, and then squared his shoulders and glared at Bale.

Sylvie grabbed Bale's hand and pulled him inside with the others, then turned back to Wydel. "We'll talk after I'm done here. Gamal hurt Jax and he might die." Her voice was accusatory, and the offended look on Wydel's face confirmed her worst fears.

Before Wydel could offer any excuses or empty words, she picked up her pace and caught up with the others. Bale continued to look back behind them as if ready to fight Wydel if needed. She wondered what she had done to earn this man's loyalty.

On their way to the healers' room they ran into the High Wizard gathering the students and instructors. Her eyes roamed over the group, lingering on each medallion, then she smiled at all of them.

"Ah, Kyril and Joelle, I presume," she said to them. "I'd heard from the Emperor of Gildan and the King of the Realm about you two before I was incapacitated by Gamal—our mutual enemy."

The two didn't recognize the High Wizard. Sylvie knew that Danijela's small stature and youthful appearance made others assume she was younger.

"High Wizard Danijela Anwar." Sylvie made hasty introductions, anxious to get Joelle in with Jax.

Joelle and Kyril appeared surprised and bowed to the High Wizard.

"High Wizard, I need to get Joelle to Jax," Sylvie said. "We can talk later."

She nodded. "I have things to take care of as well. In such a short time, Gamal did a lot of damage among the students and professors, I'm afraid."

Sylvie's mind went to Wydel and she understood far too well.

CHAPTER THIRTY

Kyril walked with the others into the healers' room in the Wizard Conclave. The building was smaller than the wizard school in Gildan, but it had a grandeur and feeling of power all its own. A raw energy flowed through its solid stone walls. Besides the man on the cot, Kyril noticed three others in the room—two were older and appeared to be trying to help the man. One a year or so younger than him stood up from a chair and gave a brief smile at the newcomers.

"I'm Jocelyn," said the young woman.

Kyril made quick introductions of their party and then Sylvie directed them all toward the injured man. A blanket was pulled up under his chin and although there was some color to his face, he appeared sick and was very still. Glancing at the two healers, Sylvie asked if there had been any improvement.

"I'm afraid not, Wizard Sylvonna," said one, a middle-aged man whose blond hair held speckles of gray. "We've slowed down the spread, but can't stop it. We've called for the king's healer from the capital, but…"

The words were left unsaid. This man was close to dying and the healer from the City of Arc probably wouldn't arrive in time. Sylvie's eyes grew watery, and Kyril realized that this man, whoever he was, meant a lot to his friend. He had long dark straight hair tied into a ponytail, and his pointed ears and slanted eyes made Kyril sure he was an elf. The man was a long way from Elvyn if that was true.

Joelle moved closer to him. "May I?" she asked the two other healers.

They looked at the young woman, and then at Sylvie for confirmation.

"Let her try," Sylvie said, choking on her words. "She may be our last hope."

Joelle brought her hands out in front of her and began running them over his body. "How long has he been like this?" Joelle asked. "Do you know the weapon that attacked him? Was it infused with an evil power? Ah, I see he's an elf. That's good."

"Good?" Sylvie whispered.

"They are stronger than we are," Joelle said. "Have you ever met any other elves? We had a few from Elvyn at the wizard school on White Island, but they stayed to themselves mostly. They aren't as comfortable out in the world outside of Elvyn as we are. I wonder why that is…"

Kyril smiled at Joelle's chatter. He knew her enough now to know that her talking was a way of distracting others while she worked. Many thought it meant she wasn't paying attention to her healing, but Kyril knew better from firsthand experience. His mind went back to the day he had first heard Gamal's voice in his head. Of course back then he hadn't known what it was. But it had tried to convince him that he could fly. He'd jumped off a wall in the gardens around the wizard school in Gildan and had broken his arm. Sylvie had saved him that day from

Bale's mocking and had taken him to see Joelle, who healed him.

That was also the day he had met Targon Quereshi, the man who had become his mentor…and the same man Kyril had to betray to save the emperor and his son. Glancing around the room at Bale, Joelle, Hasani, and Sylvie, he thought about all that had happened to him in such a short time. Ever since finding that first medallion and discovering Gamal's intentions, they had all stuck by him, even though he was a relatively weak wizard. He would even consider Bale a sort of friend at this point.

As if by thinking about him brought his attention, Bale turned toward Kyril and nodded his head at him.

Yes, it was nice to have friends.

But now, with all the medallions found, they needed to find Gamal and stop him from the chaos he was bringing to the world.

"Kyril!" Joelle called him over to Jax. She had pulled the blanket aside and exposed a knife wound in his side. It was black and spreading out up and down and around his middle.

Kyril sucked in his breath. It looked bad. "Can you heal him?"

Joelle thought about it for a moment and Sylvie stood expectedly off to the side awaiting the answer. "I'm not sure," Joelle said.

Sylvie put her head in her hands and Kyril could hear a soft sobbing.

Bale approached Sylvie, and although he didn't touch her, he stood very near to her. "There must be a way," he said. "Sylvie's been through enough."

A lump formed in Kyril's throat—he could only imagine what Sylvie had been through since leaving Gildan. She had come away from multiple encounters with Gamal and had survived a shipwreck…only to still end up in Arc with the third medallion.

"Aren't you three supposed to be powerful wizards?" Bale said, his voice growing louder in anger. "What's the use of being a wizard or having these medallions if you can't do something with them besides fighting others?"

Sylvie's head jerked up and Kyril and Joelle all looked at each other.

"I couldn't heal the headmaster at the wizard school," Joelle said, "but that was only with one medallion. Bale has a good point. We have all three medallions with us now."

"What do we do?" asked Sylvie, giving deference to Joelle's ability as a healer.

Joelle looked at Kyril for suggestions. He thought back over all that he had learned about the medallions in the three visions. "We have to use them together," he finally said. "I still don't know a lot about their use, but in all we've seen and read, they are meant to be used together to bring balance to magic."

Sylvie's whole demeanor grew hopeful for the first time. The other two healers stood off to one side, clearly not understanding what was going on. But they along with Jocelyn looked on in interest.

"If we can help, please let us know," one of them said.

"Hand me the medallions," Joelle said with new confidence.

Kyril and Sylvie drew theirs up over their necks while Joelle removed her own. They placed all three in Joelle's small hands—Joelle's own bronze one on the bottom, Sylvie's silver one in the middle, and Kyril's gold one on top. She then placed her other hand over Jax's wound. Without waking up, his body flinched in response to her touch.

"What do we do?" asked Sylvie.

"Put your hands on top of the medallions," Joelle said. "I can already feel my healing power growing."

Kyril turned to Bale. "Make sure we are not interrupted," he said.

Bale moved closer to the door and took up position in front of it.

"If any of you want to help," Joelle spoke to Hasani, Jocelyn, and the two older healers, "then place a hand on one of our shoulders and lend us any power that you are able to spare."

"We can do that?" asked one of the healers.

"The medallions augment a wizard's own powers," instructed Hasani. "If we are touching them, the medallions will have more power to augment."

Kyril thought he understood the process, but Hasani's simple explanation was better than he could have himself.

The three medallion holders held their hands on the medallion, with the four others touching their shoulders.

"I can feel it," Sylvie whispered. "So much power."

Joelle closed her eyes and Kyril could feel their power shift toward her. The three medallions began to grow brighter and brighter until it was almost impossible to look at. Kyril gazed at Joelle's hand on Jax's body. The blackness around the wound appeared to be shrinking.

"It's working," said Joelle. "I can feel the power of the medallions pulling the evil stain out of him."

Loud noises suddenly erupted in the hallway and Kyril told Bale with a look to go and see what was happening. Turning his attention back to the healing, Kyril closed his own eyes for a moment and focused on the power coalescing around them. He felt a calming presence, and then suddenly he was not in the room anymore, but instead was pulled into some type of empty space. He could see grayness around him but nothing else.

Where was he?

CHAPTER THIRTY-ONE

Kyril panicked for a moment, wondering if this was a result of the evil shadow in Jax. But then Sylvie appeared next to him, materializing out of nowhere. Next came Joelle.

"What's happening?" Sylvie asked in a pained voice. "We need to heal Jax. What are we doing here?"

"We are still healing him," Joelle said. "I can feel it working."

"I'm so glad you two arrived when you did," Sylvie said. "It seems like forever since I've seen you."

Joelle froze. "You mean…you remember us now?"

Sylvie appeared to think for a moment, and then smiled. "I do remember some things, now that you mention it."

"The power of the medallions," Kyril said. "They're bringing your memories back."

Sylvie's face grew panicked. "But I don't want that if it means diverting power from Jax. Where are we?"

Kyril looked around again. "I…I'm not sure."

"You are in the magic stream," a soft voice echoed around them.

But when they looked around they didn't see anyone.

"Who are you?" Kyril felt he recognized the voice, but couldn't place it. "I've heard the magic stream mentioned in my studies a few times."

"Show yourself!" Sylvie swirled around, readying her hands for an attack.

"You are safe here, medallion holders," came the voice again. And suddenly Kyril recognized it.

"King Anikari?" Kyril had a hard time believing the ancient king was there. "How is this possible?"

"The magic stream is a place where time doesn't flow like it does in the physical world. A few powerful wizards have moved from place to place through it in the blink of an eye."

"Like transporting with my medallion," Kyril said.

"Similar outcome but different methods," said Anikari. "In death, I am not strong enough to appear in person, as I've been gone too long. But there are those among your world that can. Their assistance will be needed to defeat the Shadow Master. But don't wait too long."

"But what about my friend Jax?" Sylvie asked. "Can we heal him with the medallions?"

Before Anikari could answer, Joelle faded in and out a bit. When she reappeared again her face held fear. "It's slipping. The shadow is returning to Jax. I...don't know what to do!"

"Align your powers," Anikari said. "True balance is only restored when the medallions are aligned."

Kyril was exasperated. "Riddles, just like the Cremelinos. Why can't you speak straight?"

"Patience, young medallion holder," Anikari said, taking no offense. "Just do as I say and your friend will be saved and you can defeat the Shadow Master. Align the medallions."

Kyril took a deep breath and glanced around. He was back in the room with everyone else. Both Joelle and Sylvie stood with eyes wide. They all looked down at Jax and saw the blackness spreading once again.

"No," Sylvie said with such force that the building shook around them.

Yells were heard again out in the hall and someone banged against the door. Kyril heard Bale's voice telling someone to get back.

"I'm going to help," said Hasani, heading toward the door.

The other two healers sat back on chairs, clearly exhausted at the effort.

Jax's face was flushed with what appeared to be a burning fever and Sylvie let out a brief sob.

"He said that we needed to use the medallions together," said Joelle.

"We are!" Sylvie cried out. "What more can we do?"

Kyril played back the memory of the conversation in his mind. That along with the memory of something that was said as the three medallions were made, came to Kyril's mind.

He took his hand off of the medallions.

"No," Sylvie said. "What are you doing?"

She reached to grab Kyril's hand back to the medallions. As she did so the windows of the room rattled with her power of the earth.

"Sylvie," Kyril said calmly but firmly as he took his hand from her. "You must trust me. Do you remember now? Do you trust me?"

Sylvie's eyes blinked and her pupils grew larger. "I remember some…" she said. "I remember Gildan and saving the emperor. A fire at the wizard academy, and…" If it wasn't for Jax's condition she would be ecstatic to begin remembering her past life, but all of it would mean nothing to her if Jax died.

"Trust me, please."

She nodded slightly and removed her hand from the medallions also. The door behind them rattled again and began to open, only to have it pulled shut amidst a loud wail.

"Bale?" Joelle said with a quick glance to the door.

"Let him be for now," Kyril said before turning his attention back to the medallions.

On each one outside of the largest circle were three evenly spaced half circles—small bumps of metal protruding out from the medallions themselves. Kyril turned them slightly so that the three bumps on all three medallions sat directly on top of each other. They fit together like a puzzle.

"He said to align the medallions," Kyril said.

Before he was finished talking, the three medallions flared to life and a blast of power radiated throughout the room.

Joelle grabbed all three in both hands and placed them directly on Jax's wound. "Now," she told the other two.

Kyril and Sylvie placed their hands on top of the medallions and Kyril felt a surge of power flow through his body like never before.

"Wow," Sylvie whispered beside him.

"It's working," Joelle said excitedly.

Kyril could feel an evil influence amidst the medallions' power radiating from Jax's body, but, in time, the vile shadow began to lessen. Balance was being restored and Jax's wound was closing, the black tendrils disappearing.

Sweat formed on Kyril's forehead as he continued to maintain a connection to the power of the medallions. It was mind-boggling, really. Never had he supposed that such power existed, let alone that he would be a part of wielding it.

Without any warning a hot wind blew out from Jax's wound and a black shadow emerged from his body. It was taken upward into the light of the medallions. There was a soft explosion and tiny fragments of the shadow dissipated in the air above them.

At the same time, the door crashed open and Bale came running back inside. He turned, pushed it shut, and leaned against it. "There's a lot of wizard power going on out there," he said.

"Where's Hasani?" Joelle asked.

Bale pointed toward the hallway. "With the High Wizard. How is it going in here? We could really use your help."

The light from the medallions grew softer and the three wizards turned their attention back to Jax. The wound was completely closed up. Sylvie pulled the blanket up under his chin, and without opening his eyes, Jax moved his hand to cover Sylvie's.

"Jax?" Sylvie said, leaning down closer. "Jax, can you hear me?"

Jax groaned and then his eyes fluttered open.

"Oh my," Joelle said and sank to the floor.

Kyril squatted down to help her. She was still alert, but her face was pale and sweat covered her face.

"That was a lot of power," Joelle whispered. "I just need a little rest."

Kyril chuckled a bit at her simple statement. "If all you need is a little rest after that, you are much stronger than me."

Joelle smiled and patted Kyril's hand. "Of course I am."

Bale approached Jax and Sylvie, peering intently at the man.

"So this is the person you used up all that power on?" Bale said. "The world is in chaos out there, you know."

Sylvie looked up at him but didn't rise to his ire. Instead her face softened as she turned back to Jax. His hand was still over hers.

"Gamal?" Jax asked.

Sylvie shook her head. "He got away."

"You saved me over getting him?" Jax's voice came weak and low.

"And I would do it again," Sylvie said.

After making sure Joelle was comfortable and safe on the floor, Kyril moved to Jax's bedside. Bale stood on the other side, but Kyril couldn't decipher the expression on his face.

"Jax, this is Bale," Sylvie said with a smile toward both of them. "He is a friend from Gildan and one of the bravest men I know."

The remark brought a surprised smile from Bale—one he tried to hold back, but couldn't.

"You remember?" Jax asked.

Sylvie nodded her head and a big smile spread across her face. Now that Jax was looking better she let the excitement of it come out more. "Some of it. More and more all the time. Kyril and Joelle are also wizards and friends of mine."

Joelle stood up and handed Sylvie and Kyril their medallions. Sylvie removed her hand from Jax's long enough to put the chain back around her neck. All three medallion holders stood there quietly for a moment.

"Now what?" asked Bale.

"Now we put down this rebellion and find Gamal," Sylvie said with a voice firm and full of anger. "He's done enough damage."

"I'm ready," Kyril said.

"Me too," Joelle joined in, although she swayed on her feet. Bale came to her side and steadied her.

"Why don't you stay with Jax?" Sylvie said to Joelle. "Both of you need to recover."

Joelle nodded and said nothing, a testament to how exhausted she must really feel.

A slow smile spread across Bale's face. "Let's end this, wizards. I'm tired of saving you from trouble."

Kyril laughed and slapped Bale on the back. "Let's go, spymaster!"

CHAPTER THIRTY-TWO

Sylvie took a deep breath as she, Kyril, and Bale emerged from the healers' room. After seeing Jax well once again, a newfound exhilaration surged through her. She hadn't realized the depth of feelings she had for him. But now, energy surged through her body, coming from every source of the earth around her—augmented by the medallion she wore on a chain around her neck.

In front of them, however, a horrifying scene unfolded. Wizard fought against wizard. Even apprentices were in the throng. It was hard to tell who was on what side. She glanced around, hoping to find Gamal, but he wasn't there. Only the chaos he left in his wake.

Across the room, she spotted Danijela Anwar, the High Wizard, and with at least partial memories restored now, a flood of recollections and a surge of love shot between them. Danijela caught her glance and smiled before shaking the ground in front of her and causing a dozen people to fall to the floor.

Then Sylvie saw someone running out from behind a pillar and toward the High Wizard's back. He held a knife out in front of him, fire sizzling down its blade.

"No!" Sylvie called out, knowing she couldn't get there in time.

Beside her, Kyril turned his attention to where she pointed. In a flash, Kyril was gone and suddenly reappeared by the man with the knife, pushing his shoulder into him. The appearance of Kyril after he had transported caught the attacker by surprise and the knife flew to the ground while the man tumbled, just missing running into the High Wizard. The man jumped up, cowl falling back from his face, and Sylvie gasped. It was Wydel.

Tears of anger and hurt filled her eyes.

He stretched his arm out toward Kyril and a dark mass of shadowy smoke poured from his fingertips, snaking its way to Kyril. But Kyril's medallion flared to life and a golden burst of fire devoured the shadow and dropped Wydel to his knees.

Sylvie tried to run to them but kept being stopped by bits of flying fire, swinging swords, and the occasional puff of black fog. With a combination of air and water, she formed a multicolored shield in front of her outstretched hand. It spun around and blocked anything coming at her; flinging it back at her attackers. With the shield in front of her, she ran into the fray.

How many people had Gamal recruited? She hadn't realized his influence. And where had the man run off to? He had mentioned not needing the medallions now to accomplish his goal. That made her even more afraid. What other power had he amassed?

She watched as Wydel stood back up, but by now Kyril had turned and was fighting someone else. Before Sylvie could warn him, Bale came up behind Wydel and knocked him to the ground with the hilt of his sword.

"A wizard falls to brute force, just like anyone else," Bale said as Sylvie skidded to a stop in front of him.

"Thanks." Sylvie smiled and released her shield.

Bale pushed her aside and stabbed at a man that had come up behind her. "I thought you said we were going to end this," he growled. "It's too tight in here to fight properly—and too many wizards."

Sylvie looked around for an opening and saw the staircase close by. She ran toward it and climbed up enough steps to see out over the fighting. It was still hard to tell whom was fighting whom. She didn't want to hurt innocent people—but Bale was right; it needed to stop.

She glanced at a floor-to-ceiling window beside her, saw the fountain outside, and got an idea. She called upon the power of the medallion and it sprang to life, bathing the area around her in a silver glow. Water from the fountain obeyed her summons. It flowed to the ground and snaked across the yard and under the hallway door toward the fight. She thought of the earth around her and dug deeper. There was an underground river here. And she pulled from it. Water began filling the hallway.

The entire process had taken less than a minute, but already the fighters were sloshing around in water up to their ankles. The fight was slowing, and more people were falling to the ground. Soon the High Wizard joined Sylvie, and without even having to share plans, struck her hands out over the crowd with a blast of cold wind. And the water at their feet began to freeze.

Sylvie smiled at her mentor. It felt good to be with her once again. Everything she had learned had been from her. Besides learning how to control her powers, Danijela had taught her how to think for herself, reason things out, and use all the resources at her disposal. But the biggest thing she had taught her was that to accomplish something you usually needed to work together with others.

"Together?" the High Wizard said.

Sylvie nodded her head, and within a few short moments everyone—except the two of them—were stuck up to their ankles in ice.

"I'm not sure how long I can keep this up," the High Wizard said. "Water is not my forte. If you want me to reshape stone, that I can do."

"I think this will do for now," Sylvie said. With a small, precise blast of fire, she let loose Kyril, Bale, Hasani, and several guards that Danijela said would be loyal to them. She let the rest stand frozen for a moment trying to decide how to tell who was on which side.

"Don't blame them," Danijela said. "Gamal deceived them, just like he has done to all of us at times."

The High Wizard was right—except about one person. Sylvie marched down the stairs until she stood in front of Wydel. He had tried to get up but was frozen in place on his knees.

"Someone you knew?" Bale asked.

"Someone I thought was a friend," Sylvie said. "But he betrayed us all and allowed Gamal to get away."

"I'm sorry," Bale said in unusual softness. "I know how hard it is to find a good friend."

More memories came rushing back to her in that moment. She remembered heading out from Gildan with Bale and being captured in Cyrene. Bale had risked his own life to make sure that she got to safety. And now once again he was at her side fighting.

"Oh, Bale!" She threw her arms around him.

He stiffened at first, then hugged her back.

"I'm so sorry," Sylvie said. "You must have been so worried about me, and I didn't even have any idea who you were!"

Bale pulled back and smiled. A small tear slid from the corner of his eye. "I thought you were dead, Sylvie. And I thought it was my fault. I couldn't live with myself knowing that."

"I'm glad you came," Sylvie said, then turned to Kyril and Hasani who had just joined them. "I'm glad you all did."

Wydel grunted and struggled to get up, but he still couldn't move. The ice in the room was beginning to melt and, with a wave of her hand, Sylvie sent the water back outside. The High Wizard's guards were separating people and marching them away from the room. It would take a while to separate out who had willfully rebelled, who had been caught up in Gamal's lies, and who was fighting for the High Wizard.

Bale reached down and lifted up Wydel by the collar of his shirt. His burgundy robe hung torn off one shoulder. His blue eyes smoldered as he looked at those in front of him, but stopped as they focused on Sylvie.

"How could you?" Sylvie said. "I thought you were my friend, Wydel. I trusted you."

Wydel sneered, his face twisting into something horrible. "He is more powerful than you, Sylvie. The Shadow Master will rule, and all of us wizards of the mind will rule with him. You can't outsmart him."

Bale punched Wydel in the side and the man collapsed slightly and winced in pain. Normally Sylvie wasn't one for revenge, but she would have liked to have been the one to have punched him. Bale raised his eyebrows at her as if asking if he should hit him again.

"He deserves it," Sylvie said at last, "but we must be better than him."

The High Wizard walked up to them with two guards in tow.

"Oh, Wydel, what have you done?" Danijela asked with a drawn face. Turning to Sylvie, she spoke in an authoritative manner. "I'll take him now. He will be stripped of the ability of ever becoming a full wizard and won't see the light of day for many years, I suspect. We will send him to the prison in Arc. There, he will have many years to contemplate his role in this rebellion."

The guards pulled him away, but Wydel turned his head. "His power is greater than yours, Sylvie. You'll never beat him."

Just then Joelle approached them all. The three medallions glittered, reflecting the sunlight coming in through the windows.

"But his power is not greater than all three medallions," Joelle said. "We were born for this."

Wydel paled and stumbled. The guards held him tighter and dragged him away.

"He befriended me here," Sylvie said. "When I couldn't remember anything and had no friends except for Jax—he and Jocelyn accepted me. And it was all a ruse." Anger rose up within her once again. "Let's go find Gamal; it is time for him to pay for what he's done."

CHAPTER THIRTY-THREE

After the fighting was over, the entire Wizard Conclave had, for the first time ever, gone on lockdown. No one was allowed in or out of the school, and for now all students had to stay in the buildings where they were housed. Sylvie had thanked Jocelyn for her help and promised that everyone would know how important she had been in freeing the High Wizard. She was already a promising wizard of the heart..

The rule to stay put, however, didn't apply to Sylvie and her friends as she wasn't truly a student anymore and her friends were here to find Gamal. Currently, they were all sitting around a table in a small dining room, eating their evening meal. Jax was sitting next to Sylvie—he had regained most of his strength from the healing hours before. Joelle was correct; his Elvyn blood had helped him to heal more quickly.

Next to him sat Hasani, who had been continually pestering the half-elf with questions about where he had come from and what abilities he had. Jax was polite and answered as truthfully as he dared without giving too much away. He and Sylvie had told the group about their time on Vorwyth Island, but neither had mentioned anything about the SpeedStone that was now back in Jax's possession.

Across from these three sat Joelle, Bale, and Kyril. Earlier, Danijela had spent some time with them and had given orders to the servants to bring anything the group needed. But, having been absent from running the Conclave for a few weeks, she was now off trying to put things back in order.

The group finished eating and conversation grew quiet. Sylvie knew what was weighing on their minds and was just about to broach the subject when Joelle jumped in first.

"So, about Gamal…" Joelle said. "What do we do now?"

Sylvie was surprised how Joelle had anticipated the exact words she was about to speak.

"Sorry," Joelle said to her. "I didn't mean to read your intentions, but they just came to me; I'm still learning to control it."

Sylvie smiled at her best friend. She had known something was missing over the last weeks, and it wasn't until she had her memories back that Sylvie realized it was her best friend.

"I keep forgetting you can read people's intentions," she laughed.

"I try not to all the time," Joelle said. "But it's hard—I mean, look at Jax here! He wants to stay with you, but he doesn't know if you want him to, now that you have your old friends back."

Jax gasped and Sylvie turned red. The others in the room snickered.

"Now all Hasani wants is more information for that head of his," Joelle continued.

"What about Kyril?" Bale smiled.

Sylvie shook her head. Those two were always at each other. Before Kyril and Bale had worked together to save Emperor Alrishitar and his son, Bale and his friends had mercilessly teased and bullied Kyril. She knew that Kyril looked at him as a friend now, after all they had been through, but the two still seemed to enjoy poking at each other.

Joelle turned to Kyril who tried to keep his face neutral.

"Watch out, Bale," Joelle laughed. "Kyril likes you, but he just might punch you one of these times. You can be frustrating at times."

Bale's eyes went big and he peered at Kyril. "That's what you're intending?" He rolled his eyes. "That I'd like to see."

Kyril only shrugged, looking a bit sheepish.

Everyone laughed again, even Bale and Kyril.

"Back to Gamal," Kyril said after the fun died down.

Bale leaned forward, growing more serious himself.

"Now, wait," Joelle said glancing over to see Bale, "you didn't ask me about Bale."

"Let's move on, Joelle," Bale said in a voice that brooked no argument.

"Fine," she said, but she looked concerned. Sylvie would have to ask her about it later.

"Gamal can't be far," Sylvie said. "The High Wizard and I injured him—and besides, I think he still wants the medallions. Either way, he is planning something and we need to find him."

"A trap then?" Bale said. "We use the medallions and set a trap for him to come to us."

The group generally appeared to agree, but Sylvie had something else in mind.

"I would rather we surprise him," Sylvie said. "I don't want any more harm to come to the school."

"But how do we find him, Sylvonna?" Hasani asked.

"I think I can find him," Sylvie said. "My medallion allows me to sense people and their conversations from things of the earth they have touched. I need to go back to the window he jumped from and see if I can decipher any last thoughts he had of where he might be going."

"Well, let's go," Bale said, the first to jump up.

The rest got up from their chairs and followed Sylvie toward the door. Before exiting the room, she turned her head and saw Bale and Joelle exchanging heated whispers. She wondered what that was all about.

As they walked down the hall and up the multiple flights of stairs, the Wizard Conclave was eerily quiet. Sylvie could now remember most of her time here before she had gone to Gildan. There were still a few holes, but her memories of the school were fond. She hated the thought that Gamal had infiltrated all three wizard academies in the northern kingdoms—Arc, Gildan, and the Realm. They had to stop him.

As Sylvie came to Gamal's old room, she put her hand on the wooden doorframe. Without warning, her silver medallion flared and her mind was filled with memories of others who had touched that same spot. She saw flashes of Gamal coming and going with some of the other wizards and professors of the school. Then she growled.

"Sylvie, are you all right?" Kyril stepped over to her.

"It's Wydel," she said. "He'd been working with Gamal the entire time, it seemed. Each time I had shared something with him, Wydel would meet with Gamal here in his room. Working with me to get the High Wizard out was only a ruse—they figured she would tell me where the medallion was."

She shook her head to clear those traitorous thoughts away. It was hard to stay focused. Too many people had touched that door frame throughout the years. It did seem that the most recent came to her mind slightly easier and more clearly, but it was still very disorienting. She felt the world suddenly spin around her.

"Catch her, Jax!" Joelle called out and Jax—the closest one to Sylvie—caught her, preventing her from falling to the ground.

"Thanks," Sylvie said, looking up at him. He held her a moment until she had steadied herself. "Too many memories there."

Jax set her upright and she walked forward again, careful not to touch anything else of stone or wood until she made it to the window where Gamal had jumped from. She hoped not as many people had actually touched the molding around the window. She had to try and concentrate better.

The others gathered around and she stepped forward, trying to remember exactly where Gamal had touched before he jumped out the window. The glass was still broken and a warm wind blew her blond locks over her eyes. She pushed her hair aside, but it did little good. Closing her eyes, she tried to remember.

She had been with Jax on the floor when she'd heard a noise. Looking up, she saw Gamal get off the ground. He was hurt and stumbled to the window. Before jumping, he had placed his hands on either side of the window molding to steady himself. Sylvie, now doing the same, focused her mind on the most recent memory that the wood held.

She could feel the echoes of Gamal's thoughts in the darkness behind her closed eyes. In his apparent pain, they were a bit scattered.

The elf is stronger than I thought. He hummed with power that I've never felt before.

Wydel warned me of Sylvie's plan in time. He will be a good asset to my new empire.

I must get away from Sylvie. She is not strong enough with only the one medallion—but my black medallion is not strong enough either...yet.

I'll transport there.

Sylvie gasped.

Where? She thought. Where would Gamal go? He wanted the medallion. At least he had before. But what were his plans now?

As if in answer to her questions, Gamal's inner voice came to her mind once again.

I'll jump out the window.

In the back of her mind, Sylvie heard the crashing of the window and just before Gamal let go of the window molding, a scene—strong and clear—opened up in her mind. If Gamal's powers were like Kyril's, he wouldn't be able to transport anywhere he hadn't been before.

She saw brief flickers in the residuals of Gamal's thoughts. Green grass waving in the breeze up against the sea, and hundreds of tents speckling the land. Men and women milled around. She sucked in her breath as she realized it was an army. In her mind, Sylvie knew that Gamal's hands had left the window edge and he was now falling down through the air. The memories were fading. She tried to grab hold of his thoughts again—she had to push through his pain to do so. Pain, she found, that she was glad she and Danijela had inflicted on him.

Still in Gamal's recent thoughts, she looked off to her right and saw the beginning of a mountain range. To her left, she spotted hundreds of sails coming into a bay.

"West Port!" She recognized it from her brief time there.

And then it was all gone. She snapped her eyes back open and found that both Jax and Bale were holding her from jumping through the window herself.

"That was close," she mumbled as they pulled her back in. "I'm still getting used to this."

"The power of the medallions takes some time to control," Kyril said.

"Yes," Joelle agreed. "I remember ending up in the women's bathroom when you tried to transport the first time."

Kyril turned red and shrugged his shoulders.

"You mumbled 'West Port,' Sylvie," Hasani said, his dark braids blowing in the wind. "Is that where Gamal has gone? It's at least a two-day ride from here."

Sylvie thought for a moment before answering. "He wasn't strong enough to beat me—but I couldn't beat him either. We were at a standstill. But he has an army growing on the coast. Wizards and non-wizards, I assume. He is north of West Port on a grassy field just south of the rise of the coast mountains of Finn."

"I can use the medallion," Kyril said with bright eyes. "We can't wait two days. He must be getting stronger each day."

"How many can you transport with you?" Sylvie asked.

Kyril looked around at the five others in the room. "Not all of us." He shook his head as he spoke.

"I need to be there," Bale said. "I vowed to kill that man."

"You'll get yourself killed," Joelle said, her eyes appearing worried.

Bale's vehemence surprised Sylvie. She was afraid that his mind was taking him down a dangerous path he wouldn't come back from. She too wanted to destroy Gamal, but Bale's vengeful attitude was not healthy.

"But the three medallion holders are needed to defeat him," Hasani said. "Before mealtime, I spent some time in their library here. It's marvelous." His brown eyes held excitement. "Of course, I've read and studied much of the same in Gildan, but there were a few older books in the smaller room. There is still not much information, but the balance of power was mentioned multiple times. And that balance must include all three disciplines."

"Great, we have our own encyclopedia here," Bale mumbled.

"Thank you, Bale Nabhani." Hasani nodded his head toward the junior spymaster. "I'll take that as a compliment."

Bale rolled his eyes, but for once didn't rise to an insulting occasion. Instead, he took a step toward the door. "If I start now, I can ride through the night and all of tomorrow and…"

"Wait Bale, there may be another way," Jax spoke. Sylvie whipped her head around and caught the meaning in his eyes. She shook her head at him slightly. The SpeedStone was something sacred to him and his island. She didn't want him to feel he had to use it. He became exhausted each time he used it.

"It's the only way, Sylvie," Jax said with a smile. "It may be the reason I am here."

Sylvie grabbed his hand. "The reason you are here was to help me get to where I needed to be. You don't have to do this."

"Do what?" Joelle asked, confused. "Am I the only one lost here? The three of us need to get to West Port and stop Gamal. Kyril can take us. If the others can follow on horseback and get there before it's over, great, but we need to do this now that all three medallions are together. And we need to do it quickly."

Sylvie smiled at her friend. She was remembering more about her all the time. Joelle was always one to think out loud, but she was right. As if on cue, Jax reached into a pouch and pulled out the stone. It shone brightly, sitting in his slender hand. It was so striking that even Bale walked back to join the group.

"What's that?" asked Joelle. "It's beautiful. I've never seen anything like it before. Does it do something? Where did you get it?"

After every question, Jax opened his mouth to answer, but couldn't get the words out before the next question rolled from Joelle's lips.

"Joelle," Kyril said with a look of exasperation. "Let him answer."

"Oh…" Joelle's green eyes flicked with embarrassment. "Of course."

"It's a…" Jax began

"…orange garnet SpeedStone," Hasani finished. "Of course, I've read about the stones of power, but never thought I would ever see one."

"What does this orange pebble have to do with us getting to West Port?" Bale asked, clearly feeling in the dark.

"It's a SpeedStone," Jax said. "With it, you can travel very fast. I'm not sure what transporting is, but it only took us half a day to get from West Port to the City of Arc."

The others stood quietly in a moment in surprise.

"Kyril can transport three of us—himself, Joelle, and me," Sylvie said. "I've seen the spot where Gamal is in my mind. We can scout things out and begin to make plans. Jax can you bring Bale and Hasani with him using the SpeedStone. Is that too much?"

"I can try," Jax said.

"If so," Sylvie continued, "you should arrive by morning. We'll all meet together, and based on Gamal's position and strength, we will assess the situation and then do what we must."

All stood looking at her with bewilderment on their faces.

"Oh," she realized, "I'm sorry. I didn't mean to take charge. It's just that…"

Kyril laughed. "No problem, Sylvie; as a wizard of the earth, you're the closest we have to a battlemaster. Your strategy sounds perfect. You are more powerful than the rest of us here."

"But I'm not enough," Sylvie said to Kyril. "We need all three medallions. Do you have any idea of how we need to use them to defeat Gamal?" She looked expectantly at her friend.

She remembered now befriending him the prior year. He was the lonely, shy apprentice with hardly a friend. Now he had grown more confident—so much so that he was trying to save the world with the rest of them. "You are the wizard of the mind."

"Not yet," Kyril said with a frown, "but I'm thinking on it."

"Good then," Joelle said with a clap of her hands. "Sounds like we at least have a plan to get there."

"Just don't do anything reckless until I get there," Bale said with a friendly smirk. "I suppose you'll need me to save you again if you do."

They all laughed and headed out to gather their things. Sylvie let the rest of them go downstairs while she turned toward Danijela's room on the other side of the hallway from where Gamal had lived. Danijela was happy to have heard that Gamal hadn't taken her rooms.

Sylvie smiled as she knocked on the High Wizard's door. She needed to talk to her about something before they left. As the door opened, Sylvie glanced back down the stairs and caught Jax looking back up at her. She smiled—and most likely blushed—then waved and turned back to the door. He was part of what she needed to talk to her former mentor about.

CHAPTER THIRTY-FOUR

An hour later, Kyril was standing with his friends near the practice fields in the back of the Wizard Conclave. Jax had just pulled Sylvie aside for a few moments. Kyril could tell that they had grown close by the tender way they spoke and his hand on her arm. He was happy for her. She had been a great friend to him and Jax was lucky to have someone like her to care about him.

Bale stood off to the side with Hasani but kept glancing at Sylvie. It was hard to read what he was thinking. He had appeared to have taken a liking to Jax—something that wasn't hard to do. The man was friendly, loved adventure, and truly seemed to care for their mission. And his SpeedStone had definitely come in handy.

The High Wizard had come out to see them off. Kyril watched her speaking with Joelle out of the corner of his eye. He thought it a bit amusing that she was so small for someone so accomplished, but even in Gildan, he had heard of the famed and mighty Danijela Anwar, High Wizard from the Kingdom of Arc. She was among the handful of the most powerful wizards in the western continent—which worried him in their present situation.

"Why the frown, Wizard Kyril?" Danijela said to him.

Kyril jumped—he hadn't seen her approach.

"I'm a bit concerned," Kyril admitted, "and honestly, afraid."

"You are smart to be so," she said with a smile. "You have more sense than I did when I was your age."

Kyril found it difficult to imagine the great High Wizard at his age.

"I'm not that old, you know," she said, swatting him on the shoulder. "I'm only in my thirties."

"I…uh…" Kyril tried to cover up what he had been thinking.

"No matter," Danijela said. "I've heard great things about you from Mezar."

Kyril choked for a moment. He wasn't used to hearing someone refer to their emperor on such a casual basis.

"I'm sorry," she said. "I forget that your kingdom is more formal than here. The revered and honored Emperor Mezar Alrishitar speaks highly of you and your potential. He said you have a good mind and kind heart."

Kyril felt his face flush.

"But that doesn't mean you shouldn't be worried," the High Wizard continued. "It seems that from the beginning we all underestimated the power of this new Shadow Master."

"And that's what worries me," Kyril admitted. "Our emperor didn't notice his growing power, but he had men kill the headmaster of the wizard school on White Island, and he—pardon me for saying—seems to have bested you also."

The High Wizard nodded her head and took a step closer. "Yes, you are correct, but…" All pretense of friendly banter was now gone. She held his eyes with her bright blue ones.

They were so close to each other that he could see specks of blue—a sign of her great powers—in the whites of her eyes.

The others in their party gathered around. The High Wizard still stood directly in front of Kyril, looking up at him, but she spared a glance to both Joelle and Sylvie before continuing. "…but you three have the medallions. Three ancient artifacts that are made specifically to bring balance back to magic. The power of the earth, heart, and mind. And they chose each of you three for a special purpose. They have brought each of you a unique special power—transportation, seeing others' intentions and thoughts, and reading signs and portents of the past—but these are not the true powers of the medallions. These are only side gifts to aid you in your quest— bonuses, if you will. The real power of the medallions comes when they are used correctly together. Don't forget that. Only together can you defeat Gamal."

At this point Danijela took a step backwards and Kyril let out a breath of relief. For such a small woman, her words held much power.

"Will it be enough?" Joelle asked. "Will the three of us be enough?"

"You have more than three, Joelle," Hasani said from the side "All of my knowledge is at your disposal. I will do all I can for you…" He looked around the group. "For all my friends."

"As will I," Jax said. "Though you are all new to me, I see how much you care for Sylvie. Any friend of hers is a friend of mine. I may not have magic like you, but as an elf, I do have my own tricks."

Sylvie raised an eyebrow at him and he only smiled—though a bit mischievously.

"And someone has to watch over all you magic wielders," added Bale.

Kyril slapped the man on the back. "We love you too, Bale."

The sentimental quip caught everyone by surprise and laughter ensued.

"You will do well," the High Wizard said. "I don't think Gamal could have anyone at his disposal that is as powerful as six good friends. Good luck. I will do what I can from here."

"Well, let's do this," Kyril said with a look at Sylvie and Joelle. Then, turning to Jax, he nodded his head. "You should find us north of the Bay, if what Sylvie says is correct."

Jax peered at Sylvie seriously. "I can find her wherever she is."

Sylvie blushed.

The three medallion holders grabbed hands and prepared.

"Hasani," Joelle said. "You take care of those two, now."

Bale grunted and Jax smiled, not taking his eyes from Sylvie.

"Ready?" Kyril turned to Sylvie. Then he said to Joelle, "Just keep your mind blank. I don't want to end up somewhere strange again."

Joelle squinted her eyes at him in mock anger, but then smiled. "Fine."

Kyril thought about his medallion, and it flared to life. He linked his thoughts to Sylvie and saw their destination in their shared mind. He could see a field of tents and chose a small copse of trees on the next hill.

Bright light engulfed all three of them and they transported away.

Kyril put his arm forward to stop his fall and slammed his fist into a tree. He heard a gasp behind him, then Joelle cried out, "duck!"

Without thinking, Kyril squatted and pulled Sylvie and Joelle with him to the ground. An arrow stuck into the tree above them. He let go of their hands and rolled to the side as another arrow hit the dirt nearby.

Turning around, he spied two men on horseback approaching. Beside him, Sylvie brought her right hand up and with a flick of her wrist, the ground in front of the horses buckled and the two riders flew out of their saddles.

The three wizards ran up to the men and grabbed their bows. One rolled and tried to stand, but Joelle smacked him hard on the side of the head with her staff, sending sparks flying into the air. The other man lay still from his fall.

Kyril and Sylvie took their remaining weapons while Joelle checked them for injuries. Pulling away, she nodded.

"They'll be fine," she said. "Just out for a while."

"But they'll report to Gamal," Kyril said.

"Not if you take them somewhere else," Sylvie said.

Understanding, Kyril moved the two together and thought of the cave they had been in days before. His medallion flared and he grabbed the two by the arms. In a matter of moments, he stood in a dark cave. The remnants of a burnt-out fire stood off to the side and blankets and pouches of food were against the cave wall. His brow furrowed at the memory of their capture and Henry's greed.

He was back with Sylvie and Joelle in a moment.

"Where did you take them?" Sylvie said.

"To a place that Joelle and I know well." Kyril laughed and Joelle joined in.

"I see I've missed some adventures. I haven't even heard how you found the second medallion!"

"Let's take a look at the camp and then find a place for the night," Kyril said. "Then we can fill you in while we wait for the others. Do you really think they'll be here by morning?"

Sylvie's eyebrows furrowed. "I hope so."

The three of them walked quietly up a small hill. The sun had recently set and a slight ocean breeze made the air more comfortable than farther inland at the Conclave. As they came to the top of the hill, Kyril was the first to peer down onto a small flat grassland that extended to a slim sandy beach, and then the western Blue Sea. Golden clouds floated over the sparkling water that held outlines of ships anchored off shore.

"There's more than I thought," Sylvie said.

Kyril agreed. There must have been two hundred tents and hundreds of men and women milling around the camp. A larger and more colorful command tent stood separated from the others.

"Gamal," Joelle said.

"What's that darkness?" Sylvie pointed past the command tent.

Kyril squinted, but couldn't quite tell. There was a wavering of the air and a blackness that appeared to be darker than night—and a little smoky. A small crowd of people mingled around it, but he couldn't discern anything specific.

"I can check it out," Kyril said with a hand on his medallion.

"No, that's too dangerous," Joelle said. "We said we would wait for the others."

"I'll just pop over real quick," Kyril said. "And then I'll come back."

Joelle shook her head, but Sylvie pursed her lips as if thinking strategically.

"It would be helpful to know," Sylvie said.

"I can do it," Kyril said to Joelle. "There's a group of trees I can hide in there. I'll go there and see what is going on and then come right back."

The other two weren't particularly comfortable leaving him on his own, but they would be taking too much of a chance of being caught if all three went. They walked back down the hill and then Kyril readied himself to transport.

This time, he did so without running into a tree, landing right where he intended. After a few deep breaths, he snuck through the trees, getting as close to the darkness as he could. He peered around the tent and gasped.

In the middle of the evening air was what could only be referred to as a rip. It was as if the air itself had torn in two, and through the widening fissure a dark gray fog oozed out. Five wizards were spread out in front of it, all holding objects in their hands and sending what Kyril guessed was evil magic into the tear.

Two people walked by and stopped directly between him and the fissure, partially blocking his view. He slunk back before they could turn around and see him—but he could tell by the back of his bald head that one was Gamal.

"Everything is ready, Master," came a woman's voice. It was Myna; he recognized her from White Island. She had been one of the people that had killed the headmaster there.

"Good. Good," Gamal said. "My shadow wizards are doing well." He waved a hand toward the five wizards that stood in front of the fissure. "The artifacts we secured from each of the wizard schools are speeding up the process, just as we planned. Soon the magic stream will be opened and available for our use."

"What about the medallions?" the woman said. "You still don't have them."

Gamal and Myna continued walking, so Kyril slipped behind the next tree to try to follow them. His foot stepped on a brittle stick and it snapped. Heart pounding, Kyril dropped to the ground and froze. He hoped the low light would keep them from noticing him.

"What was that?" Gamal asked, glancing around.

There was silence for a moment, then Myna answered, "Nothing, Master. Just an animal, I'm sure. What about the medallions? When will you have them?"

Kyril couldn't see Gamal's expression, but he could feel the man's beady eyes looking into the forest behind him. Kyril made himself as small and still as he could. He hoped that neither his medallion nor the mark in his hand wouldn't begin to glow—something that happened when he was around the black shadow medallion that Gamal usually carried with him.

"I feel something," Gamal said, and Kyril could hear him walking closer.

"Master," came a new voice. "New recruits from Cyrene are here and awaiting your direction. The troops are ready."

Kyril listened to Gamal breathing deeply, then heard his footsteps retreat. "Wonderful. Get them some food and tell them I will meet with them later. Tomorrow we begin. Tomorrow is the day the world changes."

Kyril's heart beat so loud and hard he wondered how Gamal and Myna couldn't hear it. Something big was happening, and based on the little he had seen, it wasn't going to be good.

"And the medallions, Master?" came the woman's insistent question once again as they walked closer to the fissure.

"They are of no use to me now," Gamal growled. "Those three children won't figure out what's happening until it's too late. With the artifacts I've retrieved instead of their medallions, along with my shadow wizards, these troops, and the magic stream, no one will be able to stop us. It is time for the wizards of the mind to rule what is rightfully ours."

Their conversation faded as they walked away and Kyril had to strain to hear any more. But it was enough. He wrapped his hand around the medallion and transported back to Sylvie and Joelle.

"Let's go," he said as soon as he was standing once again in front of the other two. He didn't know where they should go, but he knew they couldn't get caught. "We need time to plan."

"What did you see?" asked Sylvie.

"Later," Kyril said as he began walking—and then running—down the hill.

Joelle and Sylvie caught up to him, and the three ran for at least fifteen minutes. They found a small creek and followed it through some grasslands until they reached another copse of trees far enough from Gamal's camp that Kyril hoped they wouldn't be discovered.

After taking a few deep breaths and drinking some water, Kyril told them about what he had seen. They sat, looking astonished, as he spoke.

"And you said the hole in the air went into the magic stream?" Joelle asked.

"That's what Gamal said," Kyril answered. "And the wizards he had doing it were using artifacts that they stole—we missed that all along. I think he did want the medallions, but he was also stealing ancient magical artifacts from each school. When he couldn't get the medallions, he just decided to use the artifacts to get what he wants. To have so many in his possession is dangerous. He could be very difficult for us to take down."

"But what does he want?" Sylvie said, clearly frustrated. "Why is he opening holes to the magic stream?"

No one had a clear answer, and after discussing what he had seen for a while, there was no other information they could come up with.

"We need to rest so we have our full magic at our disposal," Joelle said.

"But he has a small army," Kyril said. "Hundreds of them—and many of them wizards."

"And we have the three medallions," Sylvie said.

Kyril shook his head nervously. "But will they be enough?"

CHAPTER THIRTY-FIVE

As the sun rose early the next morning, the three wizards woke up refreshed. They had each taken turns on guard during the night, but nothing had happened. With some fresh food from the pack they had brought with them and the little sleep they did get, they felt as refreshed as they were going to be.

Sylvie could feel power pulsating through her from both the medallion and the land around her. She'd been the last one on watch duty and was antsy to get going.

"How long will we need to wait for Jax and the others?" Joelle asked.

Kyril only shrugged his shoulders. The three were farther away from the coast than Jax and the others would be looking. She was afraid that they wouldn't find them and would get caught by Gamal and his troops.

"I think we need to go back and assess the situation again," Sylvie said. "We need to see more of what Gamal is doing."

The other two agreed and soon they were jogging back to the hill where they had first seen the camp the night before. It was a clear day, and as they crawled quietly up the last few feet of the hill, Sylvie felt the warm sun on the back of her head. Looking west now, they could see the entire camp, and her stomach dropped.

"It's bigger than before," Sylvie said.

The number of ships and troops had at least doubled from the night before. They needed an army of their own to contend with this. All three slunk down and were quiet. Running off in search of a few medallions with the hope of banishing one man had sounded doable—had even held a sense of adventure, but now…

"How?" Kyril whispered. He left the rest of his thoughts unsaid. Even Joelle stayed silent.

A small tumult in the camp caught their attention. From the south ran a dozen horses moving swiftly toward the camp. Some of them held additional riders.

"Jax," Sylvie gasped.

"And Hasani and Bale," Joelle added, bringing her hands to her cheeks. "They've been caught."

"This is bad," Kyril said.

Then an explosion shook the ground and their attention was taken back to Gamal's tent where the fissure had been the night before. A tall column of gray wizard power flew straight up in the air and stayed burning—a beacon for all to see.

"We need to get closer," Kyril said.

"They will not have him," Sylvie growled. "We need to rescue them first."

"But we have no chance," Kyril said. "There are too many of them. Our main purpose is to stop Gamal. We need to do that first. Then we'll rescue them."

Sylvie shook her head and began sprinting toward their friends. As each foot hit the ground, the earth around them shook. She *needed* to save Jax.

"No, Sylvie, get down!" Kyril shouted at her. "You're giving our position away!"

"Sylvie," said Joelle, "we need to stay together. Remember what Danijela said: only by working together can we defeat him."

Sylvie slowed her steps and turned back at Joelle's words. Her medallion dimmed and the ground stopped shaking.

"They'll be all right," Joelle said. "Bale will take care of them. But Kyril is right—we need to go after Gamal first. If we don't stop him, nothing else will matter."

Sylvie felt torn in two, her heart and mind at war. She walked toward Joelle and Kyril, but glanced back in the direction of Jax. Thinking that he might come to harm, after all he had done to help her, brought tears to her eyes. She wiped at them angrily.

"Gamal has a lot to pay for," she growled at the others.

Looking back at camp, they spotted a few men pointing at them.

"So much for surprise," Kyril said, grabbing their hands.

They were on the other side of the camp in a small copse of trees in the blink of an eye. In the daylight, it would be much harder to stay hidden than when Kyril had come down the evening before. Sylvie crouched down low behind a bush and the others did the same. Then she turned to the camp, and her jaw dropped open.

There were now at least five fissures ripped into the air. A wizard stood in front of each as they grew wider and wider. Only a gray nothingness was on the other side.

Dread settled into Sylvie's heart. It was even more terrifying up close. What could they do?

"What if we can take out each wizard one at a time?" Sylvie proposed.

Joelle spun her staff around. Sylvie had never seen her more serious before. She shook her head, realizing how much harder it must be for Joelle to fight these people than herself or Kyril. Joelle was a healer—a fantastic and caring one at that. Sylvie's background as a wizard of the earth was more in line with combat

"What if we take three out at once?" Kyril offered instead.

Sylvie smiled. "Why, Kyril, you're getting brave these days. What do you have in mind?"

"Well, I've been thinking about it," Kyril began. "If we take one out at a time that leaves the rest to focus on us together, but if we each take one, then their attention will be divided. The wizards left will have to try and maintain the openings of the others."

"I like it," Joelle said, "but there are more people here to worry about than just these wizards and their openings. We'll be completely surrounded in moments."

"Not if we transport in and out," Kyril said with a pat on his medallion.

"Where's Gamal?" Sylvie peered through the trees. "We need to find him."

"He'll come once we start attacking," Kyril said.

Finally, they all agreed on a plan. Kyril grabbed their hands and they transported.

In the blink of an eye, they appeared in the middle of three of the openings. Upon arriving, Kyril shot a bolt of fire toward one of the wizards. The man ducked but continued pouring power into his opening.

"Behind you," yelled Joelle, and Sylvie spun around to face three soldiers.

With a wave of her hand, the ground buckled around the soldiers, bringing them to their knees. By this time, Joelle had begun swinging her staff at one of the other wizards. He tried to fight her and maintain his hold on the opening, but he couldn't do it. Instead, he turned to fight Joelle head-on.

Sylvie took on her own wizard. The woman was twice her age and held a strange carving of a creature in her hand. She turned and pushed her palm out toward Sylvie. A screaming hiss filled Sylvie's head and she collapsed to the ground, covering her ears. Two people grabbed her from behind and pulled her up. She kicked out at them and scrambled to get away. Jumping up high in the air she spun around and kicked them both in the shoulders, then rounded back on the wizard. This time, Sylvie brought rocks out of the ground and spun them in the air in front of her.

The woman tried to use her artifact on Sylvie again, but Sylvie used one of the rocks to knock it out of her hand, and then threw her to the ground. The now shimmering—and still dark gray opening, however, wasn't closing. Out of the corner of her eye she saw Kyril struggling with a wizard. He was beating Kyril down badly. All of a sudden, Kyril blinked out of existence and transported behind the wizard. The man spun around, but Kyril was there to meet him and he knocked him to the ground.

On her other side, Joelle was spinning her staff around—colors of magic flying beautifully off of its ends. She seemed to anticipate every move before it was made, and was wearing down a group of wizards.

While the other two held their own, Sylvie approached the fissure with the intent to try and destroy it, but as she got closer she saw something inside of it. Through the grayness, there appeared to be a small room. She began walking closer when suddenly she was hit from behind, and fell through the opening.

"Sylvie!" she heard Kyril call out, then his words were cut short.

She landed on her knees then stood up and looked around. The room was made of rough gray stone, and stood about eight feet wide and a bit longer. There was a door to the side and she slowly approached it.

After opening the door, she climbed a single stairway. Dagger out in front of her and ready to call upon her powers if needed, she came to the top of the stairs and ventured out into the rest of the building. It appeared as if it hadn't been used in a while. She found a small window and tried to look outside, but it was too dirty. Instead, she chose a door and opened it very carefully.

She was met with a cool breeze, and stepped out a bit farther. There were buildings of varying sizes of an architectural style she had never seen. People walked the streets but paid her no attention. She stopped a man on the street.

"Sir, this is going to sound strange," Sylvie said, "but what city is this?"

The man pushed her away and continued walking. He must think her crazy. Finally, she spotted a few children playing. They had fair skin and brown hair, and acted like any child would. She approached them carefully.

"What city is this?" she asked again.

One of the young boys screwed his face up as he looked up at her. "You crazy?"

Sylvie wondered if maybe she was. "Humor me."

"You have pretty hair," said one little girl.

"Thank you," Sylvie said, then turned to her instead. "Maybe you can tell me what I need to know."

"This is Cassian, silly," the girl said. "Don't you know where you are? Are you new here?"

"Apparently," Sylvie said under her breath. With a quick nod of thanks she ran back into the house. She was in Cassian, the capital city of Alaris. How could that be? Cassian was a thousand miles south. What was Gamal planning?

She ran down the stairs to the fissure again. Without checking first, she leaped straight through it—headlong into a group of soldiers back on the battlefield in Arc. She put her hands up to battle, but was faced by three other wizards who'd been waiting for her.

She couldn't see Joelle or Kyril anywhere, but a slew of enemy bodies lay moaning and groaning on the ground, and two of the fissures were unattended. She smiled inside despite her situation. Her friends had already done a lot of damage, and Kyril must have gotten Joelle away to safety.

She could try and fight her way out, but the odds of her survival wouldn't be great, and she needed to stay alive to save Jax.

The crowd parted in front of her and Gamal came strutting forward. "You got here quicker than I would have expected—you and your little friends." Gesturing behind him, Gamal presented Jax, Bale, and Hasani.

"Are you all right, Sylvie?" Hasani asked.

Sylvie nodded her head.

Bale unsuccessfully pulled against the man that was holding him.

Gamal walked up to Sylvie and held his hand open. In it sat the orange SpeedStone.

"Oh," she gasped.

Gamal sneered and then put it in his pocket.

"That's mine," Jax said, as he pulled against his captors.

"I've heard rumors of these out on the isles of the sea," Gamal said. "It might come in handy during my conquest."

As if to emphasize his words, troops of men and women arrived in an organized fashion and began lining up in front of each of the openings in the air. Sylvie groaned and suddenly felt sick with a new realization.

Gamal only laughed. "Smart one, you are, Sylvonna, and powerful—but not as smart and strong as me. I just wish your other two friends had come with you to watch this."

It was then that Sylvie realized that Gamal thought she had arrived with Jax, Hasani, and Bale with the SpeedStone, and had no idea that Joelle and Kyril were close by. Well, at least they had one thing going for them.

This close to the ocean, Sylvie could feel the power in the water there and began to reach out to it, careful not to alert Gamal or his soldiers. Let them think she was docile.

Gamal walked around the semicircle of the five openings and inspected them carefully, then went to a spot out in front of them and raised his hands up in the air. Each fist held an artifact—one was a small carving of a gruesome creature, the other a small dagger she supposed was infused with magic of some sort. A dark gray fog filtered out of each one. The ground rumbled and Sylvie felt her powers slipping. She redoubled her efforts and her medallion began to glow. But Gamal didn't notice—or didn't think he should care.

In the middle of the small field, lightning came from an empty sky and another crack in the air appeared in front of Gamal. This one was black rather than gray, darker than midnight on a cloudy night. A black that seemed to pull light from the air around them into it.

Even the sun appeared to dim, but Sylvie had now pulled a huge amount of power into herself and held it in reserve until the proper time. She looked around for Kyril and Joelle. Why weren't they here? It would have to be up to her.

A loud screech came from Gamal's new fissure, and an ugly black creature walked out of it. It was hideous, and by far the most horrendous thing she had ever seen. It was twice the height and width of Gamal. It had a vaguely human head, but dark horns hung down from the top of its head and dagger-like teeth filled its mouth. Its skin was a thick black hide covered in scales.

"Shadow Master," the beast said to Gamal, and Gamal smiled back. "You have summoned me?"

The soldiers holding Sylvie, Jax, Bale, and Hasani had their attention on the creature rather than the four of them. Sylvie glanced at Bale and he nodded to her. He was ready. Jax held his body taut and ready for a fight.

With the soldiers distracted, Sylvie let loose a large portion of her power, sending fire toward those that held her three friends, and buckling the earth for everyone else. She fell to the ground and her captor behind her tried to keep from falling over her. She kicked behind her and caught him hard, and he went down with a groan. Suddenly, other wizards threw their own lightning and air at Sylvie—was she their main focus? Sylvie brought up a defensive shield of light like she had done in the Wizard Conclave. It spun in the air in front of her, pulling power from the earth around her, and the attack of the wizards had little effect on her.

The hideous creature that Gamal had brought forth growled and moved over to allow another one out. This one was smaller than the first, but its face was more beast than man. Also with black hide, this one had spikes along the back of its arms and legs. Its eyes and nose were small, as most of its face was taken up by a giant mouth full of dangerous looking teeth. It snarled at Gamal, but then bowed its head to him.

Over the din, Sylvie suddenly heard a voice singing. It was beautiful and pierced her soul with joy. She jerked her head around looking for the source while still holding back the soldiers and wizards. And then she saw Jax—and he had never looked so beautiful to her before. His long dark hair was out of its ponytail and blew around him like waves on the sea. His head was lifted toward the trees and his face was glowing with joy. Many of the soldiers around her dropped their swords and other weapons and stopped attacking Sylvie and her friends.

"It's a beautiful song," said one.

"It reminds me of a forest near my home," said another.

The tree branches at the edge of the field began to sway in unison, and a power of peace and joy filled the air. Sylvie remembered Jax humming once on the island and another time in her vision of him with Gamal. His voice must hold some kind of powerful song magic.

"What is this?" Gamal called out. It took him a moment to find Jax. "Shut that elf up," he ordered.

At that moment, Jax held his hand out in front of him and Gamal howled in pain. A bright orange light came out from between his fingers and the SpeedStone burst out of his fist and flew back to Jax.

The soldiers around Jax still stood in awe of his singing. But the creature that Gamal had released had no such feelings and with a giant leap began running toward the elf.

CHAPTER THIRTY-SIX

"Jax!" Sylvie yelled out in warning. The monster would be upon him before she could get there.

As if out of nowhere, Bale jumped between the attacking creature and Jax. He stood with his sword out ready to defend against the creature.

"Bale, move!" Sylvie screamed as she ran forward, already readying another spell of fire. It felt as if the power was endless inside her right now. "He's too big for you."

But Bale didn't move, only stayed in the creature's path. When the creature was nearly upon him, he dropped to the ground flat on his back, and it passed right over him. With the legs of the creature barely passing him by on the right and left, he lifted his sword and stabbed it directly into its belly.

The hideous beast stopped in its tracks and bellowed an other-worldly screeching sound. Bale rolled out from under it as the creature reached for him.

Sylvie couldn't attack the monster with any magic without taking the chance of hurting Bale, so she watched helplessly. Without warning, the beast picked up Bale in the air and swung him around. Now, however, Sylvie had her chance. She focused and let loose a spear of white-hot fire that flew out of her hands and directly into the chest of the beast. It howled again and threw Bale up in the air toward one of the gray fissures.

Sylvie ran toward him to help, but, before she could get there he rolled through it and disappeared.

"One down," Gamal roared, black smoke pouring from his hands once again. He was trying to open another black fissure for more monsters to arrive. Sylvie took stock of the situation and decided it was time to take care of Gamal, once and for all. Then she would go after Bale.

Pulling upon the never-ending strength of the Blue Sea close by, she raised her hands up in the air and the sea surged. She twirled her hands and formed a spinning wheel of water, which hovered above the heads of Gamal and the soldiers. Another beast was just exiting one of his great black fissures in the air when Sylvie dropped it down on Gamal. The water swept the evil wizard off his feet and sent him flying through one of the smaller openings that his wizards had created—the same one that Bale had gone through.

"No!" Sylvie shouted and tried to pull back the water, but it was to no avail. Gamal was gone, but so was Bale.

"Sylvie!" Hasani came running to her side. "Where are they? What's on the other side?"

Sylvie shook her head. "The one I went through went to Alaris. I have no idea where that one goes."

Hasani shook his head with a look of disbelief. "You mean he found a physical way to travel through the magic stream?"

"I suppose," Sylvie said, then turned around at a noise behind her. A dozen wizards—backed up by a hundred troops—now surrounded them. Two of them held Jax by the arms.

"Get him back!" commanded a man. "Get Gamal back or you and your friends die."

One of the creatures roared and swung its arms, knocking down some of the soldiers.

Before Sylvie could even think, Jax disappeared from in front of her and she felt him grab her hand and pull her away. Everything blurred around her, and the figures of the soldiers and wizards moved in slow motion as Jax maneuvered her through them using the SpeedStone.

They ended up on top of a nearby hill. Joelle and Kyril jumped up in surprise.

"Hasani and Bale are still back there."

Kyril disappeared and returned in a brief moment with Hasani in tow.

"What about Bale?" Sylvie asked.

"I didn't see him there," Kyril said. "Where is he?"

"He went through one of the openings in the air."

Joelle stood up quickly. "What? How? Where do they go?"

"They go to other kingdoms," Sylvie said. "Soldiers are lining up. I suspect that Gamal is sending them in to conquer those nations along with the shadow monsters he's pulling from somewhere. We don't have long." She looked around her at the strange markings on the ground and her frustration rose. "What are you two doing drawing pictures on the ground? We need you down there."

"We figured it out, Sylvie," said Kyril.

Sylvie watched Hasani walking around and nodding his head, excitement growing in his eyes.

"Yes, yes," Hasani said. "I see what you are doing. You are recreating the pattern of the medallion on the ground."

"What?" Sylvie yelled out. "We need to fight."

A shout echoed back down below in Gamal's camp. They all turned and looked. Coming out of the opening was Gamal, but Bale was still nowhere to be seen.

Gamal roared, and the line of soldiers began moving forward toward the openings.

"We're too late!" Sylvie shook her head. "He's going to win."

"No he's not," Joelle said as she finished drawing a half circle at one edge of the last outer circle.

Sylvie took a moment to look over the ground. Three concentric circles with six lines coming from the center covered a significant area. Three of the lines reached the edge of the outer circle. At these three points stood three small semicircles.

"One for each of us to stand on," Joelle explained. Then turned around to face the field below them. "They're coming."

"Who's coming?" Kyril peered over the field.

"Gamal's wizards," Joelle said firmly, still watching down below. "And they intend to kill us this time, I'm afraid."

"Then we have no time left," Kyril said. "Get on your spots."

While Kyril moved to one spot, Joelle moved to another. Sylvie looked down below once again. "We need to rescue Bale."

"Sylvie!" Kyril called out, and his medallion sent forth a burst of power. His voice was louder and deeper. "Get to your spot on the circle. This is the only way we can defeat him. Do it now!"

His voice reverberated through the air and both Hasani and Jax swayed on their feet. Sylvie had never heard such a command come from Kyril. But she recognized its power and could do little but obey. With tears in her eyes she moved into position.

"I'll go and find him," Jax said, and before anyone could argue, he sped away using the SpeedStone.

Sylvie tried to cry out but he was gone before she could. Her heart broke thinking that Jax, who scarcely even knew Bale, would risk his life to save him. She crumbled inside even more when she realized he couldn't really defend himself down there against Gamal and his forces. A sweet song and a stone wouldn't save him this time. Now she had lost two friends.

Turning to Kyril and Joelle with tears streaming down her face, she faced her duty. "This had better be worth their lives!" The ground shook around them with the force of her own words—or was it the army approaching the hill?

Both of her friends cringed, but Kyril was the only one who spoke—to Hasani. "Keep the army from us for as long as you can, then get yourself to safety. Someone needs to tell Emperor Alrishitar and High Wizard Danijela if we fail."

Hasani nodded, then turned with hands raised, to face the onslaught. Against Gamal's full might, the scholar wizard of the mind wouldn't last long.

CHAPTER THIRTY-SEVEN

Kyril opened himself up to the magic of his medallion and a bright golden light shot out from his position toward the center of the circle. Joelle followed and her white light joined his, and Sylvie's silver light met the others. A brilliant glare formed in the middle of the circle.

As the three powers of the medallion met, Kyril felt a jolt inside of him and everything became clearer. He could hear the army approaching and could sense the evil creatures down below.

"So much power," Sylvie said to his right. "I could fight them all with this."

"And I could heal them all," Joelle said to his left, her voice softer than Sylvie's.

"Anikari said the medallions were made to bring balance to magic," Kyril said. "Sylvie, you must let go of your anger. You're making it unstable."

Sylvie grunted. "You left Bale and Jax to die down there, you know."

"No," Kyril said. "Gamal forced this on us. It's not my doing. If they die, they die because of his lust for power, but…" He stopped Sylvie from talking with a held-out hand—the hand that held the mark of the medallion. "I won't let them die, Sylvie. We'll save them both. But we have to stop Gamal first."

"Promise?" Sylvie asked after a brief moment.

"Yes, I promise." Kyril said. "Do you trust the power of the medallions and the charge we have been given?"

"Yes," Sylvie answered back, her voice losing some of its anger.

"Now concentrate," Kyril said as soldiers approached the top of the hill. But the army seemed to be moving in slow motion—had time slowed down in the rest of the world? "Bring our powers together."

The power was amazing, but Kyril didn't know if it was enough. "Something's missing," he said.

The magic of their medallions coalesced in the center, but it wasn't spreading around to all the circles and lines like he knew it should. Then he realized what was missing. They needed a fourth. In history in all times of great need, a fourth power had been needed. Many times this need had been met by a dragon or Cremelino, as they held the power of the spirit and the power to bind…but they didn't have one of those. So they needed to use the next best thing.

"Hasani!" he called out. "We need you."

Hasani, pacing on top of the hill as slowly as the army was moving, turned toward them. As he approached the three medallion holders, his walk seemed to accelerate.

"Stand in the middle," Kyril said. "We need someone to keep our powers centered and focused."

Hasani, always agreeable and looking for more knowledge, now stepped forward without question.

"He can't handle this much power," Sylvie said. "Without the medallion, we'll burn him out."

"It must be done, Sylvonna," Hasani said, taking his place in the middle. "We all do our part in this. I will be fine."

Lifting his hands up in the air, Hasani braced himself as all three powers struck him hard. Kyril felt a shift in the power now.

"It's more stable and firm," Kyril said. "Now, Joelle and Sylvie—bring as much to you as you can.

The ground shook, water lifted up from the sea, and lightning forked from a cloudless sky as Sylvie pulled her powers to her. A renewed sense of healing, health, and calm surrounded them as Joelle took as much power as she could.

But what did Kyril have? What could he give? He wasn't a powerful wizard in his own right. He'd only ever wanted to be accepted and to have friends. Now, looking around the group, he saw those friends in front of him—Sylvie, Joelle, and Hasani. Three friends that he was lucky to have.

A voice in the back of his head reminded him of Bale and guilt filled him. He had left Bale on his own as Sylvie had accused him of doing, but what could he do now? With the clarity that only the power of his medallion brought him, he now knew what he must do. But could he do it? Was he powerful enough?

He concentrated on the magic stream. He had been there before and tried to remember how it felt. He pictured the grayness and the power there, and suddenly, it opened up to him. It wasn't a physical fissure like Gamal had created, but a mental one instead. Still feeling his body back in the circle, he stepped inside and entered the grayness of the magic stream.

Sylvie gathered a storm in the sky around them and began to drench the hill. The attackers slid down the slope in the soft mud and couldn't get to them. Lightning came from the sky and scorched the tents in Gamal's camp as the soldiers began to enter the openings into other lands.

Kyril could feel it all happening, but he left that behind and concentrated on his own mind.

"Bale?" he called out. "Bale, where are you?"

Tiny stars appeared around him. He looked at each one carefully, trying to figure out what they were. He touched one of the brightest ones and all of a sudden found himself in the palace in Gildan—in the emperor's private study.

"Kyril?" The emperor stared at him. "What are you doing here?"

"Trying to find Bale!" The words rushed out of him—he didn't dare take time to figure out what he had just done. "Gamal has opened up fissures in the magic stream to other kingdoms and intends on sending soldiers through. Bale is lost in one of them."

Without any warning, Emperor Alrishitar moved and now appeared beside him in the magic stream, rather than in his office in Gildan.

"I'll gather the others, Kyril and warn them." The emperor said as he pulled Kyril along through the stars in the magic stream.

Finally they stopped at a group of stars that were dimmer than some of the others.

"There's Bale," the emperor said, pointing at one. "I can sense all my spymasters here."

"Why is his star so dim?" Kyril wondered. "Is he hurt?"

"No," Emperor Alrishitar said. "The more magic one has, the brighter their star."

The ground outside where Kyril still stood shook and it reverberated in the magic stream.

"You must hurry, Kyril," said the emperor. "Bring balance to the land."

And with those words, he was gone.

Kyril touched the small dim star that was Bale, and immediately found himself at the edge of a forest before a bridge leading into a big city.

Something flashed to his right and he turned as a sword rose up toward him.

"Bale!" Kyril shouted. "It's me."

"Kyril," Bale said. "I can hardly see you."

"My body is still back in the battle," Kyril said. "I came to find you."

"You came for me?" Bale asked, his eyes wide in surprise.

A brilliant flash occurred to their right and troops started pouring through a rift and into the forest.

"Oh no," Kyril groaned. "We're too late."

"Because of me?"

Kyril cocked his head to the side. He didn't know what to say. It may have been true. Kyril's searching for Bale may have cost the three medallion holders the time they needed to destroy Gamal. But it was the right thing to do. And he wouldn't feel bad about that.

"Where are we?" Kyril didn't recognize anything.

"The Realm, I think," Bale said.

"Well, let's go." Kyril reached out and grabbed hold of Bale's hand. Before he pulled him out of the magic stream he caught a glimpse of soldiers on foot and horse, racing from the city toward Gamal's soldiers that had escaped through the fissure.

Bale stumbled, disoriented, but Kyril concentrated again on the battle around them and suddenly his mind was back in his body and Bale tumbled to the ground just outside of the circle—from seemingly nowhere.

The air was now misty and the ground wet and muddy. Blasts of wizard fire hurdled toward the three medallion holders and Hasani. But Sylvie was holding up a large magical shield that—for now, at least—was keeping them safe.

"Bale!" Sylvie exclaimed. "You're safe! Where's Jax?"

"Jax?" Bale said. "Kyril found me."

Sylvie's eyes went wide with surprise, and she momentarily lost her focus. An arrow made it through their shield and pierced Hasani in the shoulder. He howled out in pain and tried to grab at it.

"It's crumbling!" Kyril cried out. "Concentrate."

"Everything we're doing is defensive," Sylvie said. "We need an offense."

Hasani tried to stand straight in the center of the circle but was hurt too badly and fell to the ground. Blood soaked his shirt and his face paled.

"I need to help him," Joelle said.

But if she moved from her position at the edge of the circle, Kyril knew their power would collapse for sure. Already without them being able to focus their power through Hasani, the strength and energy of the medallions was lessoning. Things were falling apart before they got a chance to attack Gamal.

Hasani stumbled toward Joelle, and fell to the ground before he reached her.

At the same time, they heard a loud roar down below. Trying to look through the mist and rain, Kyril spotted Gamal. He stood in the middle of two of the ferocious creatures with his hands up in the air. Black lightning shot from the sky and landed near their circle.

Kyril could feel Gamal's eyes on him, and over the din of battle his words flew on the wind.

"I have beaten you, little Kyril!" Gamal gloated. "Even now, my soldiers will be securing the rest of the continent. And now I come for you."

Gamal leaped up into the air, his dark cloak floating around him as he landed on the shoulder of one of the great beasts. The creature then began running toward them.

Joelle screamed and reached down toward Hasani, but she couldn't reach him. She made a move to step toward him.

"No!" Kyril shouted. "You can't move. Stay on your point."

"We can't win, Kyril!" Joelle began to cry. "I can't do this anymore. All this pain and hurt and these dangerous thoughts—they're going to kill me. Use the medallion and transport us away."

Kyril's heart fell. Were they really going to lose? The ground shook and at first Kyril thought it was Sylvie's doing, but he realized it was Gamal and his creatures approaching. A hundred others followed behind them, many of them wizards.

Sylvie reached her hand out toward them and the ground buckled. She called forth rocks from the earth, and they rose up in the air and pelted many of the men, but the beasts marched on. Getting closer and closer.

Hasani crawled out of the circle and another arrow from one of Gamal's on-coming soldiers stuck into his leg. He roared in pain and tried to pull it out, but fainted instead.

"Hasani!" Joelle continued to cry. "Kyril, he'll die if I don't help him."

"We'll all die if you do," Kyril choked out a response. It shamed him to say it, but it was true.

Without Hasani in the middle, their power wouldn't be strong enough. From outside the circle, Bale turned and came running toward them at full steam. He slid to a stop in the center where Hasani used to be—where the lines of power met. He held his hands up in the air and bellowed a cry that was heard across the field.

"No!" Sylvie screamed, her voice echoing over the hill. "You'll kill yourself."

"Bale, what are you doing?" Kyril said with a shake of his head. Of all the stupid things for him to do. "You can't handle this power."

"No, Bale," Joelle sobbed. "I knew you'd try to do something stupid like this. I should have warned the others. You're not a wizard."

"No, but I am a man with friends to save and an evil wizard to finish off."

Kyril knew they had no choice, but he also knew it would indeed destroy Bale. The power the three of them held was difficult for Hasani to be the focal point for, and he was another wizard. A mere human without any spark of magic couldn't do this without killing himself. It was not something Kyril had foreseen and yet, it may be the only way to stop Gamal at this point. But he couldn't ask someone to give up their life like this.

"This is my choice, Kyril!" Bale bellowed over the din as if in answer to Kyril's thoughts. "You're not the only one that can be a hero." His broad shoulders were already shaking with the strain of so much magic coalescing in him, but he kept his hands out to the sides and brought the three streams of magic together within his body. "Kill that weasel Gamal and rid the world of his ugly hide."

Kyril hesitated for only a moment longer, then nodded his head. He would honor his friend's last request.

Sylvie wailed in frustration, and she brought so much power into herself that she began to glow.

"Sylvie!" Kyril called out. "You'll burn yourself out."

"Then do something about it!" she shouted. "You're the leader of the medallions. You're the one with the mark!"

It was now or never, he supposed. Everything that had happened to him in the last month all came down to this moment. He shut his eyes and thought about his family who had died in the fire, and left him all alone with only the medallion now to remember them by. He thought about all those that had teased him when he was younger and bullied him when he was older. Bale had been one of them.

As if in response to his thoughts, Bale roared out in pain. "I can't take it much longer, Kyril—do what you must!"

Gamal and the beasts were only moments away so Kyril cleared his mind as he was taught and let it float off into the magic stream once again. There, in the timeframe of a thought in the real world he met Emperor Alrishitar, High Wizard Danijela Anwar, King of the Realm Darius DarSan Williams, and—he could scarcely believe it—Bakari, the Dragon King of Mahli. The four mighty wizards of the western continent stood and watched him as if awaiting him to speak first.

They were not solid, but he could see them well enough.

The emperor took a step forward. "My dear Kyril. Your warning helped all the kingdoms prepare for Gamal's soldiers. Most have been taken captive or killed. There are not enough left to cause any real damage. Gamal's plans for dominion have been thwarted. All he has now are those with him. You must end it now once and for all."

"But how can I?" Kyril said. "I am nobody, a weak young wizard with no family and few friends."

"Just like all of us at your age," the Dragon King said. His dark hair and braids reminded Kyril of Hasani. "You just have to do your best for the right reasons."

"Your friends are your family, Kyril," said High Wizard Danijela, a small dimple showing in her cheek as she smiled.

"And those with friends are never nobody," added King Darius.

The four mighty wizards placed their hands together and Kyril felt an increase of power roar through his entire being.

"Now take some of our power with you," The Emperor of Gildan said, "and go and defeat the Shadow Master."

The words and power of the wizards not only lifted Kyril physically but gave him the internal hope and encouragement he so desperately needed. He finally totally realized how many people were relying on him.

"I can do it," he whispered, then with new found confidence loudly roared. "I will defeat him."

CHAPTER THIRTY-EIGHT

"Now!" Kyril called out to the others and the power of the three medallions along with the wizards help from the magic stream flared to life, circling and filling all three circles and six lines that were drawn on the ground with a brilliant and glowing golden light of fire. They all now stood as parts of a giant medallion on the ground, with Bale in the center.

Kyril noticed that Bale, who had been sagging moments ago, now stood up straighter once again. The strain was apparent on his face. In the short time he had been in the center of the magic, he had aged. His once black hair now turning white and his skin had lost much of its sheen.

The power of the three medallions flowed through Bale and then up into the sky, forming a dome of golden fire over them all—stretching from the hill to a half mile out to sea.

Gamal, on top of one of the creatures, raised his hands in the air and called forth his dark shadows. They came from the fissures below and raced up the hill toward the circle of magic.

Sylvie pointed her fist toward the shadows. "By the power of the silver medallion, I send you back to where you came from."

A flash exploded from her hand and a wall of fire spread toward Gamal's evil shadows that had come out of the fissures in the air. It pushed them back down the hill, across the field and back into the black and gray cracks they had come from. With one last scream she closed the fissures in an explosion of white light.

Gamal sagged and his arms fell to his sides. But the two giant beasts that accompanied him still came forward.

"By the power of the bronze medallion…" called out Joelle, her red hair blowing wildly around her. " I close the rips and tears in the magic stream." Her staff glowed with bronze fire and she pointed it down the hill.

With a wave of her staff a narrow bronze light shot out and divided into five different streaks of light. Each one finding and closing one of the fissures that Gamal and his shadow wizards had opened.

"Nooo!" roared Gamal.

"They are of no use to you, Gamal!" Kyril called up to him. "Your soldiers have all been captured. Your plans are ruined."

"You trifle with powers you know nothing of, boy." Gamal brought his hands up again and two stone artifacts glowed brightly in them. "I will rule you all."

"By the power of the golden medallion, I call the artifacts to me," Kyril said, and with a wave of his arm and a flash of gold, Gamal's evil artifacts were transported into Kyril's outstretched hand. "These never belonged to you. And you had no right to take your vile magic and manipulate the magic stream for your gain. It doesn't work that way."

"I know how it works," Gamal said, now still sitting on the shoulders of one of the creatures a mere ten feet away. "I've studied it my entire life. I am the Shadow Master."

A boom shook the hill at his word and black lightning came down from the sky. The dome of golden light above them vanished and three strikes of lightning hit close to where each of the three wizards stood. The rest of the army stopped, afraid to get in the middle of the incredible and intimidating display of good magic versus evil.

Gamal then pointed his finger directly at Sylvie and shot a thin but powerful bolt of dark fire at her. Not wanting to leave her place on the medallion circle, she leaned back as far as she could from the waist up, but it still grazed her shoulder. Kyril could feel their shared magic weakening, but Sylvie stood back up with a grimace.

Bale growled and almost fell down, but somehow his stubborn will kept him upright. "Leave her alone!" he bellowed at Gamal.

Gamal barely spared a thought for Bale and once again readied a spell to throw at Sylvie. He must have known she was the strongest of them all. But, before he could do it, a strange sound came up from the field below. Everyone, Including Gamal, turned to look.

Kyril had forgotten about Jax, as had Gamal.

Now they all watched as the elf pulled back on his bowstring and let loose a fire-tipped arrow. At the same time a new mournful melody came from his lips as both he and the arrow sped toward the top of the hill. Both voice and flame grew louder and larger as they approached.

Suddenly, Jax appeared in front of them holding the SpeedStone in his hand. The music continued pouring from own lips; an Elvyn tune that appeared he had no intention of stopping.

Only a brief moment later the flaming arrow arrived and plunged into the chest of Gamal. The Shadow Master howled with pain and the blackness around him shifted, collapsing and shrinking.

"Jax!" Sylvie's voice pierced the din around them.

Jax turned and looked at Sylvie; the love he held for her was apparent in his eyes. He turned back to Gamal and his voice grew louder, the Elvyn song becoming more intense as it filled the air. Rather than the tune of peace and joy earlier in the fight, this one was of sadness and destruction.

The song was haunting and almost caused Kyril to lose his focus, but the three wizards held their circle and watched Gamal.

Struggling in pain, Gamal yanked the arrow from his chest and threw it to the ground. He appeared as if he would recover and continue the fight, but instead he slumped forward on the creature he was still riding. His hand ran lovingly over the scaled hide of the beast.

"Kill them," he hissed. "Kill them all."

The two creatures bellowed, and the sound stopped Jax in his tracks.

"Get away, Jax!" Sylvie cried out, taking a step toward him. "They'll kill you!"

"Hold the circle," Kyril called out. This wasn't over yet, and he knew they needed all the power they had to finish it off. Gamal's power was far more than any of them had supposed.

The creature next to Gamal reached one scaly, grotesque hand toward Jax, and Sylvie screamed again. Jax used the SpeedStone and raced around to the other side of the circle.

"Kyril," Bale whispered quietly.

Kyril turned his attention to Bale. The power of the three medallion holders still convened into him in the middle of the circle, and now Bale was on his knees, face and hair white, body sagging with the immense power that flowed through him.

How have you survived this long? Kyril whispered to himself. The man was as stubborn as ever.

On the other side of the circle, Hasani woke back up and realized for the first time what Bale had done after he had been injured. Arm hanging limp to the side, blood soaking his shirt, and leg bleeding, he began to crawl back toward Bale.

"Let me," he whispered.

"No." Bale shook his head, his voice barely audible. "It's too late for me. Stay away."

Hasani paused at the edge of the circle and the two creatures approached. Gamal thrust his hand out to Bale with one last bit of strength. A thin line of dark shadow flew from his finger toward Bale.

With reserves of strength Kyril didn't know Hasani had he reached forward and with a light of his own blocked Gamal's attack on Bale—though the effort must have been exhausting for him. It was enough to divert Gamal's attention from Bale for a moment.

"Give me your power, medallion holders!" Bale screamed in response. "Let's end this now!"

Kyril didn't want to—he knew it would kill Bale. But Bale turned his face upwards and slowly regained his footing as the black shadow from Gamal continued to try and penetrate the medallions' power around them all.

"Kyril, please," Bale begged. "Let me do this. Let me be the balance to his evil. Let me finish it my way."

Kyril's heart beat like thunder. He didn't want to make the choice. Kyril caught the eyes of Sylvie and Joelle. They all knew what this would mean for Bale and so each on their own resolve refused to release any more of their power.

"Kyril!" Bale now screamed in such mournful fury and desire that Kyril knew he couldn't deny the spymaster one last chance to defeat Gamal and his minions.

"Sylvie, Joelle!" Kyril called out to his companions in anguish. "Bale is right. Give him all the power you have. This ends now!"

Kyril thought once again about all the damage Gamal had inflicted, and all the lives that were lost because of him. The world was unstable and the three of them—no, now four of them, six if you counted Hasani and Jax—had been chosen to bring back balance and peace to the world of wizards and humans alike. It was their duty, their calling, their destiny.

And so he dug deep inside and accessed all the power that the medallion afforded him. Sylvie and Joelle did the same— although tears ran down their faces, mirroring his own—and where their powers met in the middle, Bale endured.

Tall and proud, the Gildanian spymaster stood. He had not only held off Gamal's final attack, but now he was somehow pushing it back upon Gamal himself.

Bale's body began to dissipate in a glowing gold and silver light that almost blinded the rest of them. The circle of light grew brighter and bigger pushing back all the darkness that Gamal had brought upon the world.

The creatures themselves stumbled at the edge of the circle.

"*Aaah!*" Bale screamed out, the sound reverberating to the seashore. Jax's song went silent. The creatures' growls subsided. Kyril felt as if his heart would burst with each beat.

Kyril could barely discern Bale's features through the burning brightness of power. His face was turned up to the heavens and his mouth was opened wide. Through the medallions' connection, Kyril could feel the man's anguish. It was at the same time the most terrifying yet selfless and beautiful thing he had ever seen in his life. The pain of what it must be doing to Bale's body was more than anyone could bear.

"But my soul is strong," came Bale's whispered voice to Kyril's mind. And he knew that Sylvie and Joelle could hear it also. "Thank you all. Thank you for teaching me to care, love, and to put something of greater worth above my own needs. You have given me more than I deserved and now I repay you by defeating the shadow and helping you fulfill your destinies as I fulfill mine."

Sylvie broke down and sobbed. Even Jax and Hasani, outside of the connection knew that something momentous was happening. Their faces turned toward Bale in utter amazement.

Then it all ended.

In a blinding flash of brilliance, Bale's body exploded into thousands of shards of light. The pieces flew through the air around them, piercing Gamal's body a hundred times, taking down the two shadow creatures, then flying out over the field and destroying all the wizards and leaders who had come with Gamal to take over the world.

The mercy of the light spared the common soldiers who were only following orders, but it still knocked them to the ground. For a minute, the flecks of light flew around the field. Just before they completely disappeared, Kyril heard one last final fading voice.

"Tell the emperor what I did," Bale's voice echoed in Kyril's mind. "And tell my family I did it all willingly."

The sparkles of light faded to mist and then Bale was truly gone. The light of the three medallions instantly winked out and all three medallion holders sunk to the ground in utter exhaustion.

A stillness filled the air. A stillness of peace, quiet, goodness, and balance.

And then Jax began to sing once more. The song began soft and slow and then rose in volume. It was a magic of its own, a magic of his Elvyn heritage. Colorful birds flew overhead, their song drifting down to join with Jax. Flowers suddenly bloomed in the field below, and all left alive looked around in wonder.

Joelle crawled over to Hasani and put her hands on him to heal him.

"No," he shook his head. "You need to rest."

Joelle shoved his hand away and smiled at him. "If I save the world but can't save my friend, what kind of person am I?"

A soft healing light infused around Hasani. Twice Joelle had to stop and rest, but eventually she healed both arrow wounds enough that he would be able to walk and move without too much pain.

As the song of peace, love, and balance faded away, Sylvie ran to Jax and hugged him fiercely.

"How?" Sylvie asked. "Where did the singing come from?"

Jax only smiled and shook his head, but kept one arm around her shoulders. "I'm not sure. I guess I always knew there was a power in my voice, but until I was faced with the threats of this battle, I never knew how powerful it really was."

With the other four busy consoling and talking to each other, Kyril stood and took a few steps forward. Looking down the hill over the destruction, he thought he saw one last final speck of light drifting out over the Blue Sea.

The four wizards and elf had all given much in this fight, but Bale had given his all. Kyril shook his head in amazement and a small grin slid across his lips. Who would have thought that the bully that had been the bane of his existence at the wizard academy would one day save his life—and the world?

You never know what was truly inside of anyone. You never know what potential someone has when faced with daunting and impossible circumstances.

You never know their destiny.

But give someone a chance and they just might surprise you. And that's just what Bale did.

CHAPTER THIRTY-NINE

Three weeks later, Kyril, Sylvie, Joelle, Jax, and Hasani sat outside Emperor Mezar Alrishitar's office after being summoned there together.

After the battle, all had gone their separate ways for a while. Sylvie had gone home to visit her family—along with Jax, of course. They were inseparable now. Then they had met with Danijela Anwar, the High Wizard of the Wizard Conclave, and helped to continue to root out any last vestiges of Gamal's followers there. Plus, with most of her memories intact now, Sylvie was able to have a true reunion with her mentor.

Joelle had gone home to Belor to spend time with her family. She felt she had left them on difficult terms, having just heard about her adoptive status. But they accepted her with open arms. While she was in Belor, the King of the Realm, Darius DarSan Williams, and Governor Kelln El'Han met with her and offered her a position in the capital city as a royal healer. She told them she would think about it.

Sitting outside the emperor's office, Kyril watched Hasani for a moment. The scholar from Mahli sat with a pleasant smile on his face now, but after the battle he had felt bad that he hadn't been more helpful. Kyril and the others had reassured him that his help in the library researching and his ability to remember things had been greatly instrumental in the journey to defeat Gamal and his followers. And his final act of staving off Gamal's last attack on Bale had allowed their friend to finish his final assault on the Shadow Master. Hasani had decided that he would return to Mahli soon and begin writing a history of what had happened with the Shadow Master, and to research the power of the medallions and other artifacts.

Kyril had met with Emperor Alrishitar upon returning to give him the artifacts that Gamal had stolen from multiple places. The emperor assured Kyril that he would make sure they got back to their rightful place and guarded well.

A click in front of him brought Kyril's attention back to the present. The door to the office opened and Zaidan Alrishitar, the emperor's son, greeted them. He called them inside and they went, Kyril bringing up the rear. As he entered the room, he once again felt the power of the emperor's office and of the various artifacts in the room—maybe even more now than he had before.

The emperor approached Kyril, Sylvie, Joelle, and Hasani with a broad smile and hugged each one in turn. He stood and took in Jax for a bit longer, and then grabbed him in an embrace also. They had not met before.

"And Jax Miramenor—it is always an honor to have one of the distinguished elves here in the Empire of Gildan."

Jax blushed. "I'm not sure I'm distinguished…" His slanted eyes sparkled. "And I'm only part elf," he said with a low mumble.

The emperor waved a hand in the air. "There is no part elf, young Jax. Many of us have mixed parentage in our bloodlines. You are what you make yourself to be. I've heard from Kyril about your amazing magic of voice and song. I'm very interested to learn more about you and where you are from. I've not heard of this talent before."

Jax relaxed and smiled back at the emperor.

Emperor Alrishitar led them all to the small sitting area in his office. There was a moment of silence before he spoke. Kyril saw Hasani sitting on the edge of his seat, most likely memorizing everything that was happening for his research.

"My young friends," the emperor began. "There is nothing I can say or do that would accurately show the appreciation that not only Gildan, but all the kingdoms have for you and for…" The emperor actually choked up before gaining control of his voice once again. "And for Bale Nabhani. All of you, especially Bale, have given so much already to bring balance back to our continent. I have had other contact with all the leaders, and they express their appreciation to each of you for your part in extinguishing the threat of the Shadow Master."

Upon mention of Bale, Kyril saw both Joelle and Sylvie wipe their eyes. It was still hard to believe that he wasn't there with them, and even harder still to believe what he had done.

"I have papers drawn up here." The emperor motioned for his son to bring them to all five attendees. "You five all have the right and authority to travel among the kingdoms of the Western Continent in any capacity you would enjoy. There will be lands, titles, and gold given to each of you for your service. You and your families will not lack for anything for the rest of your lives."

Another scroll sat on the desk and the emperor glanced at it. "Bale's family has been awarded additional lands and for many generations will be taken care of. I know it is nothing compared to what he gave up for us, but it is all I have to give. In addition, the non-wizard portion of the academy will now be called the Nabhani School of Learning."

"Wouldn't Bale have been surprised to learn a school was named after him?" asked Kyril. Through the tears there was joy and satisfaction for how their friend was being recognized.

The others nodded their agreement and appreciation.

"As for the three of you," the emperor said to Sylvie, Joelle, and Kyril, "I would like to ask you to take some time to travel the kingdoms of the continent and make sure that Gamal's influence is truly gone and that balance is restored fully to all the land. You can make your own schedule, but each kingdom would like to thank you personally."

Kyril had been at a loss of what he was going to do. It seemed that Sylvie and Joelle had more opportunities and family to be with. This would be a great way for him to take some time before deciding what he would do with his life.

"Would you accept this invitation?" Emperor Alrishitar asked.

"Yes," Kyril said immediately.

Joelle nodded and smiled at Kyril. "Sounds fun. I wonder where we should go first. Should we go north? No, that's my own kingdom. I'd rather go south. Oooh, I know, maybe we can visit with Hasani in Mahli and meet the Dragon King, Bakari." She turned to Hasani. "Could we meet him? Do you think he would see us?"

The emperor laughed and clapped his hands in pleasure. "Oh, I'm sure Bakari would be delighted to meet you, Joelle."

The others joined in the laugh and then Joelle covered her mouth with a grimace. "Sorry," she said quietly. "Too many questions?"

"No, my dear," the emperor said. "We learn by asking."

"Then I must be learning a lot," Joelle said with bright eyes and a snort.

Kyril almost choked with laughter. It was cathartic to laugh—it was a much-needed relief after the past few months. It would be good to still have Joelle around.

"And you, Sylvonna Hickory?" the emperor asked. "I know the High Wizard has plans for you eventually, but could you spend a year and travel first?"

Sylvie fidgeted and peeked over at Jax, sitting next to her. He reached over and placed his hand on hers and squeezed. She gave him a questioning look and he smiled and nodded his head.

"Yes," Sylvie said. "If Jax can come with us." Her fair skin turned red and she pushed back a lock of blond hair behind her ears.

"I can't think of anything better," Emperor Alrishitar said. "I suspect he would be delighted to visit Elvyn and learn more of his heritage."

Jax's eyes grew moist at the offer and Sylvie grasped his hand tighter.

"Wonderful!" the emperor said. "I may even send my son with you to a few places."

Zaidan beamed with delight. "It would be my pleasure."

"And Hasani," continued the emperor, "You are welcome to join them at any time. I hear you will be writing a history of these events."

Hasani nodded his head in thanks.

"Then there is only one thing left," the emperor said as he stood up. "Follow me."

Each of the five looked at each other with questions in their eyes. Where was the emperor taking them? Kyril wanted to ask Zaidan, but the young prince only put a finger to his lips—it was a secret he wasn't going to share.

The group exited the office and walked down the broad marble-tiled hallway. Kyril turned his head and looked out at the city through the windows. He had come here two years ago without a family and as a relatively weak wizard with a burned mark on the palm of his hand. He had used all the money that he had to get admitted to the academy and hadn't had much hope for his life.

Now he walked on the heels of the emperor, one of the mightiest wizards and leaders in the land. Next to him stood solid, good friends that he would do anything for. His lips spread into a wide smile.

The emperor stopped at a set of gilded double doors where two guards stood. They nodded to him and then opened the doors to the largest banquet hall Kyril had ever seen. Hundreds of people—nobles, wizards, and commoners alike—smiled up at them. The emperor ushered the five of them into the room ahead of himself and his son.

The crowd stood and began clapping as Kyril, Sylvie, Joelle, Jax, and Hasani walked down a red carpeted aisle between the tables. It led up to a dais, upon which sat a grand table overflowing with the most savory smelling meats, breads, and vegetable dishes.

Kyril's stomach rumbled in anticipation and Joelle giggled.

He had a great life. He really did.

The End

This ends the Wizard Academies series and the adventures of the medallion holders Kyril, Sylvie, and Joelle.

Other Series By Mike Shelton
The Cremelino Prophecy

About 18 years prior to The Wizard Academies read the background story of some of the leaders of the Western Continent.

A Prophecy. A Powerful Sword. A reluctant wizard.

Darius San Williams, son of one of King Edward's councilors, cares little for his father's politics and vows to leave the city of Anikari to protect and bring glory to the Realm.

When a new-found and ancient magic emerges within him, he and his friends Christine and Kelln are faced with decisions that could shatter or fulfill the prophecy and the lives of all those they know.

Wizards and magic have long been looked down upon in the Realm, but Darius learns that no matter where he goes, prophecy and destiny are waiting to find him.

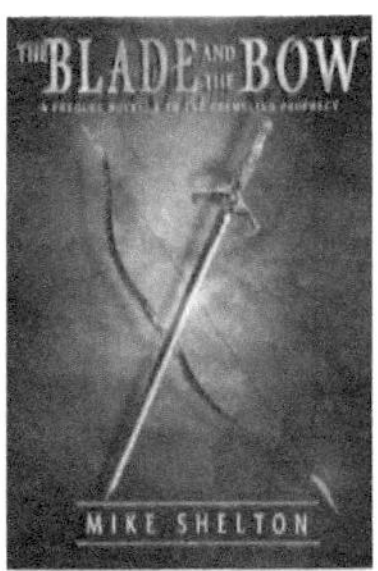

Sign up on Mike's website at www.MichaelSheltonBooks.com and get a copy of the prequel novella e-book to The Cremelino Prophecy, The Blade and The Bow.

Follow Darius and Kelln in one of their more fantastic adventures prior to The Path Of Destiny.

The TruthSeer Archives

On an island far out in the Eastern Sea join a new adventure of magic through the stones of power.

Everyone lies.
What if you could tell when they did?
What if this knowledge caused you immense physical pain?

Given a rare TruthStone, Shaeleen suffers immense agony with every lie she hears or tells. While struggling to control her new power and curb the pain she learns a powerful truth that could thrust an entire continent into civil war.

The stones of power protect the five kingdoms of Wayland - and have done so for two hundred years. Now those stones are failing and a dark power threatens to take control. With the help of her brother, and a young thief, Shaeleen sets out on a dangerous journey to gather and restore the power of all the stones.

The lies could kill her, but the truth could destroy a kingdom.

Will she succeed before the endless lies destroy her?

About the Author

Mike was born in California and has lived in multiple states from the west coast to the east coast. He cannot remember a time when he wasn't reading a book. At school, home, on vacation, at work at lunch time, and yes even a few pages in the car (at times when he just couldn't put that great book down). Though he has read all sorts of genres he has always been drawn to fantasy. It is his way of escaping to a simpler time filled with magic, wonders and heroics of young men and women.

Other than reading, Mike has always enjoyed the outdoors. From the beaches in Southern California to the warm waters of North Carolina. From the waterfalls in the Northwest to the Rocky Mountains in Utah. Mike has appreciated the beauty that God provides for us. He also enjoys hiking, discovering nature, playing a little basketball or volleyball, and most recently disc golf. He has a lovely wife who has always supported him, and three beautiful children who have been the center of his life.

Mike began writing stories in elementary school and moved on to larger novels in his early adult years. He has worked in corporate finance for most of his career. That, along with spending time with his wonderful family and obligations at church has made it difficult to find the time to truly dedicate to writing. In the last few years as his children have become older he has returned to doing what he truly enjoys – writing!

mikesheltonbooks@gmail.com
www.MichaelSheltonBooks.com
https://www.facebook.com/groups/MikeSheltonAuthor/
http://www.Twitter.com/msheltonbooks
http://www.Instagram.com/mikesheltonbooks